The Blue Scorpion

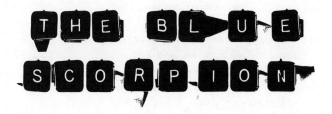

THE BLUE SCORPION

A
LOY LOMBARD
MYSTERY

JULIA LIEBER

alyson books
los angeles

Celebrating Twenty-Five Years

© 2005 BY JULIA LIEBER. ALL RIGHTS RESERVED.

MANUFACTURED IN THE UNITED STATES OF AMERICA.

THIS TRADE PAPERBACK ORIGINAL IS PUBLISHED BY ALYSON BOOKS,
P.O. BOX 4371, LOS ANGELES, CALIFORNIA 90078-4371.
DISTRIBUTION IN THE UNITED KINGDOM BY TURNAROUND PUBLISHER SERVICES LTD.,
UNIT 3 OLYMPIA TRADING ESTATE, COBURG ROAD, WOOD GREEN,
LONDON N22 6TZ ENGLAND.

FIRST EDITION: JUNE 2005

05 06 07 08 09 **a** 10 9 8 7 6 5 4 3 2 1

ISBN 1-55583-876-6
ISBN-13 978-1-55583-876-8

LIBRARY OF CONGRESS CATALOGING-IN-PUBLICATION DATA
LIEBER, JULIA.
    THE BLUE SCORPION : A LOY LOMBARD MYSTERY / JULIA LIEBER.—1ST ED.
    ISBN 1-55583-876-6 (PBK.); ISBN-13 978-1-55583-876-8
    1. WOMEN PRIVATE INVESTIGATORS—NORTH CAROLINA—ASHEVILLE—FICTION.
    2. RUSSIANS—NORTH CAROLINA—FICTION. 3. MAIL ORDER BRIDES—FICTION.
    4. ASHEVILLE (N.C.)—FICTION. 5. MISSING PERSONS—FICTION. 6. LESBIANS—
    FICTION. I. TITLE.
    PS3612.I33B58 2005
    813'.6—DC22   2005041159

CREDITS
COVER PHOTOGRAPHY BY MEL CURTIS/PHOTODISC RED/GETTY IMAGES.
COVER DESIGN BY MATT SAMS.

CHAPTER 1

Natalie Wolf was her American name, but the only trace of her was a dated photograph made when she had been Natalia Godunova. Pretty, with a thick tousle of red hair, ivory complexion, and dark, deep-set eyes, she hadn't had any trouble using the snapshot to snare an American husband, even when he'd met her and discovered she had gained a decade on a picture taken of a teenage Russian girl. Abel Wolf had brought her back to the States two years ago and set her up in a farmhouse in Buncombe County, N.C., where the police now believed they would find her body.

The Buncombe County Sheriff's Department, aided by homicide detective Lt. Mike Church of the Asheville police, acknowledged only that they knew she had gone missing on Tuesday, and they had put the word out through every news agency in the region by nightfall on Wednesday. Loy Lombard knew what they really thought; otherwise, they wouldn't have alerted the press. They thought she was dead; that her husband, Abel Wolf, had killed her; and as Lombard had so far discovered, they were probably right.

Abel Wolf was sitting at the breakfast table of his house, forking chunks of ham and eggs into his mouth while his mother explained everything to Lombard. He was a big man, late 30s or early 40s, with very little hair and a long, sad face. Augusta Wolf was a blustery bully of a woman, still robust in her early 70s, with coarse gray hair cut in uneven layers, no doubt by her own hand. Her ill-fitting polyester shirt and pants and crusty old loafers were a testimony to her frugality, and the house—cavernous in both size and gloom—was sparsely furnished with decades-old upholstery held together by oilcloth slipcovers.

"You see that boy?" Mrs. Wolf bellowed. She hadn't spoken in a normal tone of voice since Lombard had arrived. She pointed at her son, who seemed oblivious to any human presence, fixing his attention on the greasy pile of food on his plate. "He's a strange bird. I'm no fool. I can see it. Everybody in this part of the county will tell you the same thing: My son is a weirdo. But that don't make him a killer."

Lombard glanced at her watch. "Who thinks he's a killer?"

"You know who! The police."

"Why do they think so?" Lombard let her eyes wander to Abel Wolf, in his flannel shirt and bib, slurping his coffee, letting a tiny rivulet stream over one corner of his mouth. She averted her eyes to the kitchen window.

"Search me," said Mrs. Wolf. "But no sooner had he talked to the sheriff than some smart-ass detective from Asheville came out here to get his statement."

Lombard eyed Abel again. "He talks?"

"He ain't retarded!" Mrs. Wolf snapped. "He just ain't right."

Lombard leaned forward, resting her elbows on her thighs. "Look, Mrs. Wolf—"

"Call me Gussie."

"Gussie. I got here ten minutes ago, and your son hasn't said a word."

"He don't talk when he's eating."

Lombard sighed and snatched the snapshot of Natalie Wolf off the table. She wondered what degree of desperation could have forced so lovely a woman into the arms of the creep sitting across the table, and it occurred to her that maybe Natalie Wolf was still alive.

Maybe she'd had enough of the Wolf freak show and had taken off. Who could blame her? But she had vanished without a trace in the middle of the night, by Mrs. Wolf's account, and hadn't taken the car she used for trips to town.

"This is your only picture of her?" Lombard asked.

"We're not picture people," Mrs. Wolf explained. "And she took her passport and all her immigrant papers with her, including the one other picture I know of. Listen, Miss Lombard, do you want to know what it is I want, or not?"

"You want me to find your daughter-in-law."

"I want you to find the $200,000 she stole." Mrs. Wolf leaned back and folded her arms, and for the first time, Abel Wolf looked at Lombard.

Lombard's eyebrows furrowed. "Two hundred grand? From where?"

"My bunker," Abel said softly.

"Bunker?"

"I told you he ain't right," said Mrs. Wolf.

"Hush," said Lombard, waving off Mrs. Wolf. "Mr. Wolf— Abel—is that what you told the police? I have to know exactly what you told them."

"She took my money," said Abel, and Lombard noted his distinctly northern accent. "I kept the cash in my safe, in the bunker. It went missing right along with Natalie, late Monday night or very early Tuesday. I reported it immediately, and yesterday this lieutenant from Asheville came here to see me."

"Mike Church," said Mrs. Wolf. "I figure Hugh Potter called him. Hugh's a deputy. His old man, Felix Potter, was a hand on my farm. Got cancer of the nut sac and died horrible. My husband—Abel's old man—fell off his tractor and died horrible too. But not before he built that bomb shelter, what Abel calls the bunker."

Lombard nodded. "Go on."

"It's down near the creek, so we can pump water into it in case of attack. Back when the Russians were fixing to blow us all to hell, we figured it might come in handy. It's one airtight son of a bitch. Abel banks there."

"Banks?"

"I told you he ain't right. He took all his money he inherited from his old man and stuck it in a safe in there. Makes sense. He spends all his spare time in the bunker, cranking away on that computer of his."

Lombard watched Abel while his mother talked. He was hunched over his plate, his head turned off to one side as he chewed open-mouthed. He swallowed, wiped his mouth with his bib, and sat upright when he noticed her staring. He looked at her with large brown hangdog eyes. His eyes were the only halfway attractive thing about him.

"Tell me how you met your wife, Abel," said Lombard.

"I was under the impression there were women in Russia interested in finding American husbands, so I went to St. Petersburg."

Lombard suppressed a chuckle. She wouldn't have traveled halfway around the world for any woman she'd ever been with, let alone one she'd never met. "What gave you that impression?"

"I read about it online, on a Web site."

"What sort of Web site?"

"A gentleman's Web site."

Lombard's eyes flashed. She knew better, but just for fun she asked, "Porn?"

"Certainly not." His gaze moved away from Lombard. "It was a legitimate matchmaking service advertised on a Civil War Web site. I'm a history buff, you see."

"He's into Civil War reenacting, that kind of thing," Mrs. Wolf offered.

Abel looked at Lombard again. "I'm Colonel William McCandless, First Brigade commander over all Pennsylvania reserves."

"Hmm, a Union officer in North Carolina," Lombard mused.

"His kin were all Confederates," said Mrs. Wolf. "Whew! He ain't right."

"That's a minor point," said Abel Wolf.

Lombard folded her arms on the table and leaned in. "Do you travel much?"

"No. Russia was my only trip abroad. I did go to school in Philadelphia."

"Temple University," piped Mrs. Wolf. "Don't ask me why."

"I won't," Lombard said irritably. "Abel, did you graduate?"

"No," he said. "I disliked city life. I came back here after a year."

"And he never went another place, other than to those battle reenactments, until that damned trip to Russia."

"So you and Natalie didn't travel together," said Lombard.

Abel's expression darkened. "No."

"Ever socialize at all?"

His upper lip quivered slightly. "Things were just fine here on the farm," he said, gritting his teeth. "Mother, Natalie, and I enjoyed each other's company just fine."

"Speak for yourself," said Mrs. Wolf. "I couldn't understand a damned word she said. And she obviously needed plenty of time on her own." She gave a triumphant smile.

Abel's lips were drawn as though he'd just sucked laudanum, and he breathed deeply through his nose before saying, "Mother is referring to Natalie's excursions."

Mrs. Wolf started to speak, but Lombard shushed and swatted at her. Abel said, "She took the car into town sometimes and stayed gone for days. A day out turned into two, three days sometimes."

Lombard's ambivalence suddenly turned to keen interest. "You say she disappeared for days at a time? When did she start doing that?"

"Soon after she arrived here in the States and married me."

"And you have no idea what she was doing?"

"No. But I think wherever it was she was doing it is where she is now."

"How did she get there?" Lombard asked. "My understanding is she didn't take any of your vehicles. What do you drive, anyway?"

"I have a Ford F-150," said Abel. "Mother and I share it, but Natalie always drove the Buick."

"The one I saw parked out front," said Lombard. "So how did she go?"

"Now you talk like the law, laying blame on Abel!" Mrs. Wolf grumbled.

"I have to ask the same questions they ask, to come up with answers," said Lombard. "Only I don't think I'm going to have any for you." She stood up.

"Where are you going?" said Mrs. Wolf. "Look, we need some help, here. I thought you wanted to help us."

Lombard said, "I have to think about this."

"I'll pay you a pile," Mrs. Wolf said, for the first time sounding the merest bit pleading. She stood up and ambled over to the kitchen counter, on top of which sat a battered light-blue leather shoulder bag. She rubbed it and said, "This is where *I* bank. You call it."

Lombard shrugged. "Five grand to start; $150 an hour plus expenses." She put her hands in her back pockets and yawned.

Mrs. Wolf's tongue rolled under one cheek as her eyes narrowed at Lombard. She reached into the shoulder bag and withdrew a wrinkled, stained manila envelope. She opened it, licked her index finger, and began peeling out $100 bills. After she had counted 50 of them, she handed them to Lombard. "Don't spend it all in one place."

Loy Lombard and Sam McLean had met years ago in Charlotte, when McLean had been promoted to homicide detective and assigned as Lombard's partner. Since going into business together in Asheville, they had worked only one homicide case as private investigators, but it had been a big one. Their client, Sen. Jasper Slade of North Carolina, had been accused of murdering his young male lover. Slade had committed suicide— or more likely had been murdered himself—and an executive of his conservative lobbying foundation had been exposed as the chief conspirator in the complicated murder plot. Lombard and McLean had been widely praised for solving it, even though the culprits had turned out to be their own clients.

It had been gratifying but a little embarrassing, and it had called a lot of attention to their business, which was less of a private investigation firm than a security guard contracting service: a rent-a-cop shop, as McLean's 13-year-old daughter called it. Other than the Slade case, they had gotten some PI work from local lawyers in the past year, most of which involved doing background checks on witnesses and potential jurors. It wasn't as much fun as murder cases, but it paid well enough, and it kept their names on the criminal justice radar screen.

McLean was sitting with Lombard in their regular booth at a diner near their office. "Only because it's in the news," he said. "That's the only reason you've taken it. Get our names out there again, and bring in more business."

"There's nothing wrong with that," said Lombard.

"Except if she's dead, we both know who killed her."

Lombard pursed her lips. "Give me some credit, Sam. I already thought of that. But why would Abel give us five grand to find a woman he murdered?"

"Abel didn't hire you. His mother did. All she knows is there's a bunch of money missing. Well," he smirked, "that's what she says. For all we know she and Abel are in cahoots and are using you as a smoke screen to fend off suspicion."

Lombard said, "Anything could have happened to her, Sam. Natalie either ran away—"

"In what? She didn't take a car. That house is miles out in the country."

"—or she…" Lombard frowned.

"Or she's dead," said McLean. "Abel's already made it clear he had plenty of reason to kill her, if it's true she stole $200,000 from him or was fooling around with somebody else on those 'excursions' he talked about. No wonder the police are on his ass. Now, the way you've described him, he's a mama's boy, totally dominated by Gussie Wolf. Naturally the old lady would put a pro like you between the police and her boy. Whether or not there's any missing 200 grand."

Lombard sighed. "I know I'm gambling with this one. If Natalie's dead, Abel probably did kill her. I'm sure Mike Church and all the other cops are digging up everything they can on him by now. But if she's alive, we've been hired to find her and the missing loot, and that's what we're going to do."

McLean leaned back while a server refilled his iced tea. He spooned sugar into the glass and said, "So where is she?"

"Hell if I know. If she took off, somebody fetched her, and it's no doubt a boyfriend, and probably a local one. I'd say they've run off to a beach somewhere, but they'll be back, and by the time they are, I'll know exactly where to find them."

McLean shook his head. "It's just not like you to ignore the obvious, Loy. She's vanished. There are at least two possible motives to kill her that Abel admits. Are we really so hard up we'll work this loser for $5,000?"

"In cash," Lombard grinned. "But I'll give back every cent if you don't think it's worth it."

"You mean you actually care what I think?"

"Of course I do. You think I want to work this dog by myself?" she chuckled. "Sam, I have a hunch this case will turn up some good stuff. I think Natalie Wolf had an angle before she even got to the States. Abel said the stepping-out started as soon as she got here. Something strange was, and maybe still is, going on." Lombard reflected for a moment. "Abel's a sap, an easy mark for a hustler."

"Oh? You think she was a hooker?"

"I said 'hustler,'" said Lombard. "More along the lines of a con. But now that you mention it, hooking isn't too far removed from selling yourself in marriage."

"It's a world apart," said McLean. "Marrying for security is one thing. It's not the same as prostitution, Loy."

"One's just as easy as the other, as far as I'm concerned." Lombard noted McLean's frown and added, "OK, hooking is slightly *less* degrading." She laughed. "Once you see Abel, you'll agree with me. He's a sucker, and I bet we'll find he got used."

"More reason for him to want her dead," McLean offered.

"Maybe," said Lombard. "But she took her passport and some of her things."

"So Abel killed her and ditched some of her stuff to make her look like a runaway. Come on, Loy. It's all over the news. We both know what the police think, and they know a lot more than we do by now."

Lombard smiled. "Talk to Mike Church. He likes you."

That night Lombard was sitting up in bed with a novel, her favorite kind of story—an epic wartime romance, like *Birdsong* and *Dr. Zhivago*. She'd rather have died than have anybody know her eyes welled up for heartbreaking prose. Her girlfriend, Christine Campbell, lay next to her watching the 11 o'clock news. Her fat tomcat, Romeo, was curled up at the foot of the bed, maliciously eyeing Petie, a bulldog mix Chris had found abandoned on a mountain road and now took everywhere she went, even to work.

Chris was a park ranger who lived in a cabin in Madison County, a few miles north of Hot Springs. She had been spending her days off at Lombard's house on the outskirts of Asheville for more than a year, but signs of decline were showing. Chris was spending less of her spare time these days with Lombard and more time with friends in Hot Springs. Lombard realized their relationship had been built primarily on a physical attraction but, now in her early 40s, she hoped to deepen their companionship.

They had little to talk about, though. Chris had no interest in business, books, or crime. She came from a big Baptist family in the hills around Boone, and she liked sports and the outdoors. She was young and pretty, with strawberry-blond curls and a freckled face, blue eyes, and what seemed like a year-round tan. She was petite, strong, and athletic.

Lombard had grown up in New Orleans but had left at 19 to join the Navy. Both her parents were dead, she had no siblings, and she had always lived in cities, real cities, before ending up in Asheville, a town of about 70,000, three years ago. She had a tall, husky build and dark good looks, and in years past, women had always been attracted to her. But as she got older she felt less secure in her attractiveness. She had been abstinent for two years after moving to Asheville and had put all her energy into building up her business. Then suddenly she began noticing lines and gray hairs, and thinking she'd passed her prime without even feeling it slip away.

"Hey, isn't that the case you were telling me about?" Chris said through a yawn. She pointed at the TV.

The still image of a young woman with red hair and dark eyes filled the screen. A voice-over said, "Natalie Wolf was reported missing by her husband, Buncombe County farmer Abel Wolf. Mrs. Wolf vanished from her home during the night of August 29th or early-morning hours of the 30th. While the case is under police investigation, law enforcement authorities are not commenting on whether foul play is suspected. Anyone with information about Mrs. Wolf should contact the Buncombe County Sheriff's Department or the Asheville police."

Lombard picked up the remote and turned down the volume. "They didn't mention the money," she said, as though to herself.

"What money?" Chris said, nestling under the covers and fluffing her pillow.

"Nothing," said Lombard, putting her book away and flicking off the TV and the lamp. She spooned herself beside Chris and held her, massaging Chris's breasts and kissing her hair. Chris's lips parted to the soft wheezing of early sleep. *So it's come to this,* thought Lombard. *Not even a kiss good night.*

Sam McLean was a few years younger than Lombard, and with his sandy hair and frat-boy looks, he seemed even more youthful than 39. Few would have guessed he'd been married for 15 years to the same woman, Selena, who had been a stay-at-home mom before recently announcing she'd taken a job at a department store cosmetics counter. The McLeans had three kids, tended to be conservative in politics, and regularly attended a Presbyterian church.

Lombard was Catholic anytime she flew or had an anxiety attack. Otherwise, she steered clear of what she considered religious hocus-pocus. She detested any form of idealism, spiritual or political, and in the rare case that she voted, it was against an incumbent who had done or said something to piss her off.

So religion and politics were pretty much out of the question as topics of conversation between Lombard and McLean. Even rarer was any discussion of their personal lives, but now and again one of them might ask about the other's loved ones. McLean knew about Christine Campbell, and had met her a few times, so when he sat in Lombard's office on Friday afternoon to tell her about his talk with detective lieutenant Mike Church, he started by asking about her girlfriend. "And how's Chris?" he asked.

Lombard frowned. Chris had left at daybreak saying she'd be on duty the next six days. Her absences were growing longer, and her excuses were wearing thin. Lombard suspected now more than ever that Chris was seeing someone else in Hot Springs. Lombard said, "She's just dandy, Sam. Thanks for asking."

"Do you ever visit her?" McLean asked.

"I hate the sticks."

"Well, you kinda live in the sticks yourself."

"I live in the lap of civilization compared to Chris," Lombard said. "I'm within a mile of a gas pump and a gallon of milk in any direction. Chris lives within a mile of Tolkien's Middle-earth. I half expect to find long-armed trolls under the bridges. But I have made the trip a few times." She yawned and stretched. "There's nothing to do up there. We just sit around with her hippie friends playing cards and listening to somebody strum a guitar and sing little feel-good sister songs, which was tolerable until one time this girl started burning sage and invoking the triple-horned goddess or some goddamn thing. That was the last straw."

McLean laughed. "I'm surprised Chris is into that."

"She's not. Just some of the people she hangs out with. Anyway, the woods are creepy enough without that earth-mother voodoo. Got varmints too, you know."

"I hear a lot of gay people live in that area now."

"Hooray for gay pioneers, then. Let them wave the rainbow flag at the ass end of the earth. Anyway, enough about that." She picked up the old photograph of Natalie Wolf and studied it. "What did Mike Church tell you? Why is he fooling around with the sheriff's case? The Wolf farm is way out in the country."

"Mike said this fellow from Asheville named Dewey Holloway called the police the day after Abel Wolf reported Natalie missing. The man said he had a Russian lady friend he was supposed to meet on Tuesday, but she hadn't shown up and hadn't called. He had a bad feeling because the woman had been complaining that her husband was abusive and she was afraid of him. Mike asked for her name, and the man said it was Natalie Wolf. Since Mike's on a homicide task force operated by both the sheriff's office and the police, he got together with Deputy Hugh Potter, and they went out and interviewed Wolf at his farm Wednesday and decided to issue a missing person's alert. That explains why Mrs. Wolf called you on Thursday asking for help."

Lombard nodded. "A boyfriend. Like I thought. What's his name again?"

"Mike said it was Dewey Holloway."

"Where is he? What does he do?"

"Mike couldn't remember."

"Couldn't remember?"

"He wrote his number down somewhere but couldn't find it when I asked."

"The hell he couldn't."

McLean shrugged. "Maybe he's holding back. Loy, he's only talking to me at all because we're friends. He doesn't want us nosing around his investigation. You wouldn't either."

"If I lacked the basic competence to write down a potential homicide witness's—or suspect's, maybe—phone number, I'd feel blessed by the help of a private detective who knows what he's doing."

"Well, if he had the number, he obviously wasn't about to give it to us."

"We'll see about that," she said.

Lombard knew Mike Church disliked her, but she thought he at least respected her. He had been grateful for her and McLean's help during the Slade investigation—during which they had all met—but in the aftermath of the case, no fast friendship had taken off between her and Church. It had worked out all right for Church and McLean, but something about Lombard must have been off-putting to Church, who was the sort of man who probably felt more comfortable around women who were physically less imposing, less opinionated, and more ingratiating to men. Lombard was, around men, the classic bull in a china shop. She didn't mean to bowl them over; it just wasn't in her nature to be delicate.

Not that she was loud. In fact, she never raised her voice unless provoked. Lombard was not very sociable and—in social settings—almost never opened her mouth unless she was spoken to first. During one of his few attempts at friendship with Lombard, Church had invited her and the McLeans to his wife's fortieth birthday party. The booze had been flowing, and Lombard and Church both had had their share when there occurred a slight contretemps. Church joked with Lombard that it was too bad about her being a lesbian, as good-looking as she was. She had heard it all her life—had always considered it a tactless, idiotic remark—but had shrugged it off with her characteristic tolerance of drunken slips of the tongue. But when he joked there probably wasn't any danger in any man making a pass at her, since kissing her would be like kissing a guy, she fired back an offer to get Mrs. Church's opinion of her kissing. She regretted the remark only because it had been crass, and insulting to Mrs. Church, who seemed like a nice woman.

Presently Lombard was waiting for Church in a chair next to his desk at police headquarters. She had dreaded meeting him to ask for a favor, but she knew McLean didn't want to bother Church anymore, so if she were going to get that boyfriend's name anytime soon, she would have to approach Church herself.

"Loy Lombard!" Church cried with fake enthusiasm when he saw her. He was a short, stout fellow, unremarkable in appearance but for the fact that he looked exactly like what one would expect a police detective to look like. He had the mustache; the thinning, prematurely gray hair—Church was in his middle 40s—and the same lackadaisical expression whether he was looking at a mutilated corpse or reading the sports page. "Didn't Sam get enough out of me? Or have you just missed me and wanted to catch up?" He sat down behind his desk.

"Well, Mike, to be honest, this is more about business."

"And how's business?"

"I can't complain."

"So Abel Wolf's hired you to find his wife. Smart move."

Lombard narrowed her eyes. "I know by that last remark you're not commending his choice of PIs."

"Of course I am."

"You think he's hired us to throw off suspicion." She was certainly not going to tell him that it was, in fact, Abel Wolf's mother who had hired them.

"It wouldn't be the first time a killer hired you to throw off suspicion."

"Ah, don't think that exact same thought hasn't occurred to me and Sam, and in just so many words."

Church drummed his desktop with his fingers. "I have a lot of work to do. What do you want, Loy?"

"Who's Dewey Holloway?"

"Didn't Sam tell you? He says he's a friend of Natalie Wolf's."

"Yes, Sam told me. I just wonder how I might get in touch with him."

Church gave her a scornful look. "Now, Loy. This is an ongoing investigation. You used to be a homicide detective. Would you have given out a witness's contact information to a reporter?"

Lombard staved off an impulse to take offense. Church knew she disliked reporters. "I'm sorry you think of me as an annoyance, Mike. I had hoped you still regarded me as a professional case inspector, every bit as qualified to have this kind of information as yourself."

"I think you're a professional case inspector, no doubt," said Church. "But as a PI, and not as a cop working with the authorities, you aren't qualified for that information."

"So you do have it, then. You're just not letting us in on it."

"That's right." He gave her a gleeful smile. "You're a regular bloodhound, Loy. You can find out where he is. Not that he'll be able to tell you much."

"All right," she said. "The fact is we can't find a trace of anybody in Asheville by that name. At least tell me for certain whether he's in Asheville or not."

"No can do."

"It's a missing person's case, Mike," Lombard said irritably. "Sam and I have really helped you out in the past. Why can't you do me this one simple favor?"

"As far as I'm concerned, it's not just a missing person's case," he said flatly. "When a wife goes missing—leaving behind a husband with a double ax to grind—I have to consider the possibility of foul play. I'm going to be damned careful exactly what I tell anybody, including Sam, and especially including you."

"A double ax? What do you mean?"

Church stared at Lombard for a moment, as though he were hedging. "Well, I think Dewey Holloway sounds kind of like a boyfriend, don't you? And the same day he called, I found out Abel Wolf had sworn out a warrant against his wife."

"A warrant?" Lombard knew what for, and she was furious at the Wolfs for failing to mention it to her.

"That's right. He swore out a warrant against her for theft."

Lombard abruptly grabbed the armrests of her chair and pushed herself up. "You know what I think, Mike? I think you forgot to write Holloway's number down. And if you didn't, and you really are just holding back, then I think that's a shame."

Church shrugged. "You can think whatever you like."

"Some gratitude. After all Sam and I have done for you. I can't wait till the next time you ask for a favor." She stormed off without waiting for a reply, but he had one.

"Pleasure seeing you again," he hollered as she bolted down the hallway. "Don't be a stranger."

As soon as she arrived back at the office, Lombard was on the phone to Augusta Wolf, who began ranting about reporters calling her at all hours.

"I'm not a reporter, ma'am," Lombard said. "I'm working for you, right? The thing is this: If I'm supposed to work for you, you have to tell me everything."

"I've told you everything."

"Not about the warrant your son swore against Natalie for theft."

"I told you she took his money! And I told you the police knew it too."

"You didn't tell me charges had been filed!" Lombard yelled.

"What's the difference?"

"When you and the cops know something I don't know, Gussie, it makes a difference in how much I can help. You got that? Now, get Abel on the line."

"He don't talk on the phone," said Mrs. Wolf.

"Gussie, you tell Abel if he wants his $5,000 worth, he'd better get his ass on the line. I'm not gonna run out there every time I have to talk to him."

"That's *my* $5,000 worth you're talking about," said Mrs. Wolf.

"Don't you be getting uppity with me. I'll come over there and lay you out flat."

"You come right on over. And I'll give you back every cent of that money if you're going to hold back crucial information."

There was a brief pause, and Mrs. Wolf said, "I'll let it go this time. As for Abel coming on the phone, I'll have to fetch him. He'll call you back." She hung up.

Lombard slammed down her phone receiver. She liked her office phone so much better than the cordless phone at home, because she could slam this one. Somebody needed to invent a cordless phone you could slam, she was thinking, when she noticed Retta Scott, her office manager, standing in the doorway.

"How long have you been standing there?" Lombard asked.

"Long enough to figure out this case will give you a heart attack if you don't chill out," said Retta. "I heard you on the phone with Mrs. Wolf, and that reminded me. It's Friday, and the banks close at 6. I haven't deposited Mrs. Wolf's money yet. OK if I take it out of the safe?"

Lombard shook her head. "Not yet. I'll take the weekend to think it over. Let's see…Monday's Labor Day. By Tuesday, if this case hasn't gotten any better for us, we'll give back Gussie's cash and throw Abel to the…"

Retta grimaced. "Don't say it."

"I won't," said Lombard. "I'd sooner throw him in the river, which is where they'll probably find his wife."

CHAPTER 2

By Friday evening the news media had discovered Abel Wolf's affidavit of complaint against his missing wife, in addition to what was for small-town North Carolina an exotic story: a Russian bride, desperate for a better life, vanished without a trace. The media had obtained a copy of her Immigration photo, capturing the image of an attractive, thirty-ish redhead with a smug, close-lipped smile, looking off to one side. Reporters had taken aim at Abel: Cameras caught him ambling from his truck to his house, ducking from the public eye as much as possible, looking every bit the surly, disgruntled loner. For most of his sheltered life, Abel Wolf had spent his time quietly indulging private obsessions with history and weaponry, dodging the scorn and suspicion of a rural community for his oddness. Then he had gone out and found a woman.

Local fascination with the case of the "missing Russian beauty" was mounting, as was the public's ensuing contempt for her fat hick of a spouse. Asheville was a quaint, friendly town, but it was moneyed and snotty in quarters, with plenty of disdain for the likes of Gussie and Abel Wolf. By the end of Friday night's 6 o'clock news, it was clear that as far as Asheville was concerned, Natalie Wolf was a victim, and Abel a suspect.

And Lombard, trumpeted local TV news anchor Hunter Lyle the following Monday night, was yet again representing the interests of the "aloof loner," as Lyle put it, and had been retained by the Wolfs to find the missing wife. Lombard had found out about the press's knowledge of her involvement in the case that afternoon, when a reporter had tried, quite unsuccessfully, to get a comment from her. Now that all of Asheville knew of Lombard and McLean's role in the Wolf case, it was too late to get out.

Lombard grumbled aloud about Hunter Lyle as she lay on her living room sofa. "Why hasn't she found a job in a big city like she was so hell-bent on doing? She must be screwing the wrong men." She raised her glass to her lips. "Or women."

Lombard hadn't had anything to do with Lyle since their brief affair the year before, at the conclusion of which Lombard had discovered that not only had Lyle been using her for leads in the Slade investigation, but Lyle had, unbeknownst to Lombard, been married all along, to a wealthy, connected man who could help her get to the top of her career. Lyle's mussing around in the Wolf case added insult to injury. Lombard turned the channel and got up to pour another drink.

This was no night for reminders of her sorry luck in matters of the heart. No sooner had she rid herself of Hunter Lyle than she had met Christine Campbell, who was, at least, exclusively lesbian and didn't complicate things with that modern-woman, pain-in-the-ass bisexuality bullshit. But Chris hadn't called since leaving three days ago. Three days, over the weekend, and not one phone call. But Lombard hadn't tried calling her either, because she suspected Chris was spending time with a new lover. Lombard didn't want to think it, but she was too canny not to. It was all very depressing.

Lombard spied her tomcat lying on the dining room table. She sighed. "I need to get out one of these nights, don't I, Romeo?" She took a swig of bourbon and stroked the fat feline, who purred and swatted at her hand.

"We've hired a new girl," Retta said the next morning.

Lombard was sitting in the middle of the lobby sofa, her legs winged out, feet planted on the floor. A hot, steaming mug of coffee sat cupped in her hands near her crotch. She couldn't remember the last time she had been this hungover on a weekday. Something had to give. "What do you mean, 'we'?" she asked dimly, raising the mug to her lips.

"As in the company," said Retta. "You told me to advertise for somebody good at computers. Well, I found one. She's a librarian at Pack Memorial, and she knows all about Web design and information science, all that stuff we need to keep up with the competition." Retta pinched one corner of her mouth; she had a way of judging Lombard loudly without raising her voice. "Looks like you had a rough one last night."

Lombard took a deep drink of coffee and sighed. "Retta, you mind your weekends, and I'll mind mine." She began massaging her brow. "How much are we paying her? Who is she?"

"Her name is Dana Gabriel. I hired her Friday. She's smart, both bookwise and common sense, from what I could tell." Retta pulled a file folder off a credenza behind her desk. "I've got her résumé in here if you want to see it."

Lombard said, "So how much is she setting us back?"

"She'll only be working part-time nights and Saturdays, since she's keeping her day job at the library. I figured her pay at $200 a week, based on the hours we agreed on."

"Salary?"

"No, she asked for an hourly rate."

"Smart girl," said Lombard. "With the hourly rate, she can make more money by pulling a lot of overtime. Gimme that résumé."

"I'm only allotting so many hours a week, not a minute more." Retta handed the file to Lombard. "She's cute too, by the way. You'll like her."

Suddenly the front door opened, and a handsome fellow stepped inside the lobby. He was dressed in a dove-gray suit, hanging about his slender frame as only the best-quality cotton will. His shirt was blazing white, his silk tie a golden field of tiny purple fleurs-de-lis. His black curly hair was capped by a white Panama hat, his feet clad in soft leather shoes the color of dried blood. He was suntanned and grinning ear to ear. Lombard recognized him immediately.

"Tyler Rhodes," she said glumly. "How long has it been?"

"Why, Loy," he beamed, "I haven't seen you since you tried to get me indicted over a year ago." He took off his hat and sunglasses. "You don't look well," he said cheerfully.

Lombard set her mug on the coffee table and stood up. "What did you expect? I'm hungover, and I'll be 43 in November. And I didn't try to get you indicted. If anything, I kept you out of trouble."

"I was teasing," he said. He glanced at Retta and asked to speak to Lombard privately. Once they were enclosed in her office, he said, "I really am grateful to you for all you did. That's why I came here, to return a favor."

Rhodes was referring to the Slade case, in which he had been a key witness. He had provided Lombard and McLean with evidence that helped them solve the murder of Slade's lover, but he had been very close to the heart of the case: so close, in fact, that Lombard had always questioned his credibility. He had lied to them up until the very end of the case, and he had dubious connections to various radical groups that Lombard distrusted. She had never cared much for activist types, and Rhodes was a militant leftist.

He was also a hypocrite, in Lombard's view. He came from an extravagantly wealthy family, and despite his self-promotion as an idealistic champion of the underdog, he relished the perks of coming from old money. He lived alone in a beautiful Italianate home in Montford, he drove a Mercedes coupe convertible (one of three vehicles he, a self-proclaimed conservation activist, owned), and had a house in Key West. He flew to Europe whenever he felt like it, spending part of each summer in his family villa in Ibiza, hopping down to Ravello for parties when he was feeling sexy. He was a Stanford law graduate in private practice in his ancestral hometown of Asheville, N.C. Yet he had no idea whether his business broke even or not, because his entire life was funded by trusts left to him by three adoring, dead aunts. He had it made, and he knew it.

Rhodes plopped down in one of Lombard's client chairs. "Loy," he said, squirming a bit, "did I ever mention my family made its fortune in the furniture business? If you ever want a good deal on upholstery, you just wink."

Lombard sat down at her desk. "Is that the return favor you were talking about?"

He gave her a mock wounded look. "I've left several phone messages for you, and you've never called me back. I've been trying to win your favor for the longest time. I really wish we could be friends, because you're such a fascinating woman."

"You are the consummate ass kisser, Tyler. Now, tell me what you want."

"I saw the news reports last night." He looked around the room. "Wasn't that Hunter Lyle I saw on TV?" he said absently.

"I suppose it was, though she isn't getting her information from me."

"But you are involved in the scandal of the missing Russian bride, which is certain to put you in the spotlight."

"You know very well I don't care about the spotlight."

"But the spotlight is good for business, and I, of course, wish to see an interesting woman like you succeed."

"Meaning?"

"Meaning I have information you would probably find useful."

Lombard leaned back in her chair. "Now, why doesn't it surprise me that you are somehow connected to this so-called scandal, or any scandal, for that matter?"

Rhodes waved her off. "Please. This Wolf thing is hardly a scandal. So the poor Russian immigrant left her fat slob of a spouse. It'll all turn out so very banal in the end, I'm sure. But I am personally acquainted with a friend of the missing lady."

Lombard was interested. "Who?"

"Desmond Holliday. Surely you've heard of him."

"No, I haven't." She pursed her lips, wondering whether Mike Church had deliberately thrown her off with the name Dewey Holloway or if he really was sloppy enough to get the name wrong. "Who is he?"

Lombard thought she spotted pity in the way Rhodes looked at her. He said, "Desmond Holliday is the premier designer of interior decor in the region. He's been in town for as long as you have, Loy."

"Stop looking at me like I'm deformed, Tyler. Why would I know anything about that? Only rich people like you hire interior designers."

"Well, I don't hire them either, since I was born and raised with an eye for quality," he explained. "But Desmond Holliday is the social epicenter of Asheville, and I thought everybody knew that." He began inspecting his French-manicured fingernails. "Well, everyone of means."

"I'm not of means, and I don't read the society pages. So tell me about Desmond Holliday."

Rhodes stretched out his arms. "He was briefly my lover, not long after he got into town. It didn't last, since none of my affairs seem to last, for some reason." He yawned. "Anyway, we stayed friends. He's originally from Miami, though he doesn't talk much about his past. I suspect that owes more to past squalor than scandal." Rhodes sighed. "It must be dreadful to be ashamed of one's roots. I can't imagine it."

"What's his connection to the Wolfs?"

"He was Miss Natalie's very good friend. Is still, one hopes."

"No chance of his being a boyfriend, I take it?"

"I wouldn't put much past Desi, but he seems fairly solidly into younger men. He does enjoy dressing up pretty women, though, but only ones with lots of money." Rhodes smiled impishly. "You know, Truman Capote used to call those filthy rich women like Babe Paley and Gloria Guinness his 'swans.' I think Desi craves that kind of woman-object. He'd love to take a smattering of charm and good looks and money and mold it into a sophisticated woman of

the world: a first-rate, state-of-the-art, grade A–quality fag hag."
He withdrew his wallet out of a vest pocket. "I have a picture of
Desi and Miss Swan right here." He pulled out a photograph and
handed it to Lombard.

"This is Natalie Wolf?" said Lombard.

"Oh, yes," said Rhodes. "That's the Red Russian, all right." It was
a full-body shot of a redheaded woman holding the arm of a cheer-
ful-looking man with an olive complexion and thinning salt-and-
pepper hair. They looked like they could be dressed for a wedding.
Her hair was shorter in this snapshot, and she seemed plumper
than the Immigration photo making the rounds in the media, but
that made sense: Perhaps life in a new, freer country had given her
a robust, colorful glow absent in the government ID photo. In this
shot one saw her profile as she beamed at Desmond Holliday.

"How do you know this is Natalie Wolf?" Lombard asked. "When
was this picture taken?"

"I took it several weeks ago at one of Desi's outdoor parties. It
was a political fund-raiser for a friend of his. And I know it's her
because Desi says she's a Russian immigrant, and she's all sweet
and immigrant-pitiful, and how many can there be? It's Natalie this
and Natalie that with Desi. They're friends. Trust me."

"You mind if I keep this picture?"

Rhodes shrugged. "Suit yourself."

Lombard set it on her desk. "How long have they been friends?"

"I don't know."

"Mm-hmm. Have you ever spoken to Natalie?"

"No." He glanced at his watch. "Ah," he said, "look at the time."
He stood up and smoothed out his jacket.

"What are you all dressed up for?" asked Lombard. "It's awfully
hot for a suit and tie. Have you got court today?"

"I don't really go to court much. But my grandmother taught
me, a gentleman always dresses when he goes into town during the
business day."

"You came downtown just to tell me about Desmond
Holliday?"

"That's right."

"So how do I get in touch with him?" she asked.

"He's in the book. Holliday Designs and Interiors, Montford Avenue. He lives out in the country, in a fabulously vulgar mansion." He straightened his cuffs. "He's new-money to the core."

"You think he'll talk to me?"

"Of course," he said, carefully affixing his hat on his head. "Just don't tell him I spoke to you. As for the best time: You won't find Desi in town this week; he's in Palm Beach. But he is having a very swank affair at his house next Saturday night." Tyler Rhodes eyed Lombard's faded jeans and burnt-orange Hawaiian shirt. "Wear something you didn't buy at Target. I'll introduce you to Desi then. It's the only way you'll ever get him to talk to you. And you'll have a great time and meet a lot of very interesting people."

Lombard shook her head. "I hate parties. And I hate people. But I like shopping at Target, you fucking snob. Why can't you set up a meeting? Why so secretive?"

"I don't want Desi to know I've come to you, quite frankly. He'd be so angry with me if he knew. Would you want somebody dispatching a PI on you?"

"Then why did you do it?"

"Help out an old friend," said Rhodes. "You."

"Uh-huh," Lombard said, wary of his motives. She gave him a kind but distrusting sidelong look. "In that case, I'll come to the party, if you promise to introduce me to Holliday and get him talking."

Rhodes smiled broadly. "You've got a deal."

After he had left, she sat back down at her desk and eyed the folder she had been carrying when Rhodes had arrived. She opened it and scanned the résumé of one Dana Miriam Gabriel, age 31. Baccalaureate degree in English from Florida State University; master of library sciences from the University of North Carolina, Chapel Hill. Currently employed full-time as an "information specialist"—whatever the hell that meant, thought Lombard—at Pack Memorial Library. "Smart girls shouldn't need extra jobs," Lombard grumbled aloud. She examined the photo print she required Retta to make of all new hires. It was Dana's employee head shot: long, curly dark hair pulled back; horn-rimmed eyeglasses; a long, freckled nose; and bee-stung lips. She looked smart, like a plain-Jane librarian on the whole, but there was something beguiling to Lombard in her dark eyes and half smile.

"Oh, look at that," Lombard mumbled to herself. "She's a little doll."

Before their big break, Lombard and McLean's business had been called Secure Services Inc. The emphasis had been on providing security-guard and bodyguard services to various businesses and visiting public figures in Asheville and the surrounding region. When lawyers started calling for background investigations—which included snooping into the personal histories of prospective jurors as well as witnesses—they saw the potential for expanding their business and renamed it Lombard & McLean, PSI. The initials stood for "Professional Security and Investigations," but Lombard had created them for their attractive resemblance to the impressive *CSI* initials with which the TV-viewing public was now so familiar. Lombard's business had nothing to do with forensic examinations, and neither Lombard nor McLean had even learned how to dust for fingerprints in their cop days, nor attended a single police seminar on hair or blood analysis. They were hopelessly out of their depth in any matter calling for technological savvy, and that included anything to do with computers.

Lombard pointed this out to McLean as they dined at his house Wednesday evening. Lombard had met with Tyler Rhodes the day before, but contract negotiations at a plant in Hendersonville had kept McLean out of town the day before, and then McLean had had to spend all day at the UNC-Asheville campus to make a losing bid on a contract there. This was their first opportunity to catch up, and it was also McLean's birthday.

Lombard was rarely a guest at the McLeans' and only accepted their invitation because it had been a spur-of-the-moment idea of Selena's and Lombard hadn't been ready with an excuse. Lombard knew Selena disliked her and only gave the invitation out of Selena's weird sense of duty. Apart from that chilly fact, visiting the McLean household gave Lombard a headache. The kids were cute, dark-haired, and olive-complexioned like their Cherokee mother, and Lombard liked them all right. But they were noisy and high-strung and got on her nerves. Lombard was halfway through her meal when six-year-old Hannah demanded to know why Lombard didn't have a husband.

"Shut up, Hannah!" shouted Sara McLean, a tall, slender 13-year-old with long hair she was constantly tossing over her shoulders. "You're so rude! It's none of your business why she isn't married."

"Can you have a baby if you're not married?" asked Maggie, the pudgy middle girl with a lisp.

"Of course you can have a baby if you're not married, you moron," said Sara.

"Watch how you talk to your sisters," said McLean.

"And stop bothering Loy," added Selena. "You're making her uncomfortable."

Lombard smiled tolerantly and recalled what her Aunt Anna Mae would have done if she'd behaved this way around a guest: She would have smacked the shit out of her.

Once dinner was over and Selena had taken the girls away for their baths, Lombard immediately turned the conversation to business, telling McLean all about the new girl, Dana, and why Retta had hired her. "We need our own Web site, like everybody else in the business has had for a long time," she said. "I'm frankly embarrassed it's taken us this long to find somebody who knows how to manage computers. Well, Retta's decent at it, but even she's been harping for months about finding somebody with real skill." She put her napkin on her plate and sipped iced tea. "Of course, we'll probably need to update the whole system, maybe even buy new computers. That's gonna cost us."

"Well, I have good news where money is concerned," McLean said. He filled Lombard in on his discussions with the management of the Skinner Movables plant in Hendersonville, which had yielded a new contract for their security guard services. Lombard was extremely pleased to hear that. Then McLean said, "I heard something even more interesting while I was at Skinner."

"What could be more interesting?" Lombard asked buoyantly. The new contract was worth $50,000 annually, and they were locked in for three years.

"Mr. Seth Agee is an assistant manager at the plant," said McLean. "He told me the past year at Skinner has involved strikes and layoffs, so the need for security is recent. They sought our business because they knew our name."

"So?"

"It was actually Seth Agee who sought us out. He heard about our involvement in the Natalie Wolf case, did some research, and called me. You see, he had information for us about the Natalie Wolf case."

Lombard chuckled. "Witnesses are crawling out of the woodwork in the wake of this lady's disappearance. So what's his information?"

"He told me about a Russian stripper he'd seen at a bachelor's party."

"A stripper?" said Lombard. "How did he know she was Russian?"

"He said she was Russian, and she had reddish or auburn hair, like the girl in the picture on TV. He wondered if she was the missing woman."

"How would he know if she's Russian?" Lombard wondered aloud. "Maybe she had a strong accent, and accents are unusual for strippers around here, I'd guess. And red or auburn hair stands out in people's minds." She eyed McLean. "Did she happen to tell them where she was from?"

McLean grinned. "I don't think anybody at that party interviewed her, actually."

"Did any of 'em fuck her?"

"I didn't ask." McLean glanced toward the hallway, as if to make sure none of the children were sneaking around. "Anyway, what does it matter?"

"It could make a difference where to look, if she was just dancing or if she was hooking. Sam, surely you asked for the name of the club or service she worked for."

"He said he didn't know," said McLean. Lombard started to speak, and McLean cut her off. "And I did ask *whose* party. And that's when he lied and said he didn't remember."

"Well," said Lombard, "looks like I'll be paying a courtesy call on the boys down at Skinner Movables. Agee is an assistant manager, correct?"

"Correct."

"What's the general manager's name again?"

"Tony Coburn. But I got the distinct idea Agee hadn't told him anything about the stripper. Agee acted like he wanted me to let him know anything we found out about her, but to leave his boss out of it."

"Hmm. I wonder if Mr. Coburn has recently married?"

McLean looked as though he'd had an epiphany. "Well, I suppose I could check this year's marriage licenses at the county courthouse and find out if any of the names in my list of Skinner Movables executives turns up."

"Check last year as well, just for good measure," Lombard suggested, just as Selena backed into the room carrying a heavy platter. "If Tony Coburn trusts Seth Agee enough to arrange a security contract for him—"

"Then it follows he'd trust him to set up his bachelor party." McLean nodded.

"Is there cake too?" Lombard asked.

At just that moment three screaming girls came barreling out of nowhere in their nightgowns, chanting, "Cake, cake, ice cream, cake, cake, ice cream, cake…"

CHAPTER 3

On Friday, Christine Campbell was supposed to arrive in Asheville just ahead of the remains of a tropical storm that had crashed into the Gulf Coast and swirled northeast through Florida, Georgia, and Tennessee before tumbling across the mountains into western North Carolina. About the time Chris said she would be driving out to Lombard's isolated bungalow south of town, however, Lombard was headed into Hendersonville for her 6:30 appointment with Tony Coburn.

McLean had discovered that morning, by reviewing records at the Henderson County Courthouse, a marriage license that had been granted in May of that year to Anthony Edward Coburn and Misty Dawn Tittsworth, both of Hendersonville. Further investigation had revealed the 45-year-old Coburn had finalized a protracted and expensive divorce the previous March, and that Misty had turned 21 in June.

Lombard had scheduled the appointment with Coburn late out of consideration of the new and lucrative contract with Skinner Movables, on whose behalf Coburn had been authorized to accept McLean's bid. Lombard had checked her copy of the contract and made double sure that it had been signed before the close of business on Tuesday. Skinner Movables had had three business days to back out, and then it was a done deal. It didn't matter how much she pissed off the general manager by bringing up his rendezvous with a potentially murdered stripper—who was probably the subject of a massive missing person's investigation—at his bachelor party, in the aftermath of a humiliating, public divorce trial that had robbed him of more than half of everything he owned, before lawyers fees. He couldn't back out of the contract now. It was after the close of business on Friday.

The deluge began just as Lombard parked her Pathfinder in front of the Skinner Movables plant office. She climbed over the seats and fished through all the crap she kept stored in back, finally finding her rain poncho but ultimately realizing that none of her three or four umbrellas was anywhere inside her vehicle. She heard thunder rumble overhead and made her move, grabbing her satchel, dashing out of the car with her poncho held above her head, making it to the front door of the plant office inside of a minute.

She climbed the wrought iron stairs inside the warehouse and found Coburn's second-floor office according to the directions he had given her over the phone. Drenched despite her best efforts, she shook out her rain poncho, patted back her rain-slicked hair, and knocked on Coburn's door. A weary voice told her to come inside.

He was not at all what she had expected. Tony Coburn was standing behind his desk, leaning back a bit as though to work out a muscle cramp in his lumbar region. He was a top-heavy fellow with short legs and a round belly. He had frizzy red hair with gray strands popping out all over, and a freckled face with puffy eyes. He was wearing nice slacks and a golf shirt, and seemed to be sizing up Lombard's appearance. She toned down her imposing frame with light, casual choices in clothing: One almost never saw her in anything but blue jeans or khakis, and in the summer she liked to wear cotton or linen shirts that buttoned down the front and either denim sneakers or sandals. She was a creature of comfort, not style.

"Are you Loy Lombard?" Coburn asked, arching his brow.

She nodded affably and held out her rain poncho. "Sorry. This thing's dripping all over," she said as Coburn took the poncho and hooked it onto a coat tree. "I know I look a sight," she said, "but that's a heck of a storm out there." She sat down in the chair he indicated, squishing a little as she moved.

"Yeah, well, we've needed the rain." He sat down behind his desk. "So you're Loy Lombard," he said softly, as though he had expected someone altogether different.

"Yes," she said. "Thank you for making the time. I wanted to introduce myself and offer you my personal guarantee that Lombard & McLean will provide the best in security services for your company."

He stared placidly at her for a moment, swiveling his chair slightly. "Well, I appreciate that. But of course, I wasn't the deal maker. I just sign the dotted lines." He stared at her for a few more awkward seconds. "Is that the only reason you wanted to see me, Ms. Lombard? To offer your personal guarantee?"

"Actually, no," she said. She opened her satchel and pulled out the photograph of Desmond Holliday and Natalie Wolf, and placed it on Coburn's desk. "Can you identify any of the people in this picture?" she asked.

He frowned at her and reached for the photograph. He glanced at it and said, "Nope. Why?"

"Well, it so happens Lombard & McLean is providing private investigation services in the Natalie Wolf case," she explained.

"Is that right?" Coburn smiled. "Seems like I heard you were on the case. So you're being awfully thorough interviewing everybody you know or have had dealings with, I take it. Scouring the region, right?"

Lombard brought her palms together in front of her face, prayerlike, and pressed her index fingers against her lips. She reflected like this for a split second and said, "No, it's not that simple. I actually needed to talk to you personally, Mr. Coburn."

He frowned again. "Why?"

"Look at that picture again. Do you recognize that woman?"

He looked again, a little longer but impatiently, and scooted the picture back across the desk. "No. Looks like a nice-looking lady and her date on a summer afternoon."

"Well, this is the thing," said Lombard. "This is a snapshot of Natalie Wolf, the missing woman. It appears that Mrs. Wolf—and please don't repeat this—but it appears she may have been pursuing a career in entertainment in the months before she disappeared. Have you ever heard the term 'private dancer'?" Lombard noticed the color leave Coburn's face. "These days, there's all kinds of ways of finding entertainment for parties and such. Take bachelor's parties, for example—"

"What the hell is going on here?" Coburn snapped.

Lombard shrugged and raised her hands out to her sides. "She was at your party, I believe: redhead with a Russian accent. Sound familiar?"

"I sure as hell don't know what you're talking about!" he sputtered, standing up. "I've had a long day. Come to think of it, I've had a long damn year, and I don't need this shit."

"Mr. Coburn, please don't get upset. It's very important you realize I'm trying to help you. That's why I came. The coincidence of the contract and finding out about Natalie Wolf's dancing business was too much not to warn you about."

He looked startled. "Warn me?"

"That's right. I just wanted to make you aware of it. The police know about it," she lied, "and I thought I had a duty to let you know. That's all there is to it."

Coburn sat down, and his arms fell limply on his desk as he slouched forward. "Well, I don't know anything about this missing girl," he said heavily. "My God, don't tell me the police are coming after me over some missing whore I didn't even want at my party. Jesus Christ! Why me? What have I done, Lord?"

"Now, don't panic, Mr. Coburn. Like I said, I'm here to help. Lombard & McLean is nothing if not staunchly loyal to our clients. I happen to be a close personal friend of the lead detective in this case, and I can throw him off bothering you with no problem."

"How?" Coburn whined. "Tell me how. I'll do anything."

"I just need to know the name of her escort service."

"I didn't hire her!" he shouted. "That bastard so-called friend of mine Seth Agee took care of it. He planned the whole goddamn party. I didn't even want one, not after all I'd been through. One little affair. One stupid little tumble and look what happens. Misty gets knocked up, my wife finds out about it, I lose every damn thing I own in the divorce. I could have just paid child support out the ass for the rest of my life, but no. I tried to do the right thing in the end, and I married Misty." His eyes welled up. "And just for fun, just because they're my friends, some local Chamber of Commerce boys decided to cheer me up right before the wedding. And Seth Agee hired that bitch, one more woman to ruin my life. One last kick in what's left of my balls!"

"So should I talk to Agee?" Lombard asked.

"No!" he barked. "No, I'll think of it. He told me where he got her, and it wasn't any local club, that's for sure." Coburn looked ready to have a stroke. Lombard was actually getting a bit worried she had gone too far with her utterly fictitious claims based on what was obviously correct speculation on her part. He said, "I'm thinking. Um, he said he found her on a Web site. This escort service—it wasn't local—I think it was in Miami. I know because he bragged about it. But they advertised they could provide girls anywhere in the southeastern U.S., I remember that."

"So Seth Agee hired her," said Lombard. "That's good to know. That'll certainly take the heat off you. But as soon as I know the name of that service, all the better."

Suddenly Coburn sat up straight. He cocked his head to one side and narrowed his eyes at Lombard. "Just a minute," he said. "You're investigating this case, meaning you want to find this girl, right?"

Lombard casually rolled her shoulders and steeled herself. He might be on to her. "Yes, of course. We all hope to find her safe and sound."

He stood up and pointed at her. "I'm too nervous to know anything for sure right now, but I think it's pretty odd you coming in here wanting to 'warn' me about stuff you're trying to find out anyhow. Don't you think it's pretty strange?"

"I can see how a worried man might take it that way, Mr. Coburn, but I assure you I have only the best interests of my client at heart. And that's a promise." She stood up, realizing she had gotten everything out of him she could. "Thanks for your time," she said, shaking his clammy, perspiring hand.

As she walked down the stairs to the front door, Lombard half expected to hear a gun blast and a thud. She hoped she hadn't added too much stress to the man's life. He wasn't all bad. At least he had tried to do the right thing.

Lombard hadn't seen Chris in a week, and despite her nagging suspicions about Chris's life in Hot Springs, she so looked forward to seeing her. Chris was a lot of fun, and she liked many of the things that were important to Lombard, not the least of which were food and sex. They always cooked when they spent time together. If things went well tonight, they'd whip up a bowl of pasta with chopped homegrown tomatoes and fresh basil from Lombard's garden and some good-quality mozzarella, all tossed in olive oil. Chris had promised to stop at Earth Fare for some decent fish, and Lombard had picked up a movie for them to watch. And who knew? Maybe they would actually make love for the first time in weeks.

The rain was steady by the time Lombard turned onto the road leading to her house, and dark clouds brought dusk down on the countryside a little sooner than usual for early September. Chris's Jeep, parked halfway in the yard, was a soothing sight, as was the warm glow of lights in the windows and Chris's mud-caked hiking boots deposited next to the front door. Lombard walked inside expecting to find Chris watching TV on the sofa and a paper package of fish on the kitchen countertop.

Petie the dog never barked at intruders, and in fact greeted Lombard warmly with a wagging tail and slobbering mouth. She liked the mutt despite his worthlessness as a guard dog. She looked around for Chris. The TV was turned on, and Chris clearly had been lounging on the sofa—as evidenced by a glass of lemonade with melting ice left on the coffee table and the empty cradle of the cordless phone. She heard murmuring in the direction of her bedroom and crept down the hallway to check it out. Petie followed her.

Chris was sitting in bed, leaning against the headboard with her knees drawn up. She was on the phone, listening with a look of wild amusement on her face. Lombard didn't mean to spy, but something about the way Chris was sitting in bed so casually and comfortably—the way her breasts were just barely sculpted underneath the soft cotton folds of her faded T-shirt, the way her terry-cloth shorts rode all the way up the tops of her curvy thighs, and even the way the pink polish of her toenails was chipping from daily grinding against her boots—made Lombard want to lean against the doorjamb and stare for a moment. The sight pushed back any second thoughts about her feelings for Chris. She really did adore her.

"That's terrible," Chris laughed. "I would never do that! What kind of person do you think I am?" She listened for a moment and laughed uproariously. "God, you're wicked. I don't even want to know you. Who are you?" She giggled.

Lombard coughed, and Chris nearly came out of her skin when she spotted her. "Loy, you scared the shit out me!" she gasped. "Oh, uh, nothing," she told her caller. "Shut up, Petie!" she shouted nervously when the dog began yapping. She spoke into the phone again. "Loy just got home. Look, we're about to fix supper, so I'll call you when I get back, OK? You have a good weekend. Mmm, bye." She clicked off the phone and bit her lower lip. "Hey," she cooed, stretching out her legs and patting the bedding. "Come here. I missed you."

Lombard sat on the edge of the bed and stared affectionately at

Chris for a moment before leaning over and kissing her. They kissed warmly for a few seconds, and Lombard shifted to lie down next to her, gliding a hand along one of Chris's hips as they kissed. Chris relaxed into the covers and moaned softly, parting her legs so that Lombard could gently stroke her. And just as Lombard began caressing her neck and Chris let go a deep, ecstatic sigh, Lombard pulled away and looked her dead in the eye. Chris opened her eyes and knitted her brow.

"What's going on?" Lombard asked.

"What do you mean?"

"I mean, who were you talking to?"

Chris looked mildly indignant. "I'm sorry. Is that a fair question? Do I ask you about every phone call you make?"

"You might if you caught me hiding in the bedroom with the living room phone, looking like I had a vibrator stuck between my legs." She pinched Chris's crotch.

"Ow!" Chris pursed her lips and pushed Lombard away. "Stop it." Her voice was shaking just to the point of crying. "That was such a mean thing to say," she said, her voice breaking.

Lombard sat next to her without touching. "Well," she repeated, "what's going on, Chris?"

"I'm not ready to talk about it," said Chris.

"You've got somebody new?"

"Nobody new." A tear crashed over Chris's cheek, and Lombard nodded.

"Nobody new," Lombard repeated. Her surprise showed. "Is it that Willa woman?"

Chris's eyes were fixed sullenly on the floor, and she said nothing. That Willa woman was Chris's ex-girlfriend. She owned a campground near Hot Springs as well as the pub where Chris's friends socialized every chance they got. Chris and Willa had been in a relationship for more than a year when Chris met Lombard and dumped Willa like a sack of hot coals. Lombard hadn't even known Willa existed until Chris stupidly brought Lombard to the pub on one of the few occasions Lombard made the trip to the sticks, and there had ensued what Tyler Rhodes would have called "a vulgar scene." Lombard had erred on the side of believing Chris when she swore there was nothing between her and Willa anymore. Apparently, there was now.

"You stay here," said Lombard. She got up.

"I'm sorry, Loy," said Chris, her cheeks streaked with tears. "I really am sorry." She looked confused. "Where are you going?"

"I'm going out," said Lombard. "I won't be back tonight. I don't want you heading back to the cabin, or Hot Springs, if that's where you're spending all your spare time now. The weather's bad, it's getting dark, and I don't like you driving by yourself at night. Even if you planned on leaving, do me the parting courtesy of sticking around here till morning." She gave Chris a last look. "But be gone early tomorrow. And don't ever call me. By now you ought to know how I am." She eyed the clueless, panting dog. "So long, Petie."

Maddie's Bar was usually hopping on Friday nights, but Lombard didn't hold that against it. She liked the club because it showcased good music—usually jazz and blues—and catered to a diverse crowd of women and men, blacks and whites, gays and straights. Maddie's was a long walk from Lombard's office, where she planned on spending the night once she had gotten suitably bombed.

"Lady," she called out to the blond bartender, "I would like another shot of your top-shelf bourbon, if you please."

The bartender was good-looking, and Lombard was checking her out. "I'm not sure if I'm a lady or not," said the bartender, reaching for a shot glass, "but you can certainly call me Stella."

"Stella Kowalski," Lombard smiled. "You should have left that son of a bitch a long time ago."

Stella smiled as she poured Lombard's bourbon. "*A Streetcar Named Desire*," she said. "And I didn't even major in theater."

"You look a little like Kim Hunter, come to think of it."

"Who's she?"

"You don't know who Kim Hunter is?" said Lombard, a little derisively. "She played Stella in the movie. Vivien Leigh was Blanche DuBois, and Marlon Brando was your husband."

"Oh, yeah, I remember now," said Stella, patting her taut exposed belly. "Only I'm not pregnant like *that* Stella was." She shoved the shot glass to Lombard.

"Clearly not." Lombard knocked back the shot and let the burn roll slowly down her throat.

"That was fast," said Stella. "Maybe you should give it a rest for a while."

"Don't start looking after me, toots," Lombard nearly belched. "I'll get plenty of rest later. Now, fix us a fresh one. Come to think of it, just swing a hose over this way."

"We don't hose whiskey at Maddie's Bar," Stella grinned.

"Oh, right. This is a *classy* joint," Lombard said, pitching her voice higher and lisping. She tapped the bar with her shot glass. "I'm waiting."

Stella shook her head. "For what? A ride home?"

"Ooh, sassy. What makes you think I don't have a ride?"

"You came in alone, and you've been sitting alone all night."

"That's because I can't go home again." Lombard giggled. "Get it? I can't go home again? Come on, Stella. Who wrote that? I'm bringing us back to Asheville."

Stella shrugged. "Search me."

Lombard beamed. "Now, *there's* an idea."

"Easy, tiger."

"You should be ashamed you don't know that one. The one great writer this prissy little pissant town ever produced, and you don't recognize the quote?"

"Nope!" Stella went after another bar patron's order.

Lombard slouched forward, resting her chin in her palm, eyeing Stella as she glided along the bar, taking orders and pouring drinks for half a dozen customers. Stella glanced at Lombard and shook her head, smiling. She pulled down a new shot glass, poured it full of bourbon, and slid it down the bar to Lombard. Lombard wagged her index finger at Stella. "Come here, Stella."

Stella said, "What could you possibly want now?"

"I'm lonesome, honey. I need somebody to talk to."

"You seem happy enough just staring at my ass from afar."

"It is a fine ass, yet it makes a poor substitute for your charming company."

"Does that line ever work?" Stella asked.

"Never tried it before. You tell me."

Stella scrunched her face and shook her head.

"Then I'll just settle for staring at your backside. Run along now." Lombard picked up her glass and circled it under her nose. "I do enjoy the touch, though I have never goosed a stranger." She finished the glass and folded her hands on the bar. "I need to go home, but I can't." Her merry demeanor faded, and she looked suddenly despondent.

Stella patted Lombard's hands. "I'll take you home, honey."

Lombard's eyes were glazed, and her husky voice had thinned out, but the smile was still devilish. "The name's Loy. And let's have a quick toast first."

Stella sighed. "To what, Loy?"

"Why, to the kindness of strangers!"

Stella drove Lombard to her office. She told Lombard she had to make it quick because her manager was covering for her until she got back. "OK, Loy, which building is it?"

"That woman was very disrespectful, letting you drive these dangerous roads by yourself at night," Lombard said sullenly.

"Loy, we're on Haywood."

"I'm aware what road my business is on." Lombard scowled outside her window. "It's that ugly pinklike building. We've got to find new offices."

Stella parked her Honda in front and said, "OK, hot stuff. You're gonna sleep it off here?"

Lombard smiled. "Not unless I get a better offer. Say, why don't you come back around when you get off?"

Stella let go a chuckle. "Loy, if I help you go inside, you're not going to try anything, promise?"

"Certainly not."

"As in you won't try anything, or you won't promise?"

Lombard opened her car door. "I can make it by myself."

"Whoa, hang on." Stella got out and went around to the passenger side and took a good look at the car parked next to hers. "That looks like Dana Gabriel's car," she said. She peered through the car's windshield. "Oh, my God! It *is* Dana's car!"

"Small town, Asheville," Lombard mumbled. "The plant supervisor fucked the missing Russian, and my bartender knows the new girl."

"Does Dana work here?"

"Not past midnight. I knew it. She's billing us for overtime."

Stella said, "How do I get you in there? It has to be locked at this hour."

Lombard held up a set of keys. After a confusing exchange about which key unlocked the front door, Stella snatched them and said, "Come on, sweetie. Let's go see Dana."

"You're not talking to an idiot," Lombard said irritably. "I'm just a drunken fool."

By the time they got inside Lombard was barely able to walk upright. The alcohol had peaked, and it was only a matter of a minute or two before she would pass out. "Where's the new girl?" Lombard asked. Retta's desk had obviously been occupied: The computer monitor was turned on, and there was a portable radio tuned to a Latin American music program on WNCW.

The toilet could be heard flushing from inside the lavatory, and Lombard said, "I have to get on back to my office, Stella. I don't want the new girl to see me this way."

The next morning two dreadful realizations came over Lombard the instant she awoke—on her back, mouth agape, tongue dry as cotton. No, she thought, make that three, and she was pretty sure there might be a fourth. First, she was awakening to the second-worst hangover of her life, the worst having been the hangover that followed her resignation from the Charlotte police department during the same week her longtime lover had left her. That, Lombard could vaguely console herself now, had been even worse. Second, she had lost Christine Campbell for good. She had booted her out, and it had been necessary. But now she would be lonesome again.

Third—and this was truly intolerable—she had to go to that hoity-toity party tonight at Desmond Holliday's. She had promised that lying Tyler Rhodes, and she had been unsuccessful in persuading McLean to go in her place. McLean wouldn't even go with her for moral support, telling her it was bad enough one of them had to look foolishly out of place. But one of them had to go nonetheless if Desmond Holliday—a potential confidant of Natalie Wolf's—was to be interviewed.

She didn't know how long she had lain on her back on sofa cushions, her face the picture of a gaping funeral mask, as she contemplated the fiasco that was her present life before she realized the fourth dreadful thought: She couldn't recall how she had gotten here, and she certainly didn't recall laying out sofa cushions on her floor. Perhaps it was that cute young bartender she had fantasized about every time the girl poured her a drink. Lombard recalled having resisted an urge to make a pass at her. At least she hoped she had resisted. It seemed like there had been a car ride with the girl. Oh, all right, she thought. The pretty blond bartender had gotten her to the office. God bless Maddie's, she thought. How very Louisiana of them, taking care of her this way, getting her drunk and getting her home.

She rose up very slowly, feeling as though her skull were about to blow to bits in every direction. Her head was a pressure cooker; she wondered how high the temperature of her brain had grown since Chris had broken her heart. Then she felt like a pussy for thinking of the words *broken* and *heart* in a phrase concerning herself. She was merely disappointed, she told herself. She had hoped for the best, and it hadn't worked out. But business was good, and for that, she thought weakly, she was grateful.

Suddenly she spotted something strange on her desk. On the corner nearest the sofa, where she had slept, there sat a jar of ibuprofen tablets. A note had been jotted down on a piece of paper weighted down by the bottle of water next to the jar. It read, "Take three of the pills and the whole bottle of water. Then go to Friedberg's Soul Food on Lexington for the chicken soup. You'll feel like a million bucks in no time. I swear to God. By the way, I wasn't working overtime. Retta wants me to monitor the guards—you know, radio duty—on Saturday nights till the last shift is over, so what am I supposed to do? Say no? I'm new here. Be well. Dana."

CHAPTER 4

Lombard arrived late at Holliday Hill. While she stood on the porch, keeping an eye on where a valet took her car, another valet lit a cigarette and asked her who she was. She told him she was nobody but that Tyler Rhodes had invited her anyway, and asked him if he knew where Rhodes could be found. The valet told her the party was in the garden and directed her to walk around to the back porch—as the house was closed off to guests—where she would see a large reddish tent and lights on the opposite side of a hedgerow.

The porch was a deep, wraparound double-decker: It brought to Lombard's mind the stately old houses of New Orleans's Garden District or Charleston's Rainbow Row, and Holliday clearly had the same thing in mind when he'd had it built. Lombard rounded the lower porch to the back and followed a stone footpath through an opening in the hedgerow. She intended to find Rhodes and get down to business right away.

That wouldn't be easy in this crowd. There were about two dozen tables underneath the maroon canopy: some round and others oblong; some high enough for the chairs in which guests sat nibbling hors d'oeuvres and sipping their drinks, others low and surrounded with ottomans or pillows. The fabric of the pillows and tablecloths was a kind of faux silk spun in vibrant burgundies, purples, oranges, and pinks. The guests were attended by young men and women wearing white caftans and sandals, and a small orchestra played on a nearby gazebo. All of that would have been well and good were it not for the 200 or so guests themselves. Lombard couldn't have put her finger on why if she were asked, but she knew their type: socially conscious, vapid, impressed only by wealth and position. Lombard looked around for a bar, and that's where she found Rhodes.

He was perched on a bar stool sporting a black muscle shirt and raw silk pleated trousers the color of merlot. Lombard had put on a pearl linen shift she kept stored in plastic for weddings and other warm-weather special occasions, and matching slippers she'd found at Target.

"You made it," he said ebulliently when she sidled up to the bar. "My God, you're wearing stockings." He grinned. "And I must say I approve of those shoes!"

"I found all of it at a flea market," she said, and ordered a glass of club soda.

Rhodes laughed. "Where's Sam?"

"He's not coming." She noticed Rhodes's frown. "Sorry. He made plans to be raked over hot coals tonight."

"Cute. It was sporting of you to show up, though. No doubt you'll want to get down to business immediately, but I'm afraid that might have to come later."

"I hope not too much later," she said. "I can only take so much of this before I'll need something stronger than soda." She looked around her. "So far, this bar's the only thing here I can relate to. Now, where's Holliday?"

Suddenly there was a flourish of music on the gazebo, and several people rose from their seats and began crowding the bandstand. A spotlight fell on a Steinway piano, and there sat Holliday, a slightly balding but handsome man with an infectious dimpled smile. He was one of those people whose facial looks hadn't changed much since infancy; one could easily tell he'd been a beautiful baby.

As cheers and murmurs tumbled through the night air, Rhodes told Lombard evenly, "Desmond Holliday is an invention, Loy." He grinned and waved at Holliday, who waved back. "His birth name was Desiré Pedroso, Desi to his friends both before and after he changed it to the more Anglo-friendly Holliday. Before he reinvented himself, he was a Cuban refugee trying to make a name for himself in design. He got decent business with new money and celebrities, but to get to the blue blood he was after, he knew he had to lose the Latin name. At first he began calling himself Desmond Peters, which, of course, sounds dreadful. So he rechristened himself with the name of the Miami design firm that had first employed him: Holiday Interiors. Desmond Holliday with the extra *l* in his name reached the clients he'd always wanted: old-money WASPs with connections in the northeast and Europe, along with all that other trash he'd been dealing with. As the climate for spending heated up in 1980s Miami, so did Desi Holliday's business. Then disaster struck."

"How so?" Lombard asked.

Rhodes lit a cigarette and grinned. "He had a bit of a snow party one night in 1989, at a nightclub owned by some unsavory organized-crime types. Anyway, Desi was caught in a very big sting. He ended up serving three years in federal prison."

"How long has he been in Asheville?"

"About five years. He was under house arrest in Atlanta after being released from the Georgia federal prison where he'd done his time. He says he came here because he was looking for a small, inconspicuous town, yet one arty and wealthy enough to deserve him. I suspect there's more to it than that."

"Like what?" said Lombard.

Desmond Holliday finished his piano solo, and his admiring guests roared their approval, broad grins and loud clapping all around. Rhodes lifted his wineglass to his lips and said, "Like maybe he's hiding. Oh, don't look at me like I know. I don't. Look around you. Everybody here is either rich or politically useful to Desi. He's been here less than five years, and he's won over everybody worth winning over." He swallowed and shook his head. "He's a virtuoso of self-promotion."

"Fine," Lombard said wearily. "Let's talk to the climber about Natalie Wolf."

Lombard waited while Rhodes went to fetch Holliday, who was surrounded by people vying for his attention. Straight men in ties, their Junior League wives, A-list lesbians, buff gay boys, bemused patricians, overdressed patrons of art and historic preservation, and politicians flashing newly bleached grins: Everybody wanted a piece of Desmond Holliday, or at least a snapshot of him touching them. Lombard wondered how long it would take Rhodes to pull them off Holliday long enough for an interview. She glanced at her watch, sucked the last drop of club soda off the last ice cube in her glass, and casually glanced around the bar.

A woman was sitting alone. At the moment Lombard spotted her, the woman slipped off her bar stool and half turned, as though to check out the commotion near the gazebo, where the orchestra had just launched into the birthday song while two men in chef hats wheeled out a three-tiered cake with sparklers stuck all around it. Everyone else sang Desmond Holliday a happy birthday, but Lombard couldn't take her eyes off the woman sitting a few feet away from her.

She looked like imported chic. Her suit was black and tapered at the waist, cutting a thin V down her chest and flaring at her narrow hips. She was tall and slender but with a little bit of stock. She had broad shoulders, and her hands and feet looked large for a woman. She had high cheekbones and narrow glacier-blue eyes, and her silky hair—pulled back in a very tight French braid—was buttercup-yellow. She was expressionless, watching the birthday tidings as one might wait for a traffic light to change.

Lombard was still staring when a voice startled her.

"I'm sorry. I just can't get through right now." It was Rhodes. He looked in the direction of Lombard's gaze. "Loy," he murmured in her ear, "if Attila notices you staring, she's liable to cut your throat."

"Attila's a man's name," Lombard murmured back.

Rhodes nodded. "Perhaps Attila is actually a man. One never knows these days."

"That's not a man. That's a woman," said Lombard. "That is, in point of fact, a five-alarm bull dyke." She finally tore her eyes away from Attila. "Is she another foreign friend of his, like Natalie?"

"She's nothing like Natalie."

"Fill me in."

Rhodes motioned Lombard to follow him and led her nearer the canopy. "Attila is Hungarian, an old friend of Desi's from his Florida days. She lives somewhere like South Beach. Anyway, she's visiting for his birthday."

"She doesn't seem to give a damn about his birthday. She looks bored stiff."

"I don't know," said Rhodes. "I only met her the other night. Desi had a hot tub party for a few boys and his boyish blond girlfriend over there, who had just arrived for her visit. Desi wanted her to feel welcome. She didn't have much to say, but I suppose she was tired from her flight." He yawned. "Here comes Desi now."

In contrast to his bright, beady eyes and baby face, Desmond Holliday was taller than Lombard, and his dark, thinning hair was gray at the temples. Rhodes introduced them and said, "Desi, I was just telling Ms. Lombard about that orgy we had in the garden a couple of nights ago."

Holliday chuckled through clamped teeth and regarded Lombard. "Did he say your name is Lombard? Where have I heard that name?"

"She's a private investigator," Rhodes said. He lit a brown cigarette and blew smoke out of one corner of his mouth. "She just showed up here, asking for you."

Holliday frowned. "Really? Why do you want to see me?"

Lombard said, "I'm looking for Natalie Wolf. I understand you reported her missing to the police."

Holliday paled slightly. "How did you know that?"

"I used to be a cop. I have a few friends in the local department. Word gets out."

"You have friends in the police?" he asked. "Yes, I did call them about Natalie." Jittery all of a sudden, Holliday asked Lombard and Rhodes to sit at an empty table, many of the partygoers having taken to the terrace for dancing. "I was concerned about her, and obviously for good reason."

"What made you concerned?"

"I had an appointment with her the Tuesday before last, and she didn't show up. I tried calling her cell and got no answer. I thought there must be something wrong."

"Why?"

Holliday looked away, as though distracted by the spectacle of dancers, though his gaze wandered beyond them. He shrugged. "I just had a bad feeling."

"A bad feeling," Lombard echoed. "Mr. Holliday—"

"Desi." He gave her a forced smile.

"Desi, when's the last time you saw her?"

"I'm not sure. I mean, I have seen her many times, but I don't recall the last."

"How did you get to know her?"

"She came to my design studio, as a customer."

"When?"

"Months ago. I'd have to look at my date book to trace all of our appointments."

"But you're worried about her, so I take it you became good friends?"

"Yes. That's true." He shrugged again. "Why else would I call the police?"

"Why did you become close? What was so special about her?"

"She's a refugee, like my family was. And she was so lovely and eager to fit in as an American, and she had a taste for the finer things. She appealed to me. And after a while, I realized, well…"

"That she was loaded," said Lombard.

"Well, not loaded, exactly. But she could afford nice things."

"And pay cash, right?" They smiled at each other. "Did she confide in you?"

"Yes." Suddenly his voice was energized, and he looked Lombard squarely in the eye. "She talked about her husband."

"Did you ever meet Abel Wolf?"

"No."

"What did she tell you about him? You obviously knew he had money."

Holliday sighed and eyed Rhodes. "Tyler, would you please put out that cigarette while you're sitting under my silk canopy? Or go out onto the terrace with it." He gave Lombard a worried look. "All I knew for certain was, she wanted to leave him, of course. She only married him to get to America. He's so repulsive. I've seen the pictures in the news, and now I understand more than ever why she felt compelled to get away from him. Can you imagine a beautiful woman wanting to stay with a man like him?"

"I don't know," said Lombard. "So did she find a boyfriend or not?"

"Not to my knowledge. I think she would have told me if she had a boyfriend."

Lombard kept a close watch on his eyes as he talked and decided to leave alone the subject of Natalie's possible double life. "So what did she tell you?"

He added, "That she wanted to leave her husband, and she was afraid to do it."

"Why?"

"Because he kept guns, and he was violent sometimes."

"He ever hit her?"

"She never said if he did. But I assure you of this: She was afraid of leaving him, and what he might do to her if she did."

Lombard looked puzzled. "What did she spend his money on? I've been to her house. It sure as hell doesn't look like anybody's spent money on interior decor."

"She didn't buy anything from me," he said. "And I never visited her house. Of course, I hoped I would be able to help her eventually…"

"Ah," said Lombard. "Perhaps after she left her husband. I have information she spent substantial periods of time away from home, perhaps in an apartment somewhere? Maybe one you helped her to furnish?"

"That is preposterous," said Holliday. "Where did you hear that? Whoever told you that is a liar." He cut Rhodes a incriminating eye.

"I haven't said a *damn* thing," said Rhodes, putting out his cigarette.

Lombard said, "Mr. Holliday, I know she spent days at a stretch away from home. You either know where she was during those times, or she didn't tell you everything."

"Well, then, she didn't tell me everything."

"For your sake, that had better be the truth. Because wherever she's hiding out, she's got my client's money. Helping her hide would make you an accessory after the fact, which is a serious matter, and a parole violation."

Holliday pitched Rhodes a scorching glare. "You son of a bitch!"

"He didn't tell me that," Lombard lied. "I got it from a friend at the department."

"Ms. Lombard, I would *not* abet a crime. I obviously want no part of any lawbreaking! Besides, I don't think she stole from Abel Wolf. I think he's hurt her. And if she did take his money, she deserves it for putting up with him for as long as she did."

Lombard avoided eye contact with Rhodes, who watched their dialogue keenly. "So, you were her close friend," she told Holliday. "You shared a common bond in your refugee pasts, and she was pretty and lonesome and rich. Right up your alley. And she confided her fears in you, which you're being very vague about." She waved her index finger at him. "But that's not all you're being vague about."

"You can think whatever you like," Holliday snipped. "I'm telling the truth."

"Mr. Holliday, if you hear from her, you'd better call the police. But if you've done anything as stupid as help her in any way, you'd better call me instead. I won't rat you out."

Holliday looked shaken. He got up, dusted off his jacket, and gave a pained smile. "I have other guests, Ms. Lombard. Please make yourself at home. Have a drink. Dance. Mingle." He excused himself and disappeared into his house.

"Well," Rhodes sighed, "he'll be a pill tonight."

"What the hell kind of relationship do you two have?" Lombard asked.

Rhodes waved her off. "Honey, you don't want to know."

She looked at the bar, but Attila wasn't among the dozen or so people crowding around it. She searched the terrace for her, but there was no sign of the Amazon blond. Lombard remembered Attila was a houseguest, and wondered if she were with Holliday right now.

The band had just launched into a rumba. Lombard looked at Rhodes. "You like to dance, Tyler?"

Rhodes looked surprised. "Are you asking me to dance?"

"Yeah. I learned how to rumba when I was a kid." She stood up and added, "But I lead."

"No problem!" Rhodes enthused. "By all means, dip me."

Sam McLean and Mike Church shared similar backgrounds: They both had families, and they both took a fairly conservative view of politics. But there were strong differences between them, and while McLean refused to oversimplify their essential incompatibility in the same way Lombard did—she said it boiled down to the simple fact McLean was a nice fellow and Church was a horse's ass—he knew it had more to do with opposing sensibilities. McLean was an intelligent, pragmatic person who happened to prefer a commonplace lifestyle. He enjoyed having a few beers every so often with some of the men he did business with, but he also liked being married; he liked going to church; he liked staying home in his spare time doing yard work and playing with the kids.

Church may have liked the same things, but on the few occasions he and McLean had socialized, he had made boorish remarks about extramarital sex and made tacky overtures to attractive female servers and bartenders. He claimed not to be a racist, but his speech was peppered with words like "wetback," "chink," and "tar baby" when talking about people of color. And his idea of tolerating homosexuality was to besiege Lombard with salty remarks about lesbian sex and to ask for her opinion on this or that girl's knockers. He was an asshole, in short, and McLean hated hanging out with him.

Around the time Lombard was supposed to be going to the party at Holliday Hill, McLean and Church were sitting at a table in the cantina of a popular Mexican restaurant on the Leicester Highway. McLean had accepted Church's invitation partly because it was the fifth or sixth time Church had asked him out for a beer, and partly because he wanted to tighten their relationship while the Wolf case was in progress. And the Wolf case was clearly on Church's mind as well.

"So Loy went out hobnobbing at that big queer party tonight," said Church.

McLean was pouring some draught from a pitcher. "That's right." He'd just told Church about the party but didn't mention how Lombard had found out about Desmond Holliday.

"So she found Dewey Holloway after all. Or Dickey. Hell, I forget."

"Desmond Holliday," McLean interjected.

Church snapped his fingers and pointed at McLean. "That's it. I wrote it down but never can remember it right." He chuckled. "Loy gave me a hell of a time about that guy. But she got the best of me in the end, since she's going to his party tonight. I guess she found him and won him over and, by God, showed me a thing or two, huh?" He sniffed and added, "Funny you didn't get an invite."

"I did," said McLean, "but I didn't want to go."

"I should think not." Church laughed. "I'd worry if you did."

McLean smiled and dragged a tortilla chip through a bowl of salsa. He shoved it into his mouth and crunched, eyeing his watch. "Mike, Loy's going to find out a lot tonight. You know how she is."

"Reckon she'll find her any poontang?" Church erupted in wheezing laughter.

McLean shook his head and smiled. "I doubt she's looking. I think she's more interested in information about the Wolf case."

"I'd be surprised if Loy passed up any opportunity to shake somebody down for all the information she can get out of them," said Church. "I know what you want, Sam, and so I'll tell you. That snotty fag called me out of the blue a week and a half ago and told me he was worried about Natalie Wolf being dead. If he hadn't called, I probably wouldn't know she existed. I heated up the case, put the pressure on the man he says was making her life hell, and then all of a sudden Holliday didn't have another thing to say to me. Tells me he's told me all he knows." Church's face became more inflamed as he talked. "What the hell is up with that?"

"You got me."

"Look, Sam, I told you that for a reason. I want to talk business, man to man." He smiled at McLean. "Of course, I respect you. I even respect your battle-ax partner. I've had every intention of cooperating as much as professionally possible, but you know how it is when you're just digging into a case, right? Sam, I need advice."

"Why?"

He sighed. "I got a call from a fellow named Seth Agee. Ring a bell?"

McLean nodded. "He's an assistant manager at one of our plants. Why?"

"He's in a panic."

"What for?"

"Y'all just signed a contract, right?"

McLean felt deeply distrustful all of a sudden. "Yeah, why?"

"Agee called to talk about a stripper he hired for a friend's bachelor party. He says the girl he hired had a thick Russian accent and looked like the missing girl we're looking for. He said he thought he had a duty to tell us, and he sounded nervous as hell. Swore up and down he didn't remember whose party it was—he's evidently the Hendersonville Chamber of Commerce's go-to man for go-go girls—and he had no idea who she was or even when exactly he found her, only that he got her from some online agency, but he no longer has the Web address. And he thinks that agency operated out of Florida, maybe Miami." Church threw up his hands. "Now, who the hell goes all the way to Florida for a stripper?"

McLean dreaded telling Lombard how far ahead of them Mike Church was. When McLean had asked, Agee hadn't said anything about hiring the woman, only that he'd seen her at the party. "They didn't hire a stripper," he said absently. "She's a hooker."

Church nodded. "That's what I thought. But he swore to God there wasn't any of that going on."

"Did he say anything else?"

"Only that you were the first man he talked to about it, and the more he thought about it, the more he thought he ought to call the proper authorities." Church took a swig of beer. "So what do you think, since you're already privy to Agee's story? Where do I start? Should I call the feds in on this? If I do, and there's no connection between Natalie Wolf and any interstate call-girl service, I'll look about as fucking stupid as it's possible for a cop to look. But if I let it go… Shit."

McLean said, "I'd need more information before I took his story to the feds."

Church grinned. "That's what I thought you'd say."

By midnight Lombard was at home in a nightshirt and slippers, feeling proud of herself for having gotten through a party without having even one drink and for having gotten useful information out of Holliday. She relished the thought of telling Church about her find. She filled a teakettle with water, flipped the gas switch on the stove, and set the kettle on the fire.

The temperamental September night sky was threatening another storm, and winds were whipping up. A chilly breeze whistled through the open kitchen window, and Lombard cranked it closed as rain began to patter against the glass. She opened the back door and hollered for her cat, feeling a little stupid to be calling out "Romeo, Romeo!" She'd actually named him after a stud tomcat she'd known in her youth, an enormous strutting yellow stray named and fed by a few of Aunt Anna Mae's neighbors.

Wind chimes on her screened-in back porch clanged and jingled wildly. The cocoa Romeo, a trifle wet and irritated, yowled as he ambled into the kitchen, and Lombard spooned out some canned food for him just as her teakettle whistled. When she had poured her tea, she doused it with a shot of bourbon, turned off all but the stove light, and sat in one of the deck chairs of her porch to take in the storm.

Storms had always evoked a strange feeling in Lombard, ever since her childhood. She both feared and enjoyed them. Ribbons of lightning spun across the sky, followed by cracks of thunder that seemed to be shattering it to pieces. The sound of groaning winds made the hair on her neck stand on end: She remembered as a child the Irish nuns telling her it was the sound of banshees coming for the doomed. How she had loved hearing those stories of horror even then. For by the time those nuns began instilling in her a taste for intrigue and mystery, Lombard had learned plenty about the dark side.

On a chilly, storm-soaked December night in 1967, Lombard's mother died. Nobody knew at what hour. Her body was found the morning after she had left her young daughter in the care of a baby-sitter. A vagrant netting trash out of Lake Pontchartrain discovered stalled out under the bridge overpass a Pontiac Bonneville, wherein lay the nude bodies of Lola Lombard and Paul Durand, still wrapped in a lovers' embrace. Apparently, Durand had unwittingly backed his car into the embankment and left the engine running for heat. Fumes had found no escape through the embedded exhaust pipes and seeped into the car while Lola and Durand made love. They had never seen death, swathed in carbon monoxide, coming at all. They had, in the coroner's opinion, merely fallen asleep as they lay together and eventually died from the odorless poison being consumed by their lungs.

It would be many years before Lombard would force her Aunt Anna Mae to tell her the whole story about her mother. Lola and Joe Lombard had married too young, about seven months prior to the birth of their only daughter. Joe had gotten a journeyman's job as a welder on an oil rig—a good job for a family man. He was gone for weeks on end, but he was young and impulsive, and by the time he came ashore to see his family, he spent most of his time carousing with his friends. Eventually Lola began seeing a union business agent named Paul Durand, whom Aunt Anna Mae would later describe as a tough guy with good looks and bad luck. She told Lombard her mother had always had lousy luck as well. They had been the wrong two people to tempt the fates, Anna Mae said.

Lombard didn't remember Durand, though Anna Mae said he often brought her toys and candy when he visited, never staying in the house long. Lola, by her daughter's vague memory and everyone's account, had been beautiful, and that was how Lombard would always remember her: On the last night of her life, wrapped in a shiny, fire engine–red parka with matching galoshes, blowing her daughter a kiss as she sauntered into a splashy, rumbling New Orleans night.

And tonight, in a wayward point of Buncombe County two miles outside the city limits of Asheville, near an embankment of the French Broad River, lay the seminude body of another young beauty, lithe and white, her auburn hair matted wet against her crushed brow, broken eye sockets gaping under an electric sky.

CHAPTER 5

Within a few minutes of arriving to work on Monday morning, McLean knew something was wrong with Lombard. She had obviously worked that weekend, based on all the new ideas she had about how to bring in more money. Lombard was in forced high spirits, sticking to business in everything she talked about. Apart from reviewing her interview of Tony Coburn on Friday and the relevant details of her visit to Desmond Holliday's, Lombard delivered a homily for McLean on why they should start working on a home security service, once they had worked out the Wolf case. She had spent much of Sunday afternoon researching the costs and benefits of getting into home security systems. She thought subcontracting for a national or regional alarm monitoring company might be worthwhile if they could find a couple of independent technicians to sign on as employees of Lombard & McLean.

McLean wasn't interested in her moneymaking schemes today, though, and he knew there must be trouble on the home front if she'd spent most of her weekend at the office when she had been looking forward to Chris's visit all the previous week. She hadn't pointedly expressed it like that, but Lombard had always had a way of suggesting her real feelings to him with little side remarks she made. All last week there had been this or that comment on the shopping that had to be done before Chris came to town on Friday, or what tasks needed to be out of the way so she could enjoy more time at home once Chris arrived. He also knew Lombard had planned on taking Chris to Desmond Holliday's party Saturday night, but throughout Lombard's account of the event she made it clear she had been alone. And she was full of that uncharacteristic cheerfulness that always meant she was avoiding some deeply disappointing reality.

So he humored her. "Did Holliday tell you anything about Natalie Wolf that might clear up what you learned from Tony Coburn?" he asked.

She grinned. "Don't you mean 'Dewey Holloway'? Mike Church is such an imbecile to think I wouldn't get to the bottom of that one." She propped her feet up on her desk. "Nothing Holliday told me suggested a secret double life for Natalie Wolf, and I didn't try to find out either. Because I'm not ready to believe the girl who serviced Coburn's bachelor party was Natalie at all."

"Why not?" McLean was surprised. "Even I think so, Loy. She had red hair and a thick accent. Abel looks to have been swindled. It fits. What are the chances of there being two redheaded Russian hustlers in greater Asheville?"

"We don't know they're both Russian. And stripping for the Hendersonville Chamber of Commerce doesn't fit the image I have of Natalie Wolf. She was on the make, yes. She was using Abel Wolf, spending his money on the sly, palling around with Holliday. I don't think she was an angel by any means. But from the sound of what Holliday told me—even though I'm sure he was holding back something—she was his Eliza Doolittle, his fair lady. A man like him wouldn't waste his time on a skank. She might fuck a guy for money, but that doesn't mean she'd entertain a roomful of catcalling rednecks."

McLean gave his head a quick shake. "Loy, are you trying to say prostitution can be classy? What's the difference between that and stripping for a living?"

"There's a big, wide berth between the two. Scheming to shake down one sucker for his money is one thing. Shaking your tail for a bunch of horny bastards is another. Natalie Wolf did the first thing. It doesn't necessarily follow that she did the latter."

"What about the Russian accent Seth Agee described?" McLean reminded her.

Lombard shrugged, a dismissive grimace tugging her lips. "There are a lot of Eastern European immigrants these days. Russians, Romanians, Yugoslavs…" She paused and added, "Hungarians. And North Carolina's not just a hick state anymore. Charlotte and Raleigh both have international airports. You can fly direct to Paris. We're on the East Coast and primed for worldly riffraff, and we're no doubt getting our share of it. I'd need more than a description of some redheaded whore with an accent to be convinced that a stripper at Coburn's bachelor party was Natalie Wolf."

McLean smiled tentatively. "What if Mike Church was convinced?"

"He can't even remember his own witnesses' names." Lombard gave him a wary look. "Why?"

McLean told her the whole scoop of Agee's revelations to Church. "So Mike knows all about the stripper. And Agee told Mike, not me, about hiring her."

Lombard's nose twitched. "So? I already knew that by talking to Coburn. And that's why Agee called the police, you can be certain. I bet Coburn pounded him for talking to you and made him give a full report." She paused and asked, "So what does Mike think? Is he going to follow up on it?"

"He doesn't know for sure. He's actually afraid to alert the FBI."

"Oh, on some theory of an interstate white-slave racket?" she smirked. "I hope he does. I sincerely hope he reports that to those federal jerks. While they conjecture about Natalie Wolf's connection to an elusive, anonymous, and wholly untraceable South Florida online whorehouse, I'll get to the bottom of this case. Fine with me."

"Interesting, though," said McLean, "that Desmond Holliday is from Miami."

"So what? Lots of people are from Florida. It's a heavily populated state, just a few hours' drive from where we're sitting. The state line, anyway. Even the new girl is from Florida. Her résumé says she was born in Homestead, which is the last mainland point before the Keys, I'm fairly certain."

McLean smiled at Lombard's stubbornness, but he could tell she was curious about the Florida coincidence.

Lombard confirmed his hunch. "I need to get that new girl online, speaking of. She's a computer whiz. Maybe she can find that online whorehouse."

"I thought you said you didn't believe Natalie was connected to it," said McLean, "and that it was 'wholly untraceable.'"

"I'm just being thorough," Lombard said.

McLean narrowed his eyes. "You sure talk about the new girl an awful lot."

Lombard casually slid her feet off her desk and sat up straight. She affixed her reading glasses to her nose and grabbed a scheduling chart Retta had left on her desk for approval. "I just make sure we get what we're paying for, you know? Like I said, I'm thorough."

Suddenly Retta's voice could be heard on the speaker of Lombard's desk phone, announcing that Gussie Wolf urgently needed to talk to Lombard. Lombard asked Retta to put her through and left the speaker on. Lombard told Mrs. Wolf her partner was sitting in her office, and introduced them by phone.

"Natalie's dead," said Mrs. Wolf.

Lombard and McLean looked at each other. "Where?" said Lombard. "How?"

"I don't know," Mrs. Wolf replied gruffly. "Well, we ain't even sure it's Natalie, but the policeman thinks it is."

"Which policeman?"

"That Mike Church fellow. The one Deputy Potter dragged into this mess. He called the house and said they had a body, and he said Abel ought to go down to the morgue and tell 'em for sure that it's Natalie."

"Why does he think it's Natalie?"

Mrs. Wolf's voice seemed to quaver a bit. "They say she's got the same look as Natalie—this dead girl, I mean." She paused. "And they found her not too far off from the farm. Well, right close by, to tell you the truth."

Lombard asked, "Where's Abel?"

"He just walked out the door," Mrs. Wolf replied. "He's on his way downtown, just like the police detective said to do, to look at Nat— at that dead woman. They want to talk to Abel. What now?"

Moments later Lombard was sprinting out to her car, with McLean in close pursuit. "Loy, calm down!" he said irritably. "What's got into you?"

"That asshole is not going to get away with this," she panted, clicking her remote key to unlock the doors of her Pathfinder. "Get in," she said.

"Who are you talking about? Where are we going?"

"I'm talking about Mike Church, is who," she said as they both climbed into the car. "And we're going to get Tyler Rhodes, and we're going to the morgue. We have just enough time, given that Abel will take awhile driving into town."

"Why do we need Rhodes?" McLean asked as Lombard pulled quickly out onto Haywood.

She asked McLean where Rhodes's office was—McLean had visited it once, during the Slade investigation—and asked him to call ahead, and told him what to say. She prayed that smug, imperturbable playboy actually ventured into his office, at least on Monday mornings.

This particular morning was a languid, beautiful harbinger of autumn. A banner-blue sky hung over the town; the air light, fresh, and crisp as a first kiss. Rhodes was standing outside his front door waiting for them by the time Lombard pulled up curbside. He smiled vividly when he saw McLean. "What a pleasant morning this has turned out to be," he said as he climbed into the backseat.

Lombard waited until he was belted in and they were in drive before she told him the truth, not what she had made McLean tell him on the phone a few minutes before—that they wanted to have coffee and pastries with him at the Old Europe café. Lombard had wickedly used McLean as bait, and the Old Europe—with its promise of fresh, hot brioche and flavorful coffee, served on quaint sidewalk café tables on a gorgeous morning like this. She almost wished it were true.

"I need a favor," Lombard said.

Rhodes was leaning in between the front seats. "Sure, Loy." He smiled at McLean. "How are you, Sam? Long time, no see. We missed you at the party on Saturday." McLean regarded Rhodes with a genial, closed-lipped smile. Rhodes glanced out the window. "Hey," he said, "we're driving away from the café. I thought we were going to sit outside for beignets and coffee."

"Who said anything about beignets?" said Lombard. "They don't make beignets at the Old Europe."

"Yes, they do."

"No, they don't."

"Yes, they do," Rhodes insisted. "I'm positive I've had beignets at the Old Europe." He looked petulant. "Why do I have the odd feeling I've been kidnapped?"

"You have," said Lombard. "Abel Wolf needs a lawyer."

"He can't afford me," Rhodes said smugly. "What sort of trouble has old Abel gotten himself into?"

"You know good and well what kind of trouble," Lombard snapped.

McLean interjected, "Abel's on his way to the morgue to view the body of a dead woman discovered early this morning. According to his mother, the police suspect it's Natalie Wolf."

Rhodes was filing his nails. "Well, unless there's some actionable environmental issue involving the willful introduction of a decaying corpse into public lands or waterways, I'm afraid I can't be of much use to him." He put his file away and pulled out a case of Altoids. "Mint?"

"Tyler, we just need you to playact at being Abel's lawyer," said Lombard. "We'll pay you whatever your hourly rate is."

"I don't know a thing about criminal law," Rhodes insisted. "You're making a mistake. We could all get in trouble, especially me. I could lose my license over something like this. Besides, I don't need the money."

Abel Wolf was sitting in a waiting area when Lombard, McLean, and Rhodes loudly spilled into the lobby of the Buncombe County Medical Examiner's Office. He was dressed as Lombard had seen him at their first meeting, in clean but cheap, light-blue jeans and a stiff flannel shirt. His comb-over was neater than she remembered it, and his bespectacled eyes seemed to be gazing into oblivion.

Church was standing near a swinging door, talking to a uniformed police officer. He glanced in their direction, surprise evident in his eyes. "Well, look who's here!" he said in a voice edged with equal measures of cheer and dismay.

"Hello, Mike," Lombard said, all chipper. "I see Abel's on time to view the body you called him about this morning."

"That's right," said Church. "Just Abel, that is. I was just about to bring him on back, where the forensic pathologist is waiting. I'm sure you all won't mind waiting out here."

Lombard looked beseechingly at Rhodes. She hoped she had persuaded him to follow through. Rhodes glanced back at her, looking bored, utterly ambivalent about being there. He cut his eyes in Abel Wolf's direction, and a look of pure disgust flashed across his face.

But only for a second. He immediately addressed Church. "I'm sorry," Rhodes said pleasantly, "but I don't believe we've met, Lieutenant Church. I'm Tyler Rhodes, Abel Wolf's attorney."

Church looked startled. "A lawyer? Abel doesn't have a lawyer. I asked him."

"Poor Mr. Wolf has been rather forgetful in his worried state," said Rhodes. "I was just retained this morning. Therefore, I am advising Mr. Wolf not to assist you in identifying the corpse you recently discovered, nor in providing any further statements with regard to the disappearance of Natalie Wolf, or any other issue the state or county is investigating." Rhodes smiled. "Do I make myself clear, Lieutenant?"

Church's complexion darkened. His jaw was set, and his narrow eyes were burning. "Who paid your fee?" he asked, cutting a glare at Lombard.

Rhodes said, "Lieutenant, I'm terribly sorry. I don't see how that concerns you." He glanced at his watch. "I suppose we could work something out. If you let me and Ms. Lombard and Mr. McLean accompany Mr. Wolf in the identification process, I'd be more than happy to recommend that he assist in that regard." He looked squarely at Church. "But no questions for Mr. Wolf."

Fredericka Sanger was the Western Regional medical examiner. She was a Duke medical school graduate and had a Ph.D. in linguistics from the University of North Carolina, which she had obtained in middle age. She was also an expert fly fisherman, and had—with the help of one of her sons—written a manual on navigating glider aircraft. She was an attractive woman in her late 50s, of average height, slender, with close-cropped white hair and a firm, chiseled jaw.

Lombard worshiped her immediately, and patiently listened to Dr. Sanger's animated chatter about her passion for mountaineering as she and her assistant wheeled the body into the examining room where the others were waiting. McLean engaged Church in conversation while Rhodes quietly advised Abel Wolf to keep his mouth shut unless spoken to and to limit his answers to "yes" or "no," and then only after Rhodes nodded for him to respond.

"Although the police believe she was shot at the site where her body was found, I have my doubts." Dr. Sanger looked at Lombard. "There's a lot in the way of missing facial bones and tissue, leading

me to conclude she was killed somewhere else and dragged there."
She eyed Abel. "You're Mr. Wolf?"

Abel was wide-eyed, staring down at the gurney on which a human form rested underneath a plain blue sheet. He didn't look up when Dr. Sanger spoke to him—only nodded his head in apparent anticipation of seeing the corpse.

Lombard glanced at Rhodes. He looked disgusted, though at what Lombard could only have guessed. She caught his eye and smirked at him. He parted his lips to draw in a breath, pulled a handkerchief from his vest pocket, and gently raised it to cover his nostrils. Then he rolled his eyes in Abel's direction and shook his head.

Dr. Sanger said, "As a warning, she was shot in the face, and the body is in an advanced state of decomposition."

Church said, "Dr. Sanger estimates the death to have occurred sometime late Friday night or early Saturday morning, which would be more than a week after Natalie Wolf's disappearance." He eyed Abel and added, "After the theft complaint was made by Mr. Wolf. After he hired a PI to track her down. And the body was found in the Apple Creek RV Park."

"Where's that?" McLean asked.

"Next door to Wolf Branch Farm," said Church.

Dr. Sanger stood on the side of the gurney opposite the others and pulled the sheet lengthwise to reveal the whole body. "She was found partially nude," Dr. Sanger hastened to add. "We cut off the panties and a bra. No other clothes, and she was barefoot."

Lombard had seen a lot of dead bodies in her days as a police investigator, but she had never gotten used to the repugnant odor of decomposing human flesh. This body had not yet withered: It was still readily distinguishable as female, though the face had been annihilated, and elsewhere the skin had turned a bluish-gray with spots of black decay breaking out all over. What little hair still clung to the remnants of skull was matted and soiled and devoid of color.

Abel's eyes were wide around, his mouth hanging open. He

looked less shocked than excited, like a kid ogling a dirty magazine. He made a disconcerting spectacle of himself as he looked over the entire body as though he found the whole thing fascinating. Everyone else glanced at each other and the floor. It was disturbing.

"I can't tell if it's her or not," he said suddenly. He looked eagerly at Dr. Sanger. "Flip her over."

"Goddamn it," Church said disgustedly. "What's the use of that? Think you might recognize her by the size of her ass?"

"Well, I can't tell by the face," Abel replied, not in the least perturbed by Church's scathing tone. "Look, it's all smashed in. How could I?"

Lombard took a deep breath and looked up at the ceiling, praying the idiot didn't say anything incriminating.

Dr. Sanger called for her assistant to help her turn the body. Rather than turning it all the way over, they used straps to pull it up on its side. Dr. Sanger looked at Abel from across the gurney, as though she knew why he wanted a look at the backside. "See anything, Mr. Wolf?" she asked.

Lombard noticed it right away. She looked expectantly at Abel, who pointed to the area between the shoulder blades. His voice suddenly trembled, and his eyes flooded with tears. "There. That's her. That's Natalie." He cried out, breaking into piteous sobs, "That's her blue scorpion!"

Lombard had decided Abel Wolf was in no condition to drive himself home, and was at the wheel of his pickup truck while he sat despondently by her side. McLean followed in her Pathfinder, with Rhodes happily accompanying him. "Jesus," Rhodes said, "I almost got choked up back there, didn't you, Sam? It really was very affecting. That poor fellow seemed genuinely grief-stricken."

"He was pretty broken up," McLean agreed.

"But he did act very strangely before he spotted that tattoo," said

Rhodes. "He seemed almost depraved in his enthusiasm to look over this dead, rotting body." He shuddered exaggeratedly. "For a minute there I thought he was fantasizing something really sick."

McLean sighed. "Yeah, that was pretty weird."

They passed through the gate of a split-rail fence surrounding the Wolf farm and drove through a poplar grove to the rambling, plain white farmhouse Abel shared with his mother. McLean watched sympathetically as Abel lumbered out the passenger door of his own truck. Gussie Wolf came outside as he stepped onto the front porch, escorted by Lombard, and began talking to them.

"Can you hear what they're saying?" Rhodes asked.

"No." McLean noticed Mrs. Wolf's expression harden as Lombard spoke to her. Lombard patted Abel on his back as she spoke and put her arm around his shoulders as he began shaking. When he began crying again, Mrs. Wolf drew her lips in a fierce scowl and barked something at him. He seemed to stumble a bit, and Lombard tightened her grip around him and shouted back at Mrs. Wolf.

"Is Loy actually comforting him?" Rhodes asked incredulously. "She seems positively maternal right now."

"She always feels sorry for grieving people," said McLean.

"Mrs. Wolf doesn't seem the least bit grieving," Rhodes observed. "Look at her and Loy. They're yelling at each other. Let's roll down the windows and listen."

McLean ignored Rhodes. Abel walked through the front door as Mrs. Wolf stood by, holding the screen open for him, though she was pointing at Lombard and seemed to be laying down the law. Lombard was facing away from the Pathfinder with her hands on her hips, though McLean noticed her profile as she turned her head to one side and looked down at the ground with a stony expression. She looked up again when Mrs. Wolf stomped inside the house, and the screen door clapped shut right ahead of Mrs. Wolf slamming the front door. Lombard walked back to the car.

"I'll ride in the back," McLean said hastily. He jumped out and gave Lombard the driver's seat, and climbed in back. "What were y'all yelling about?" he asked as she turned around in the driveway.

"I wasn't yelling. She was," said Lombard. "She's a battle-ax, that old broad is."

"That's what Mike Church calls you," said McLean.

"Not like that old bitch. She berated Abel over grieving for his dead wife, even after I described the shape Natalie was in when he had to ID her." Lombard casually described the confrontation. "She told him he'd been taken in by a thieving whore, and she wished she knew who'd killed Natalie so she could reward him. Then she called Abel a blubbering sissy and told him to get his ass in the house, and for me to get the hell off her land if I was going to take up for him." She paused and pulled out onto the main highway. "She's about the most cold-blooded hellion I've ever met, and God knows I've met a few."

McLean was leaning in between the front seats, just as Rhodes had done earlier. "So Mrs. Wolf is glad Natalie's dead. That makes the puzzle a little more interesting, though I suppose we're off the case now that she's been murdered. Our job was to find her alive."

"Actually," said Lombard, "while she was cussing me, Gussie Wolf said we're not off the hook. She wants us to find the money Natalie took."

"Good God, Loy," Rhodes piped in, "if Natalie has only been dead for a couple of days, like Dr. Sanger said, then she was alive for quite some time after her disappearance."

"Ten days," said Lombard.

"What if old Mrs. Wolf tracked her down and shot her? Wouldn't that be just perfectly Shakespearean?"

Lombard blew a deep breath through pursed lips, signaling McLean to shut Rhodes up. "Loy," McLean began, "I think, at this point, we need to talk to Abel about hiring a lawyer for real. I have to admit the same thought occurred to me as what Tyler just said. I think Mike's gonna be all over Abel Wolf now, especially since the body was found so close to the Wolf farm."

"Well, I've had all the criminal practice I care to with this little escapade," said Rhodes.

"I'll call Sig Mashburn when we get back to the office," McLean offered.

"Yes," said Rhodes, "Sig Mashburn is an ace criminal defense lawyer, if you're into that good-old-boy country lawyer schtick."

"Oh, my God," Lombard muttered, "not Mashburn again."

"Oh, come on, Loy," said McLean. "We know him, and he's one of the best lawyers in the state. I'll call Mashburn, and you talk to Abel about it, OK?"

Lombard's eyes stared straight ahead at the road. She was very quiet and looked to be deep in troubled thought.

After a few silent minutes they approached the Asheville city limits. Rhodes asked brightly, "Can we go to the Old Europe now?"

Lombard was sitting in McLean's office while he spoke to Mashburn on the phone. She hoped Mashburn wouldn't be interested in the case, but she knew better. The Wolf case was the hottest thing since Jasper Slade, and, not coincidentally but by design, Mashburn was being handed the chance to follow up his infamous representation of Jasper Slade with that of Abel Wolf. He loved the spotlight and would jump at the chance.

Lombard thought of Mashburn as a vain, arrogant, greedy, sexist boob. His only redeeming qualities were his charm and wit, and a grudging but reliable sportsmanship. Lombard never wanted to see him again after enduring his bullying and interfering all through the Slade case, but even she had to admit Abel Wolf would be hard-pressed to find a better lawyer.

McLean hung up the phone. "He hedged at first, said he had to check his calendar for all his out-of-town conferences and speaking engagements." He grinned. "He dropped a few big names, mentioned an appearance here and one there, and then decided he could do it if they cough up the money. But there's one hitch."

"What?" said Lombard.

"Abel has to call him. He can't call Abel. It's against ethics."

"Fine. I'll talk to Abel about it tomorrow, after he's had a chance to rest. I'll have to sell Gussie Wolf on it too, you know," she added uncertainly, "but I'll tell her she's as much in need of counsel as her son." Lombard slumped in her chair. "I wish I still smoked."

"I'll see if there's an autopsy report tomorrow," said McLean. "And Mike promised to talk to me about ballistics tests."

"Ballistics? Based on what?"

"I don't know yet, but Mike says ballistics proof was found at the scene. He's hinting in a big way that we're wasting our time on this case."

"Sanger didn't mention anything being found on the body. Surely it was dumped after being shot somewhere else. Seems like somebody would have heard gunfire. Those RV parks have campers around the clock this time of year."

"I don't know," McLean said. "I have to wait and see what Mike says."

"I hate depending on that bastard."

"Well, that bastard doesn't have to talk to us," McLean reminded her. "I think it's right nice of him to give me the time of day, after that stunt we pulled with Tyler Rhodes."

"He must want something from us, then."

"Always," said McLean. "Just like we always want something from him."

Around 6 o'clock, as she was preparing to go home, Lombard realized she'd misplaced her cell phone. It wasn't in her shoulder bag, where she always stored it unless she had it out in the car. She looked around in the Pathfinder and didn't find it there either. She retraced the past several hours in her mind and realized the last time she'd had it out had been at the Old Europe café, where she and McLean had ended up with Rhodes after all his cajoling and pouting about it. It had been the least they could do, since he refused to take any kind of payment for stepping in to help Abel

Wolf avoid police questioning. Still, he had kept them there for more than an hour, holding forth on his radical worldview, until Lombard had to excuse herself to another table to call Retta and let her know they were running late. She'd probably set the phone on the table and forgotten to pick it back up when they left.

So she stopped by the Old Europe on her way home, hoping employees had found the phone and put it aside for her. She parked on the street, hurried into the café, and asked. As she waited for the server to check on it, she let her eyes wander, and when she looked through the open door to the outdoor café, she lost all thought of her cell phone. Lombard couldn't believe she hadn't noticed her on the way in. There, in as clichéd a spot as a café named the Old Europe, sat Desmond Holliday's mysterious Hungarian visitor, Attila.

Lombard quickly ordered a cup of coffee and went outside. She sat at an unoccupied table next to Attila, who was alone and apparently unaware or uncaring of anybody else's attention. She was sitting up with her legs crossed, taking in the fresh mountain air. She had on a long-sleeved crimson knit shirt and bone hemp slacks. Her blond hair was pulled back in the same severe French braid, and apart from her diamond earrings, the only striking thing about her was her large, glossy black sunglasses. She was sitting more or less facing Lombard, and might have been looking just past her without noticing her or might have been staring her dead in the eye. She raised a glass of red wine to her lips, took a sip, set the glass on her table, and startled Lombard when she abruptly spoke up. "Have I met you before?"

Lombard felt warm all of a sudden. Pretending to be distracted, she replied, "Um, no, I don't think so."

"I'm sure I've seen you before," Attila said. Her voice was a soft, velvety contralto, slightly accented. "Are you a friend of Desmond's?"

"Oh." Lombard smiled and affected a sudden realization. "You must have seen me at Desmond Holliday's party Saturday. But we didn't meet. I'm Loy Lombard."

Her face perfectly serene beneath her jet-black shades, Attila said nothing for a few seconds. Lombard found it difficult to look at her, what with her sunglasses concealing her eyes, and Lombard hated not being able to read somebody's eyes. She felt like she was the one being examined for a change, and she kind of liked it.

The server appeared with Lombard's coffee and her cell phone, which someone on the earlier shift had placed in the lost-and-found box. Lombard put the phone in her shoulder bag. "So," she said awkwardly, "I wasn't there as a guest, exactly."

"Really?" Attila slightly trilled her *r*. "I remember you now. You came alone."

Lombard resisted smiling. So Attila had noticed her. How flattering. "What's your name, if you don't mind?" she asked.

"Attila."

"Hmm. Isn't that a man's name?"

"Yes, it is." Attila smiled for the first time. "Attila is my last name. My first name is Mari. But I find I get more accomplished using my surname." She sipped some wine again. "I get tired of explaining my name, but with you I don't mind."

Now, this was out-and-out flirting, Lombard decided. And it was working. She was surprised at how charming she found Attila. She had always preferred soft, feminine women, and not much about Attila was either. In fact, sizing her up, Lombard thought Attila could best her in a fight. Maybe.

"So if you weren't Desmond's guest, exactly," said Attila, "what were you doing at his party, all by yourself?"

"Trying to find a missing person."

"That sounds interesting. Are you a police inspector?"

"No, I'm a private inspector, so to speak."

Attila slowly removed her sunglasses and set them on the table. She stared at Lombard. "Who are you trying to find?"

"Nobody, anymore." Lombard took a drink of coffee. "The person I was looking for is dead."

Attila's brow creased. "How tragic."

"Didn't Desmond tell you about his missing girlfriend?" Lombard asked.

Attila shook her head. "Why would he?"

Why indeed, thought Lombard, realizing that Attila hadn't mentioned being a houseguest of Desmond Holliday's. And Lombard didn't want to betray having noticed her before today. "I don't know. I thought maybe you were a good friend of Desmond's since you were at his party."

"Hundreds were there. They can't all be good friends." Attila reached into a thin black clutch and withdrew some cash. She set it on the table and said, "But I'm staying at Desmond's house, just while I'm in town."

"If you're staying at his house, you must be a pretty good friend."

Attila didn't look at her. "We have a mutual friend. That's all."

"Well, expect him to be upset when you get home," said Lombard. "News of her death will be all over TV right about now."

"In that case, maybe I'll stay out longer," Attila said as she got up. "I dislike places of mourning." She looked at Lombard again and said, "I'm not sure how much longer I'll be in town, but perhaps we'll see each other again." She abruptly turned around and walked away.

Lombard watched Attila's tall, angular frame disappear around a corner. A strange feeling came over her. She couldn't pinpoint why, but she knew Attila had been lying to her, and she knew she would see her again.

CHAPTER 6

The Wolfs were each sitting in their respective vinyl reclining chairs in the den, which looked to have at one time been an old-fashioned, roomy kitchen pantry. Lombard was sitting uncomfortably on the edge of a third reclining chair Mrs. Wolf had referred to as "Natalie's chair" when she offered Lombard a seat. Then she'd grumbled about how much adding a third recliner had cost them just so Natalie could sit with them and watch TV. The old room smelled of tobacco—Abel Wolf was a cigar fancier—and the hickory of its creaking hardwood floor. A mantel clock ticked away the seconds and chimed every quarter hour. It would have made a quaint setting were it not for the gargantuan big-screen TV crammed into a corner, swallowing up a quarter of the space. With that and its three overstuffed recliners, the cramped room was one of the weirdest Lombard had ever seen.

In the flurry of news reports since the previous day, it had quickly emerged that Natalie Wolf's body had been found in an RV park abutting Wolf Branch Farm. If the pressure on Abel Wolf had been difficult prior to his wife's body being found, in the aftermath it was unendurable. Lombard found it fairly easy to persuade the Wolfs to get a lawyer. Even Gussie Wolf had turned grimly quiet in the day since she had ordered Lombard off her land, and nodded her head compliantly with every offer of a reason why a lawyer had become necessary. Lombard told them to expect things to get a lot worse before they got better; based on her experience as a police detective, the investigation into any possible role the Wolfs might have played in Natalie's death was just gaining steam.

"They won't find anything on us," Mrs. Wolf said.

"Good," said Lombard. "Because if they find one thing linking you or Abel to Natalie's death, you can count on charges."

"If there ain't any charges yet," Mrs. Wolf asked, "how come we need to hire that lawyer?"

Lombard snapped her fingers. "Listen up, Gussie. You need to put Sig Mashburn between yourselves and the police. You need that buffer. They'll have to go through him to talk to you if you so much as mention his name. Same goes for the news media. They'll bother him instead of you. Even if there are no charges, hiring Mashburn will at least buy you a little bit of peace for a while."

"He'll cost a pile, won't he?" Mrs. Wolf frowned.

"Yeah." Lombard sighed. "That reminds me. I'm quitting your case, Gussie, nothing personal. Chances are, I'm not going to find the money she took, and frankly, I'm not the least bit interested in finding it since she's turned up dead." Lombard reached into her shoulder bag and pulled out an envelope. She handed it to Mrs. Wolf. "It's a check for the amount of cash you gave me, minus the few hours of work Sam and I put into it. Also, you'll find a termination agreement. Look it over, and if you're satisfied with the amount in the check, sign the form for my records."

Mrs. Wolf ignored the envelope. "How much will that lawyer cost us?"

"A lot more than this, even if no charges are filed." Lombard set the envelope on the footrest of Mrs. Wolf's recliner. "You'll notice I threw in a few expenses, but I didn't charge gas mileage since what little travel was involved covered business I had anyway."

Mrs. Wolf didn't seem to hear Lombard's last sentence. "And if charges are filed? How much will he cost us then?"

Lombard shrugged. "Call him and ask."

Mrs. Wolf gave Lombard a stern look and eyed the envelope. She bent forward and picked it up. She opened it, removed the check, and ripped it in quarters. "I'll tell you when to quit this case, lady. You look after Abel and me and find out what happened." She crumpled the termination form and pitched it into a wastebasket.

Lombard was not relieved in the least. She had shown up intent on passing command of this sinking ship to Sig Mashburn. She was deeply suspicious of the Wolfs and didn't fault public opinion for its judgment of them. Natalie Wolf had disappeared with Abel's money, had been the target of a criminal warrant he'd sworn against her, and her body had been found within a mile of the house they'd shared together. Lombard got a headache when she tried to think of some way to distance the Wolfs from Natalie's fate. She wanted out. "Gussie, I can't help you," she said.

Mrs. Wolf glanced at Abel, reclining in his easy chair with his eyes fixed on a blank TV screen. "What do you think, Abel?"

Abel raised his eyebrows and said, "I'll go along with whatever you decide, Mother."

"I say we give her a cut, then."

Lombard was taken aback. "Gussie, there's no way."

"Ten percent of that 200 grand, if you find it," said Mrs. Wolf. "And if you don't, you keep the 5,000 I already paid and bill me for overtime. I know you'll look for it, Loy Lombard. You want to work this murder case, but you're afraid Abel or me had something to do with it. Well, there's my offer. Surely you ain't so high and mighty you won't take a chance on our innocence for 20,000 bucks. It's the only chance I've got of getting my money back." Mrs. Wolf began chuckling. "Besides, sounds like I'll need it to pay the damned lawyer to keep us out of jail."

Sam McLean kept his appointment with Mike Church despite what Lombard had announced that morning: They were getting off the case. She had calculated the number of hours they had spent working on the case, multiplied them by 150, and deducted the amount from $5,000 before sitting down at Retta's desk to write a check to Gussie Wolf. She'd said she was on her way to Wolf Branch Farm to give them their money, put them in touch with Sig Mashburn, and wash her hands of them once and for all.

She'd seemed resolute, but McLean would believe her when and if she came back to the office with a signed termination agreement. In the meantime, he had an appointment to keep, and based on what he was finding out, he hoped Lombard had succeeded in withdrawing from the case.

Church showed McLean a photograph. "We downloaded this picture off an e-mail sent to us from an FBI agent in Raleigh." The photograph showed a gun lying on a white cloth. "It's a 1938 Luger with an extended barrel. Beautiful piece of German weaponry, hard to find in good condition, let alone firing condition. Very rare."

"Who owns it?" McLean asked.

"This particular model belongs to the agent. I found his name registered to it and asked him to send me a picture. I wanted to see what a mint-condition model looks like." He put the photograph down and gave McLean a somber look. "Sam, I found his name along with all the other names registered to a gun like that in North Carolina. So far, we've found four. One of them is Abel Wolf."

McLean said, "So the shell casings you found near Natalie Wolf's body—"

"Match this type of weapon, and her injuries are consistent with a long barrel."

"But you can't say for sure they were shot out of a long-nosed 1938 Luger."

"Yes, we can. Our ballistics man couldn't make heads or tails of the fragments we gave him, so we sent them off to the FBI lab. That's how we got a match."

"You got it back pretty quick."

"It's a murder case, Sam. First priority. I've got the FBI ballistics fellow's name if you want to talk to him. He'll be a witness."

"That's all right," said McLean. "I'll let the lawyer talk to him." He cast his eyes at the floor.

"Sit down, Sam." Church patted a chair near his desk, and McLean took a seat in it. "Look, I'm telling you this for a reason." Church sat behind his desk. "You're a friend of mine—well, I like to think of you that way. You need to get out of this case. Your client is the only suspect. He had the motive, the opportunity, and the means. He did it."

"Have you all got a search warrant yet?" McLean asked dimly.

"We're working on it. Everything I've told you will be in the news once we've got a warrant for Abel Wolf's arrest. I don't think it will be long. But if you and Loy work this case in his favor, I'm afraid this'll have to be the end of the road as far as cooperation between us, at least as far as the Wolf case goes."

"Just one more thing, Mike."

"What?"

"Did anybody at the RV park hear gunfire?"

Church gave McLean a blank look.

"Come on, Mike. If you found shell casings, she must have been shot where she was found." The phone on Church's desk rang. McLean persisted. "How far away was the body from the nearest camper? That wasn't in the news."

Church answered his phone on the fourth ring. After a few seconds he grinned at McLean. He didn't say anything to his caller for a couple of minutes other than an intermittent "Yes, sir" or "Mm-hmm." Finally he said, "Loud and clear, counselor. I appreciate your call."

He hung up, leaned back in his chair, and folded his hands on his belly. "That was Sig Mashburn. He's been retained by Abel Wolf's mother to represent him in the investigation of the Natalie Wolf case, and called to let me know that a written invocation of Abel Wolf's Fifth Amendment privilege against self-incrimination will be hand-delivered to my office no later than 5 o'clock today." He cocked his eyebrows. "I wonder who talked him into doing that."

McLean stood up. "Thanks anyway, Mike."

"I thought that curly-headed dandy you and Loy dragged into Dr. Sanger's office was his lawyer, but I guess that was just another one of Loy's bullshit maneuvers." Church shook his head reproachfully. "And to think I was trying to do you a favor, friend to friend."

McLean smiled sheepishly and made for the door. As he walked down the hallway to the front exit, he heard Church call out behind him: "Get out while there's still time, Sam. Don't let Loy make you look like a big ass all over again."

Lombard parked her car in the Apple Creek RV campground and sat quietly for a few minutes, watching the campers. She got out and walked up to a small concessions store and bought a hot dog. She asked the cashier if she'd heard anything about the body found there a few nights earlier.

"Yes, ma'am," said the girl, a plump teenager with braces. "It's all anybody talks about. Nobody's allowed to go near where they found it, but I heard a couple of boys got caught snooping around for bullet shells last night."

Lombard had just bitten off a mouthful of her hot dog. "Hmm," she hummed, chewing quickly and swallowing. "Did anybody hear a gun go off the night they think she got shot?"

"Nobody I know of heard anything," said the girl. "Hey, are you a cop?"

"Not exactly. Tell me something. Is there some kind of a list of who all was camped out here that night?"

The girl rolled her shoulders. "I don't know. Nothing detailed. You pretty much just show up, pay a camping fee, and set up camp."

"Surely there's list of names somewhere, for security purposes."

The girl disappeared into a room behind the concessions counter and came back with a large, bald man wearing a Worldwide Wrestling Federation T-shirt. He looked like he could be the girl's father. "It's like I told the cops," he said without introducing himself. "We keep a list of names while the campers are here. Once they leave, we chuck 'em."

"Fair enough," Lombard said. "So I take it you have a list of campers here *now* and how long they've been here, right?"

"Right. And some of them have been here since Friday, but you ain't going to annoy them. Reason *numero uno* being, you ain't a cop, and reason *numero dos* being, nobody heard nothing anyway. Nobody heard nothing, nobody seen nothing."

"Why is Friday important?" Lombard asked.

The bald man looked at her like she ought to know. "Because that's how far back the cops made me check. And, uh, that's when the dogs started barking."

"The dogs?" Lombard finished her hot dog.

"Yeah, people bring their dogs to camp. Gotta keep 'em tied, though. The whole damned camp went dog-crazy Friday night—well, I guess it was technically Saturday morning. About 3 A.M. They all started barking like crazy. Kept it up for about half an hour, but you know how dogs get going and can't quit."

"Nobody saw anything unusual?"

"Not a thing. Well, not till the next day." He pointed to the empty napkin in her hand. "Here, I'll throw that away for you."

"Thanks," Lombard said. "So who found the body?"

"Some New Jersey dude with an Airstream that left later that day. The cops have his name, and he was in the papers."

"Yeah, I think I saw that," Lombard said affably. As if on a sudden thought, she introduced herself and said, "Say, I don't suppose you could show me around the site where the body was found, Mr., uh—"

"Just call me Chet. And no, I can't. The police still have it cordoned off." He pointed through an open window to an area east of the concessions store. "It's down by the river. You can look at it if you promise not to touch anything. If I find the punks that were messing around there last night, I'll kick their scrawny asses."

Nobody heard a car or a truck, and nobody saw a thing unusual the night the Apple Creek campground went dog-crazy. Lombard spent a couple of hours walking around the campground, getting various accounts, both hearsay and firsthand, that fairly consistently followed Chet's narrative. The only thing new Lombard learned was that the campground was named for a creek and some apple trees on the west end of the campsite.

The east side of the several-acres-wide campground abutted a bend of the French Broad River. This was where Natalie Wolf's body had been found. A grove of sycamores shaded the spot several yards from the river's edge where yellow tape closed off a perimeter for homicide investigators. Of course, Lombard ignored Chet's warning and stepped over the tape as soon as she ascertained that she was alone. She crept around the grass, nettles, and moss-covered stones of the damp, rocky earth that had been Natalie Wolf's last natural resting place before a cold laboratory slab and then the crematorium that was scheduled to consume her remains later that week.

Lombard left the police perimeter and followed the shoreline. She discovered nothing unusual. No drag marks, no leavings—of course, the police would have scoured the area. Then she looked across the river, scanning the opposite bank along its edge. She spotted something in the distant south that compelled her back to her Pathfinder to retrieve her binoculars, which she found crammed in the back with all her other junk. She drove back across the campground to the shoreline and got out. She scanned the opposite riverbank with her binoculars this time and found the spot she'd noticed earlier. It appeared to be a boat launch, with an asphalt path rising up out of the water to what Lombard believed would lead to a public road.

Chances were the Wolfs would know exactly whose property it was and what road led to the spot. And if Lombard had to, she'd rent a boat and launch it off the Apple Creek campground or Wolf Branch Farm. Checking it out would be easy enough, but it would have to wait until later.

As soon as Lombard left the campground she drove to

Hendersonville and the Skinner Movables plant. She had called ahead and confirmed Seth Agee was in his office. Arriving just before 4 o'clock, she caught sight of a small, youngish man sneaking out a side door of the plant.

Guessing his identity, she cried out happily, "Hey, Mr. Agee? Is that you? Hello! I'm Loy Lombard, from Lombard & McLean." She reached him just as he landed on the bottom step of an iron fire escape.

He offered a pleasant hello and tried to brush past her. "I'm sorry. I just got an urgent phone call and have to get right home."

Lombard gently blocked him. She was half a foot taller and could be intimidating even when she was acting friendly. "Oh, this won't take but a minute, Mr. Agee."

"Call me tomorrow," he said curtly, nudging past her.

"Whoa! Not so fast. Now, do I have to go bothering Mr. Coburn again? I certainly hope not!"

Agee stopped mid stride and turned around. "No, that won't be necessary."

"We haven't been properly introduced."

"Well, I'm Seth Agee, and I'm scared shitless." He looked like the kind of fellow who was pale and plaintive even when not frightened. He had a hawk nose and wide mouth, which was presently fixed in an agonized grimace.

"Aw, what's wrong, sugar?" Lombard said soothingly.

He shouted, "I just feel like I'm in trouble for some reason, and I want to go home and go to bed."

His panic was almost infectious, and Lombard was stunned. "OK, calm down," she said, gently shushing him. She slowly drew nearer and clasped his right hand. She led him to a spot underneath the fire escape where they probably would not be noticed. "What's wrong?" she asked. "What are you afraid of?"

Agee seemed to have composed himself somewhat and looked embarrassed. "I can't talk to you. I've talked too much. I talked to the police," he said, laughing like he was amazed at himself. "The *police*! That was my second mistake."

"What was your first mistake?" Lombard asked.

Agee looked very young. He smiled. "Paying for love," he snickered.

"Paying whom?" Lombard pitched him a sidelong look. "Are we talking about Natalie Wolf? Is that what you think?"

He let go a caustic chuckle. "Think? Yeah, I think so. That picture, I don't know. It's got to be her, though. And now she's dead, right? I heard it on the news."

Lombard nodded. "What are you so worried about? Nobody thinks you killed her."

"I've tried contacting her for days," he said. "I thought, maybe it's not the same girl. Maybe there's another foxy Russian redhead." He nodded his head. "But it's her."

"It's who, honey?"

Agee sighed. "It's Nadine." He smiled. "That was her pro name, I guess."

"Natalie, Nadine," said Lombard. "A double life."

Agee gave Lombard a guarded look. "Look, Sam McLean seemed like a nice guy. Can I trust you? I mean, I did just sign a contract worth a shitload of money to you, so surely I can trust you, right?"

"Of course you can."

"I would never hurt Nadine. Or Natalie, I guess." He closed his eyes and opened them again, shaking his head slowly. "Tony's ready to have a fit. OK. My problem is kind of international, OK? Whatever. I've said enough."

"No, you haven't," said Lombard. "What do you mean?"

"I mean, I need a drink or some smoke, real bad, and a really good night's sleep. Look, it was a pleasure doing business with you." He walked backward and threw a hand up in salute. As he turned around, he shouted, "Fuck! North Carolina! I was simplifying my life when I came here. Who would have *ever* thought?"

"Who would have ever thought what?" Lombard asked, bewildered.

He turned around again. "That a chick with a Russian accent

and a bitching blue scorpion on her back would ever land in a place like western North Carolina." Agee blew Lombard a kiss, flashed a peace sign, and made quick tracks to his car.

McLean was just about to leave the office when Lombard sauntered in after 6 and told him he'd need to sit down for the news she was about to give him. He was astonished by what she told him. "And here I thought we were off the case, and I was even glad," McLean said. He leaned back in his chair. "She had a blue scorpion tattoo? It has to be her, Loy. It has to be the same person."

"If not, it's a hell of a coincidence," said Lombard. "And I don't believe in coincidences."

"Yes, you do. You said the two redheads and the two accents were coincidental."

"I never said that."

"Yes, you did—"

"Look, all we knew before today about Natalie Wolf and the bachelor party girl were that they both had reddish hair and accents. That's not weird, not like having the same tattoo in the same spot. That makes it clear we're talking about the same person, especially in a community as tight as this one."

McLean smiled. "So now you're convinced."

"Now I'm convinced." Lombard looked troubled. "But it doesn't explain why she died, or even come close to revealing who murdered her."

"Or, where the money is."

Lombard shook her head. "Old lady Wolf is absolutely certain we'll find that money. I don't know why she's so sure. Whatever outfit Natalie was working for is bound to have it."

"What do you mean, 'outfit'?"

Lombard said, "Her pimp, or madam, or CEO, or whatever the hell they're called nowadays. She was certainly working for somebody, if Seth Agee and Tony Coburn are to be believed." She glanced at her watch.

"By the way," she said, as if on a sudden thought. "I'm curious about something. When Agee told you about the dancer, what was his attitude like?"

McLean shrugged. "Private, a little shy. Like he was getting something off his chest."

"Hmm. He acts like a hunted man now. I haven't seen anybody that paranoid in a long time. Another thing, I think he was screwing her on the side. He said he'd been trying to contact her lately. That tells me he had more invested in her than one bachelor party."

McLean dreaded bringing it up, but he finally said, "Well, that reminds me of my talk with Mike Church, speaking of our other hunted man, Abel Wolf." He gave her the details of the type of gun used to kill Natalie Wolf and the fact that Abel was one of a handful of men in the country who possessed such a weapon.

Lombard shrugged it off. "So they've got paperwork. They've got no gun."

"They just might find it," said McLean. "They're getting a search warrant."

"We'll see if they find a gun. They'll need one for a comparison. Otherwise, they've got nothing."

"Even with nothing else, that registration puts Abel in a bad light."

"He's been in a bad light all his life," said Lombard. "That doesn't make him guilty of murder."

The front door opened, and a young woman stepped inside. She had long curly dark hair pulled back in a ponytail, and black horn-rimmed glasses. She was dressed in a sweatshirt and jeans, and was carrying a backpack. She looked surprised to see anybody sitting in the front office past 6 o'clock. "Hi. I'm Dana," she said in a mellow voice. She sneezed. "Jeez, allergies. They're killing me." She sniffed and cut a glance down at her vintage track shoes. "Sorry about my appearance. It's the AC. It's like a meat locker in here at night. And I didn't expect to be meeting my bosses now."

McLean noticed the twinkle in Lombard's eye, though her tone was autocratic when she asked Dana, "What did Retta tell you to do here at night?"

"Well," Dana replied, "I'm supposed to check on the guards at the top of every hour by radio, right? Which is fine, you know. This is only my third night, but I can tell you it gets lonely in here, and hearing those folksy voices roger me back is a welcome sound." She seemed to be trying not to stare at Lombard. "Anyway, um, Retta said you want a Web site, and she gave me your logo and some basic stats, and I'm working on a design for your home page, just for a start."

Lombard asked, "How would you like to put that on hold and do some investigative work instead, just for a start?"

McLean glared at Lombard, but she didn't look at him.

Dana looked surprised. "Sure. What do you want me to do?"

Lombard told her to sit down, and Dana sat on the lobby sofa. "So you're from Florida," said Lombard.

"Yeah. Tallahassee."

"I thought your résumé said Homestead."

"Birthplace, yes. But I was brought up in Tallahassee."

McLean noticed Lombard had the same look she used to get when they were homicide partners in Charlotte, during suspect interrogations. "Your résumé says you're 31," Lombard said suspiciously. "You look younger."

"Thank you."

"No, I should be thanking *you*."

"What for?"

"For the care package last Friday night."

McLean didn't want to hear any more. "Loy, Selena's expecting me. I best be—"

"Wait a minute, Sam," said Loy, swatting him back in his seat. "Dana's going to help us out, and I want you to be in on it."

"It's Dana."

Lombard looked at the raven-haired young woman. "I'm sorry?"

"It's Dana, with a short, flat *a*," she said. "You said *Dayna*, but it's pronounced like *Danna* with two *n*'s. Dana," she repeated, "just so you know."

"Sorry," said Lombard.

"Don't be. I should be sorry. It's the bane of my existence. But I refuse to yield to a long *a*."

Lombard smiled broadly, nearly laughing.

"So what am I gonna do?" Dana asked.

Lombard stood up and walked over to the sofa. She sat next to Dana and said, "We need help I think you can give us. You know we're investigating the Natalie Wolf case, right?"

Dana nodded. "Yeah."

"I'm going to tell you a story," Lombard said, "but you have to keep your mouth shut outside the office. OK?" When Dana nodded again, Lombard gave her the history of Lombard & McLean's investigation of the Wolf case, including the information obtained from Coburn and Agee that confirmed their stripper was the same person whose body had been found in the Apple Creek campground and who had been Abel Wolf's mail-order bride.

McLean was livid. Without thinking he blurted out, "Loy! What are you doing?" He glared at Lombard, his eyes demanding an explanation.

Lombard calmly looked at him. "What's your problem?" she asked quietly. She turned her attention back to Dana. "So this is what I want you to do for me. Find a Miami or South Florida–based escort service doing business in North Carolina, or in other Southeastern states. According to our sources, this outfit trucks whores out all over. Real high-dollar jinks going on here. My suspicion is they could have girls working in all the various states being paid by a centrally located pimp outfit in the Miami area. Coburn and Agee did business with them as recently as last spring. They've got to be in business still."

Dana looked skeptical. "But from the sound of it, there could be a very good chance the girls—and this girl, in particular—were sort of, like, subcontracting."

"Which means?"

"Which means connecting them to this outfit would be difficult to impossible, and that's if I'm able to find the outfit you're talking about."

Lombard looked either annoyed or smitten. McLean knew she had the same look either way, and it bothered him. "Just see if you can trace it, OK?" She got up and went back to Retta's desk and grabbed her shoulder bag.

"So, basically," Dana said, "I'm being paid to catalog the complicated galaxy of Miami-based porn-slash-escort sites. Right?"

Lombard shrugged.

"You realize it would be easier to chart all the asteroids in the Milky Way?"

"So pretend you're an astronomer," Lombard said, grabbing her car keys.

Lombard decided that, for the time being, she was just going to have to tolerate seeing Hunter Lyle, who was the local news anchor, all over the TV screen every night. Abel Wolf's case was the constant focus of the area's media. After a while it didn't bother Lombard all that much to have to watch the shameless hussy's nightly yammerings about the Wolf case. She had to stay abreast of what the public was finding out.

She'd missed the 6 o'clock news and now lay on her sofa to await the 11 o'clock report with a nice, tart, icy glass of bourbon mixed with the merest splash of club soda. She had opened some of her windows for the cross breeze of cool air flowing from outside and was nestled in a quilt with her cat curled up at her feet. She felt positively cozy.

The phone rang. She pointed at it and said, "No. Shut up." But it persisted, and late phone calls usually meant important news. She picked up.

The voice on the other line asked her if she wished to change her cell phone plan. A telemarketer, at this hour. Lombard dismissed her the usual way, by asking her if she had on any underwear. That normally got rid of them in a hurry, although male telemarketers all too often liked to play along for a while. But to date nobody had made it past the part where Lombard asked them to count the bite marks on their thighs. Only seldom did a company make the mistake of calling Lombard's domicile twice.

Five minutes after the telemarketer had hung up in a panic, the phone rang again. Surely to God, Lombard thought, the idiot wasn't calling back. The TV news was just starting. She quickly picked up the phone.

"What now?"

There was silence on the other end; someone was listening but not talking.

"Who is this? Is this the girl I just talked to? Well, sugar, you can put your panties back on. I'm done playing."

Then someone, or something, spoke to her. She nearly dropped the phone, and devil's fingers tickled the back of her neck as she slid up out of her comfortable spot and pressed her back against the cushions as though to separate herself from the sound—a garbled, guttural hiss. "Leave it alone," it said. Her goose bumps dissolved the instant she realized it was an electronically scrambled voice. "Leave it alone," it repeated.

"You have the wrong damn number," she said in as contemptuous a voice as she could muster. She hung up and noticed her cat had scuttled off the sofa.

The news was already in progress, and her heart was pounding. Hunter Lyle's delicate face smiled at the camera, her light-red hair an unwelcome reminder of the latest murder victim in Lombard's life. Then Lyle's smile vanished, and she announced that a fiery car crash had claimed the life of an Asheville man, and cut to a reporter on the scene. The reporter voiced over footage of a burned-out vehicle at the bottom of a steep ravine just outside of Hendersonville. The accident had occurred late in the afternoon as the driver was apparently leaving work and returning home to Asheville. Next of kin had been notified, and it was confirmed the victim's name was Seth Thomas Agee, 32, of Asheville. There had been no witnesses, and the cause of the accident had not been determined.

CHAPTER 7

When Lombard learned about McLean's last meeting with Church,
she knew there would be a search warrant, and she told Gussie
Wolf to call her as soon as the police showed up. Two days later, on
Thursday, Church and Deputy Hugh Potter arrived early at Wolf
Branch Farm with a search warrant. Lombard missed Mrs. Wolf's
call by half an hour, but as soon as she got the message she headed
out to the farm. When she got there, she noticed a Lexus SUV with
a license plate reading SIG LAW.

Mashburn was nowhere in sight, but Mrs. Wolf was sitting on
the front porch stairs. Clad in an old gray jersey and bib overalls,
feet planted on the next lower step and knees flaring out on either
side of her bulky frame, she looked childlike. The hard creases of
her forehead were pinched tight by her scowl. She looked somewhere between enraged and mournful.

"Took you long enough," she said in a low growl. "That lawyer's
already here."

"I got here as soon as I could," said Lombard. "Where is everybody?"

"Down in the bunker." Mrs. Wolf's eyes were moist. "Can't do
nothing," she almost whispered.

"What's that?" Lombard said distractedly, eyeing the empty cruiser and Lexus.

"I said I can't do nothing about 'em." She cocked her head in the direction of the bunker, off to her left. "They just come in here with that piece of paper that says they can look all over my place, digging around, scratching around in my personals. Abel's too. Ain't nothing for 'em to find. Don't know what they're after. They won't say."

As a cop Lombard had served a lot of search warrants, and she had treated the occupants of the places she'd searched with the same kind of indifference with which she knew Mrs. Wolf was being treated now. Invading people's privacy was disrespectful whether one had a warrant or not. No sense in pretending. "Well, Gussie, it would look pretty silly of them to act friendly, don't you think? It's not a friendly job." She was surprised to notice a tear stain on Mrs. Wolf's cheek. "They haven't seized anything, have they?"

"Not that I know of."

"Where's Mashburn?"

"He's follering them around."

Lombard arched an eyebrow. "They're letting him get away with that?"

Mrs. Wolf sighed. "I guess so."

"In that case, they shouldn't mind if I join them." Lombard headed off in the direction Mrs. Wolf had indicated, loping down the hillside behind the farmhouse, into a glen through which a narrow stream flowed out of a sickly pine thicket. An aluminum lean-to, facing the creek by a few yards, shaded a plain, flat door that looked to be some sort of metal with a vinyl covering, open to a subterranean set of stairs. Inside Lombard could hear muffled laughter. Careful not to call attention to herself, she crept into the space below.

"Boys, if you find any loose cash laying around," said the unmistakable, gravelly voice of Mashburn, "stuff it in old Sig's pockets." There was more laughter. Mashburn was around 50. But for his graying hair, he could have passed for his early 40s. He was tall and broad-shouldered, a formidable physical countenance, and he could be a bully when he wanted to be. But most of the time he charmed judges, lawyers, clients, and cops alike with his self-effacing wit. Lombard was not easily charmed by overbearing lawyers, and when she landed at the foot of the steps of Abel's bunker, she anticipated Mashburn's usual dose of flattery.

The bunker was barely seven feet from floor to ceiling, with a cracked concrete floor and brick-and-mortar walls, lit by a single bulb dangling on a plastic-coated electrical cord. The room into which the pine-slab steps descended was about ten feet by ten feet, and it contained what Lombard thought was a military-type chest on one side. On the other side of the cramped space was a tiny desk with a Macintosh computer on it and an old wooden swivel chair. There was a narrow tunnel leading into a second room, and standing in its middle was Mashburn in a gray worsted suit and scarlet tie. He appeared to be watching whatever activity was going on in the next room.

The room's overpowering musty smell caused Lombard to sneeze, and Mashburn turned in her direction. He looked a little irritated. "What are you doing here?" he said.

Lombard wiped her nose with tissue she'd pulled out of her back pocket. "That's a hell of a way to greet me, Sig, after all this time. I thought maybe you'd missed me." She walked up beside him and peered into the next room, where Church and a tall, skinny deputy were stooped over a pine table on which was spread an array of guns and knives. Underneath the tabletop six sliding trays were hinged to the legs, giving the table the look of a wooden tool chest. Each tray was stacked with varying sizes of cigar boxes.

"Didn't Gussie Wolf tell you I was coming?" she said brightly.

Church craned his neck and glared at her. "This is police business, Loy. You'll have to wait outside."

"Who's gonna drag me up those steps?" she asked. "As long as Mr. Slick here can stay," she said, pointing at Mashburn, "I don't see why I can't."

"He's Abel's lawyer—"

"That doesn't give him the right to witness a search," she said.

Church said hotly, "Fine, then, both of you, get the hell out!"

"I ain't going anywhere," Mashburn said smoothly.

"Neither am I," said Lombard.

"I'm gonna have you both arrested for obstruction of justice!" Church wailed.

"Hell, Lieutenant," Mashburn said, "what are you getting so excited about? Calm down." He winked at Lombard.

Church gritted his teeth, pointing his index finger at Lombard. "She just always gets…" His tongue got tied for a second, and he practically spat out, "Under my skin! She gets under my skin, and she does it on purpose!"

Deputy Potter, a gangly, slack-jawed fellow with permanently arched eyebrows, tapped on Church's shoulder. "This one's pretty," he said, handing him a nickel-plated .38 special.

Church examined it for a few seconds. "My daddy had one just like it," he grumbled.

Mashburn motioned for Lombard to follow him, and withdrew to the next room. "Loy," he said very softly, "you're busting up my momentum."

"What momentum?"

"Give it a rest," said Mashburn. "I know it pained you to get me involved in this case, but here's a fact-check: I can get more out of Mike without you around than with you. And that's best for Abel Wolf, wouldn't you agree?"

"No, I wouldn't."

"I should have known better," he sighed.

"What have they got so far?" she asked. "Anything?"

"They've been opening up boxes, looking for an antique Luger .38. He's got a gun cabinet at the house with all his rifles, and a bunch of handguns stored down here. But they haven't found his Luger. Abel told me he had one, said it should be in here."

"That's right," Lombard remembered. "Sam said one was registered to him."

"Just like the one that killed Natalie Wolf."

"So have they tried to talk to Abel?"

Mashburn smiled. "They know better than to try, now that I'm in."

Twenty minutes later Church and Potter were gone with only Abel's computer in tow, having failed to find the Luger. Lombard and Mashburn returned to the farmhouse and asked to see Abel. While Mrs. Wolf went to find him, Lombard left Mashburn waiting at the kitchen table and sneaked into a room next to the den, apparently used by Abel as a study, in which he housed his gun cabinet. She was looking over the rifles when it occurred to her to retrace the search done earlier by the police in that very room.

A roll-top desk was opened, and all of its various drawers and cabinets were loosened, their contents scattered about the desktop. She looked at a bookcase next to the desk and scanned the titles of dozens of clothbound books, most of them vintage history texts. Abel had an apparent affinity for military and crime history. She noted with envy his copy of *Playboy's Illustrated History of Organized Crime*, published in the 1970s and now out of print, a copy of which Lombard had once owned and lost in a domestic breakup. Other books were more ghoulish, such as one devoted to cannibal murderers. Abel was a very strange man, she thought, chuckling once as she pulled that volume out of the bookcase.

Suddenly she noticed a small glass jar in back of the empty space. It looked like a medicine bottle, dark-brown in color with a black cap, with an oblong object floating in some sort of fluid. Puzzled, Lombard picked up the bottle and shook it. She was closely examining it when the floating thing slowly spun to a stop. Lombard brought the jar closer to her eyes and let go an involuntary groan. The thing had a nail and a knuckle, and shreds of tissue clinging to its jagged end.

She heard voices in the kitchen. Abel was talking to Mashburn. She slipped the jar into her shoulder bag and went to join them.

"You did what?" Sam McLean shouted the next day as they had lunch in their regular booth downtown. "Where is it now?"

"In my safe box, at home," said Lombard. "Abel has a safe too, down in that bunker. He'd be in a lot worse shape right now if he'd stored that thing in it. Mike and that goober deputy cracked it right open, but there was nothing inside the safe. I think that's where the fat freak hid his money that Natalie stole."

McLean was incensed. "Loy, you've done some illegal things before, but this is totally off the mark."

"I know," she said, biting into a sandwich. "I feel awful about it. It makes me sick that Church is too incompetent to find evidence like human body parts in a suspect's own house."

McLean leaned across the table. "This is wrong on a lot of levels, including one that could land you in jail. It's tampering with evidence. That's a long way past the obstruction-of-justice charge Mike threatens you with almost every time he lays eyes on you." He glanced over his right shoulder and kept his voice low. "It's also morally wrong. That's human remains, for God's sake. And it's weird to boot. Why would you want to have that thing sitting around in your house?" He leaned back and narrowed his eyes at her. "Oh, wait a minute. It isn't at your house. I know you better than that. You're way too easily spooked for that. It's in your desk at the office." He stood up and grabbed his windbreaker off the coatrack near the door.

Lombard looked startled. "Sam, wait! Where are you going?"

"You know good and well where I'm going, and where I'm going after that," he said, scrambling for the door.

Lombard chased out onto the sidewalk after him. "No! Aw, Sam. Don't. Look, if Mike gets his hands on that thing, Abel's as good as fried."

"So what does that have to do with us finding the money we've been hired to track down?" McLean said.

"We're never going to find that money! It's long gone. We're going to find out what happened to Natalie, though. That's really what we're after."

"It's what you're after, Loy. And it's obvious by this point that Abel killed her and kept a trophy." He started walking. "It's in that drawer you keep locked all the time, right?"

"Yes, damn it," she said. "And I'll unlock it, but you listen to me. I said stop!" He stopped and faced her again, glancing at his watch. "I agree it's some sort of trophy, but I'm not sure it was taken at the time of death. Dr. Sanger's report doesn't mention any missing body parts other than the face, and none of us noticed it missing when Abel ID'd the body."

"What are you getting at?"

"I think Abel took the thumb *after* the autopsy."

McLean rolled his eyes. "Loy, that's impossible. He couldn't get away with it."

"Yes, he could. Natalie's body was delivered to a mortuary for cremation, and both Gussie and Abel Wolf attended the cremation two days ago, on Wednesday. I checked into it yesterday." She told him about a visit she had paid the day before to the crematorium she'd seen listed in Natalie Wolf's newspaper obituary. "The mortician is C.S. Blanchard, of Blanchard Brothers Mortuary. Gussie Wolf's maiden name is Blanchard—they're relatives. Mr. Blanchard confirmed that Abel was present while the body was being prepared for cremation, but of course I didn't ask, 'Oh, by the way, did he cut off any of her extremities as a keepsake?' " She took a short breath. "Blanchard said he let Abel watch because he's always hung out at the mortuary, since he was a kid. He even worked there once in a while, though his job dependability was sporadic, according to Blanchard, who admitted Abel's always had a morbid fascination for dead bodies. So see? It's plausible he hacked it off at the funeral home."

McLean stared at her for a moment. "Why the hell would he do that?"

"Because he's a fucked-up freak. But that doesn't make him a murderer." Lombard looked imploringly at McLean. "Don't you wonder about this Agee connection? He knew her—*knew* her, Sam—as Nadine, an alias similar to her real name. It has to be the same woman to have so unusual a tattoo: a blue scorpion. He screwed her, in all likelihood, on a regular, paying basis. And he was scared witless the day I talked to him, minutes before his death."

"Yes. Coincidences are always strange."

"But he was afraid, Sam. And that phone call I got—"

"Wasn't related," said McLean. "Even you told me it just creeped you out."

"I don't believe Abel killed Natalie."

"You just don't want to believe it. Neither do I." McLean turned around and headed back to the office.

"Don't do anything foolish, Sam!" she shouted as he rounded a corner. "I'll unlock the desk drawer as soon as I clear out the bill back here, sugar. Lunch is on me."

During his interview with Mashburn, Abel had said he had no idea how his Luger had gone missing, and reacted more with outrage at its having been stolen than with a guilty man's characteristic nonchalance. He'd insisted Natalie must have stolen it along with the money, though he hadn't checked his guns to see if any were missing or, in any case, hadn't noticed it missing among his several dozen sidearms, kept in velvet pouches in individual boxes stacked in the trays of his gun chest.

Lombard had sat quietly through that interview, paled by shock at her gruesome discovery and her misgivings about stealing a murder victim's body part. She had immediately rustled through the obituary notices to find out where Natalie's body had been taken, and raced to the Blanchard funeral home to confirm her strong hunch that Abel had somehow managed to get access to his wife's body before her cremation. Her suspicion vindicated, all she'd had to worry about afterward was her moral certainty that holding on to Natalie Wolf's remains was terrible.

Her lunch with McLean had made her feel even worse, so she decided not to return to the office for a while. She needed to check out that boat launch she'd spotted from the shore of the Apple Creek RV campground the previous Tuesday. And she needed to avoid McLean lest he shame her into turning over the ghastly evidence she'd stolen.

She drove out to the Wolfs' home and discovered that the constant stress and shock and police disruption of their lives seemed finally about to break them. Gussie and Abel's bickering could be heard before Lombard reached the bottom step of the front porch. Abel answered the door. Lombard had the impression it was something he was unused to doing. He looked agitated and was breathing heavily through his mouth; sweat trickled down his temples. His plaid shirt looked damp, and he smelled. Abel apparently wasn't the sort of man who handled pressure well.

"Mother wouldn't answer the door for you," he said, snarling a little. "She says you're not looking for the money."

"Of course I'm looking for it," Lombard said coolly. "That's why I'm here. I want to find the getaway route Natalie used after taking the cash. I need your help, though."

Lombard didn't want the Wolfs to know her real reason for finding the boat launch, any more than she wanted them to know she'd visited the site where Natalie's body had been found. If she had to pretend to be looking for stolen cash in order to solve Natalie's murder, then that was how it would have to be. Either way, she was getting paid, and besides, Abel would thank her for it when his name was cleared. Assuming, she grudgingly acknowledged, he wasn't the killer.

The Wolfs rode with Lombard in her Pathfinder to a clearing along the banks of the French Broad River where it flowed past their land. Lombard hadn't told them she'd seen a boat launch on the opposite bank, only that she wanted to see theirs if they had one. Mrs. Wolf hadn't seemed very enthusiastic about the idea and asked Lombard repeatedly what difference *how* Natalie Wolf left the farm made in tracking down Abel's fortune. Lombard hadn't been able to answer her and, frankly, couldn't even resolve for herself why she suspected a boat had been used to dump Natalie's body at the campground. But if the campers were to be believed, there were only two ways the body could have arrived without somebody seeing something: from across the water or from next door on Wolf Branch Farm. Lombard preferred the former theory.

"Here it is, rickety and rotten," said Mrs. Wolf. She waved an arm out over the small pier of dark, decaying wood, fastened loosely to blackened piles.

Lombard wouldn't have dared try to walk around on it, let alone use it to disembark a boat. "This looks more like a dock to me," she said.

"There used to be a canoe moored to it," said Mrs. Wolf. "We got rid of it a long time ago. Abel hasn't got any interest in boats."

Abel added nothing; only slouched near the Pathfinder, squinting in the hazy sunlight. Lombard said, "So you never had a motorboat, or a place where you could back a boat into the water?"

"You mean like with a trailer?" Mrs. Wolf asked. She looked deeply suspicious. "I still don't see what difference any of this makes. You ought to be tailing that feller the lawyer talked about, that Desmond Holliday. Sig Mashburn says he ran around with Natalie and is into all kinds of double dealing. Why ain't you after him?"

"I am, Gussie," Lombard said peevishly. "Never mind why I need to know this. I just need to know." She grabbed the binoculars from her car and brought the boat launch on the other side of the river into her sight. "Who owns that property over there?" she asked, handing the binoculars to Mrs. Wolf.

Mrs. Wolf raised the binoculars to her eyes. "It used to belong to a logging company, as far as I know. But the loggers moved, abandoned it. I'm not sure who owns the land. What's the big deal?"

"See that paved path dipping down into the water?" Lombard asked. "That's for putting boats in the water, right?"

"I guess so." Mrs. Wolf handed Lombard the binoculars. "I'd say the launch was used by loggers to carry timber by boat."

"Do you know how I get to it?"

"Can you swim?"

"I mean by car, Gussie."

Mrs. Wolf said she didn't know, but Lombard was sure she was lying. A woman like Mrs. Wolf would know who owned property adjacent to hers and would know how to get on it. At first she blamed Mrs. Wolf's refusal to cooperate on the old lady's evident and justifiable belief that Lombard was hedging the investigation on something that had nothing to do with finding her missing money. Perhaps Mrs. Wolf was just being stubborn, or perhaps she had darker reasons for stalling Lombard's investigation of the boat launch.

Lombard felt safe returning to the office around the close of business. If McLean were still around, he'd be in a hurry to leave, as he always was on Fridays at 5 o'clock. He didn't take their business nearly as seriously as she did, she told herself, and had probably blown off early. No doubt he'd left her to put out the late-afternoon fires that always swept their desktops on Fridays: all the phone calls to return, all the papers and checks to sign. What was he so mad about, after all? Who the hell did he think he was, in fact, to judge her so harshly, as hard as she worked compared to him, and as devoted as she was to the successful development of their business as the best in the region? By the time she parked her car out front, she was fuming.

His car was still there. By God, she just hoped he asked her about opening that desk drawer. He was on his way out when she walked inside. She pursed her lips, arched her brow, and brushed past him without speaking.

"I let Retta go early," he said, not getting a response. "And I signed all the checks." She opened her office door. "And I didn't go near your desk, except to put the paychecks on it," he added.

She kept ignoring him and went inside her office, slamming the door behind her. She thought he'd left when, as soon as she sat down at her desk, she heard him say loudly, "Hello, Ms. Gabriel. What brings you here? I thought you had Fridays off."

Lombard jumped out of her chair and smoothed her hair back before casually opening her door and stepping outside. The only person standing in the lobby was McLean, grinning ear to ear. "Did you happen to see any messages for me on Retta's desk?" she asked, as though she had meant to come out anyway.

"No," he said, beaming. "I think everything's under control, Loy. Go home. Have a nice weekend." He turned to leave.

"There's a lot of work needs doing," she said.

He turned around and gave her a conciliatory look. "Loy, I'm still in this case with you, neck-deep. I might as well be, since we'll both end up losing our licenses over the…" He hesitated. "The thumb. But I'm not going to preach on it anymore. You've made up your mind. God help the fool who tries to make you change it." He raised his chin up. "Now, tell me what you want me to do this weekend, and I'll do it."

"Good," she said. She explained her theory on how Natalie Wolf's body had come to be dumped at the campsite, and Gussie Wolf's information on the boat launch across the river. "I'd like to find out who owns the land now, and how to access that boat launch, and if anybody knows if it's still used and by whom. That's all."

McLean saluted. "Yes, ma'am. Frankly, I'll enjoy it. It's going to be a beautiful weekend, and I think the girls would like to go on a picnic. Apple Creek has a picnic ground. I'll mix business with pleasure that way."

"Suit yourself," she said, and went back into her office.

Then she heard him again. "Hey, Ms. Gabriel. How are you?"

Lombard shouted, "Not funny, Sam! I'm not gonna jump every time you say 'Ms. Gabriel.' So knock it off."

Her door opened, and McLean peered inside. "She wants her check."

Lombard shrugged. "Then give it to her."

"They're on your desk." He pointed.

An envelope bearing Dana Gabriel's name was on top of the stack. Lombard snatched it and went outside, feeling as though the blood vessels of her cheeks were popping into tiny flames when she realized McLean hadn't been bluffing this time. She handed Dana her check and said, "It was on my desk."

"Thanks," said Dana. She either hadn't heard Lombard's remark or was kind enough to act as though she hadn't. She leaned against Retta's desk. "Um, do you have a few minutes? I thought I should bring you up to speed on the Miami Vice project, as I've christened it. I hope you don't mind."

"Not at all," said Lombard. She took pains not to look at Dana's figure. She had an ordinary face with a long, thick nose her black-rimmed glasses made appear even larger. Her black, tangled hair just touched her small shoulders. She was petite and thin but buxom, and her soft cotton T-shirt and jeans made rather a show of her beautiful shape. Lombard kept her eyes on Dana's glasses, whose thick lenses made any fair judgment of her eyes impossible. "Have you already found something?"

"Well, it's what I was afraid of," Dana explained. "There's just so much. It's unreal. Miami's a hot town in more ways than one, you know. So every other escort service out there—whether it's high-dollar or low-rent—uses the Miami name. Or Hollywood. Hollywood is hugely popular. If there's one Hollywood Ladies service, there are a million. It's crazy. And there are so many search-engine hits on North Carolina availability for Miami escorts, probably because 95% of them are run out of trailer parks from Boone to Wilmington. You see what I'm saying?"

"I see." Lombard took a few seconds to let it sink in. "I hadn't thought of that, but it makes sense. I'm surprised I hadn't thought of it."

"So where do you want me to go from here?" Dana asked.

"Oh, I don't know," Lombard said, falling into a chair. She reflected for a moment. "It's a dead end, anyway. A waste of time." She looked at Dana. "Just work on our Web site. It's far more practical at this point."

Dana frowned. "Say, you can tell me to shut up since this is none of my business. But you look bummed out. If you gave me some way of defining my search a little more narrowly, I might still come up with something."

"I'll think about it."

Dana checked her watch. "Well, I need to get going if I'm going to make it to the bank before 6. I'll be back tomorrow for my Saturday shift." She stood up straight and looked as though a thought had just come to her. "Didn't you tell me Abel Wolf met Natalie through a kind of Web-based matchmaking service?"

"Yes." Lombard practically heard the flashbulb blow up in her head. "My God, Dana. I can't believe we hadn't thought of that."

"Right," Dana smiled. "You would have. You've got a lot of stuff on your mind. Anyway, it's worth a look."

Lombard looked at McLean. "Did we ever think to ask for the name of the agency Abel went through?"

McLean shook his head.

Lombard laughed. "He said he got it off the goddamned Internet! Why didn't we think of that connection?"

Dana promised to look for a connection between the bride service and the escort service as soon as she got the Web address Abel had used. Then she left.

Lombard and McLean stood in her wake, looking blankly into the empty space Dana had occupied. McLean said, "Smart girl."

"Mm-hmm."

He nudged Lombard. "She sure is stacked, huh?"

Lombard gave him a withering look and retreated to her office.

CHAPTER 8

For days Lombard had worked late every night and fallen into bed almost as soon as she'd gotten home. She was deeply invested in the Wolf case, though she'd saved some of her determination for the personal purpose of forgetting about Chris. She had been badly disappointed, but there was nothing to be done about it. There would be no parting words, no mutual examination of how things had gone wrong, no dialogue or coming to terms. She'd been fucked over, and that was that. Lombard would try to wipe Chris from her heart, her mind, her life. There was no such thing as closure; there was only erasure.

If the past were any indication, though, she would eventually wallow in self-pity over it. Only there wasn't time for that right now, so tonight she was leaning back in her bathtub, knees bent, arms dangling out the sides of the tub, watching as the shower head pelted her overheated body with tiny blue baubles of frigid water. Beads of water seemed to evaporate on her flesh; it couldn't get cold enough to suit her, and it wasn't a hard-enough spray. She mumbled something about old plumbing as she reached out for her very stiff bourbon on the rocks. The crank-out window's opaque lower pane was tilted at a narrow-enough angle to conduct a cool September night breeze right down on her.

Naturally, the phone began ringing almost as soon as she had begun to relax. She ignored it, as was her habit, letting her voice mail pick up. The phone issued two more sets of rings during a 30-minute interval, the last set—which happened to correspond to her glass going dry—prompting Lombard to climb out of the tub, put on her robe, and go into the kitchen. She pushed her glass against the ice-maker bar, filled it up, and sauntered into the dining room to the liquor cabinet. She had just poured it full when the fourth set of rings ran right through her.

She picked up the phone and said, "This better be good."

Without introduction Sig Mashburn said, "I need your help."

"What sort of help?" said Lombard.

"You've got to calm Abel down. He called me a few minutes ago saying the police had taken something of great value to him. He was beside himself, but he wouldn't tell me what it was."

Lombard bit her lower lip. She wondered if she should tell Mashburn the truth. "Is he at home?"

"Yeah, and he's threatening to call the police. He's out of control. I'm calling you to ask that you calm his ass down before he runs over to Mike Church and spills his guts. I don't know what he'd tell Church, and I don't know if you could talk him out of it, but he's in a state."

"Should I go over there now?" she asked.

"No, I think I've subdued him for the night. I'm flying down to New Orleans tomorrow for a conference, though, and wanted to ask for your intervention while I'm gone. Say, while I'm at it. You're a New Orleans girl. Got any tips for me on fun stuff to do, outside the tourist bullshit?"

Lombard gave him the name of a couple of good off-the-beaten-path restaurants she'd found the last time she'd visited. "Stay out of the Quarter," she told him. "Nothing but pickpockets, termites, and drunk sorority girls showing their tits."

"That doesn't sound so bad. I'll leave my wallet in my hotel room. Now, you look after Abel. Make sure he keeps his head on straight."

Of course she would. After they'd hung up, she phoned her voice mail, expecting to hear a message from Abel, or perhaps Mashburn had been trying to call earlier. There were no messages, but her caller ID box indicated two of the calls had come from the Wolf residence, the most recent was from Mashburn's residence, and one was anonymous. She decided against calling the Wolfs, since they'd obviously reached Mashburn, who had apparently soothed whatever panic Abel Wolf was going through over what Lombard herself had stolen. It was all too strange, the hour was too late, and she'd had too much to drink to deal effectively with the situation anyway. It could wait.

She kicked back on the living room sofa, threw the quilt over her, and turned the TV on to the History Channel. She wanted to see a war movie tonight, one without romance, and she intended on falling asleep on the couch in the dim light of the muted TV. The bed would seem a little too empty on this particular Friday night.

When the phone rang again, she thought of muting it too. If it was Abel or his mother, she'd beg them off until tomorrow. If it was anybody else, she'd be annoyed.

Static silence, just like the weird call she'd gotten a few nights earlier. "Who is this?" Lombard demanded.

"Leave it alone," the electronic voice again demanded.

"You leave it alone," said Lombard. She slammed the phone down, then picked it up, clicked it off, and slammed it down again. She was so shaken up, she got up and made sure all the blinds and curtains in the house were drawn. She scowled at the caller ID box for a moment before scrolling through the numbers. The source of the call—as it had been the last time—was anonymous.

McLean was ambivalent about his assignment on Saturday morning. He would have been content on such a sweet early-fall day to be tinkering in the garage with his Mustang, or at best in the driveway, so he would be able to get some of the fresh mountain air. Instead, he was dragging his family to a picnic at the Apple Creek campground in order to investigate the boat launch. McLean didn't think he would find out anything unusual, but he would be able to humor Lombard that work on this losing case was getting done.

He wished he had come alone. He'd made the mistake of telling Selena the picnic idea was a means of mixing business with pleasure. Selena had always resented McLean's allegiance to his work, and she always blamed Lombard for work-related invasions of McLean's family life. She hadn't spoken to him the entire ride to the campground and only broke her silence to scream at the girls for fighting.

They had just finished lunch, and McLean was watching his younger two girls play with some of the "RV kids," as his eldest daughter Sara called them with evident condescension. Having nothing to do with them or her family, Sara was sprawled out on the picnic blanket, resting on her elbows, reading a teenage mystery novel.

McLean wondered if he'd had the chance to screen that book yet: He'd found that a lot of these so-called young-adult novels were too racy for any daughter of his, especially at Sara's age. Screening normally consisted of reading the back cover and quickly scanning the first few pages for any sign of sexuality or moral ambiguity. Better not to bother Sara now, though. She was getting more and more irritable with everyone in the family and would likely bite his head off if he asked her any nosy questions.

He glanced at his watch and decided to make his move. He'd offered one of the campers with a canoe $20 to row him downriver the half mile or so to that boat launch. The man—a friendly granola type named Arlie with a long silver ponytail and gray beard—had agreed but had declined to accept any payment.

Selena had brought the girls' swimsuits and would be taking Maggie and Hannah wading in the creek. Sara agreed to go along only if she could sit under a tree with her book and be left alone. McLean estimated he should be back in an hour, and he left with Arlie.

They were about halfway to the boat launch when Arlie—after having made conversation about the weather before graduating to water quality and finally coming out as a die-hard environmentalist—asked McLean what he was up to. "Is there any particular reason why you have to check out that boat launch?" he asked.

McLean said, "I'm doing some investigation."

"Really?" said Arlie. He was a lanky, tanned fellow, shirtless under a warm noonday sun, with a wide grin under wider dark shades. He seemed barely to move even as his arms pitched his oar in a steady rotation to propel the canoe. "Cool," Arlie said, though he was apparently too cool to ask for any details.

They arrived at the boat launch, which consisted of a worn-out asphalt lane crumbling into the water. It was overgrown with weeds and vines, yet a car or truck could easily use it to put in a canoe or even a motorboat. McLean took out his camera and snapped a few shots of the boat launch and one of the smiling, waving Arlie because he asked McLean to.

Arlie tethered the canoe to a weathered post, and the two men climbed out—McLean in his hiking boots, Arlie in his flip-flops. McLean wasn't sure what he wanted to do next, so he decided to follow the path of the asphalt lane for a ways and see if there appeared to be anything worth scouting. Lombard had told him she was interested in how the boat launch connected to the nearest public road, but she was primarily interested in who owned the land.

There was no ready evidence of ownership, and the lane itself appeared to wind through a thickly wooded area for quite a way— longer than the hour McLean had allotted himself and promised Arlie. They had walked nearly a quarter of a mile when McLean decided he and Lombard would simply have to come back. Poor Arlie was in those flip-flops, though he seemed not the least bit perturbed, and had in fact stopped more than once to point out a particularly old poplar tree.

"Man, that one has to be more than a hundred years old," he wondered aloud, pointing to a thickly overgrown grove.

McLean peered into the grove in feigned, indebted interest—he felt he should act impressed since Arlie had been such a good sport—but he really was anxious to get back and had given up on finding anything useful for Lombard. Then something caught his eye, something past the enormous poplars. Roughly 30 yards from where they stood was a cabin in the middle of a clearing. It was small, made of logs, and rigged with a long, deep heart pine porch.

McLean pointed it out to Arlie. "When I was a kid," he said low, "I lived on a farm, way out in the country. I used to love to find these old cabins or beat-up old farmhouses. Something about being raised in the country—you can always tell if there's life in a cabin, no matter how still and abandoned it looks." He smiled, pointing at the cabin. "Somebody's living there."

"Wow," said Arlie. "That's heavy. I think there's somebody in there too."

"Were you raised in the country?" McLean asked.

"No. St. Louis."

"Then how do you know somebody's in that cabin?"

"Because there's a Mercedes parked next to it." Arlie pointed at a black SUV gleaming about 20 feet behind the cabin on a gravel path.

His face burning with embarrassment, McLean led Arlie nearer the house in a cautious, roundabout way, trudging through leaves and sticks but staying well within the grove. Arlie had removed his shades and intuitively kept quiet, with one bushy eyebrow cocked. McLean heard a crack. It could have been a tree branch snapping or the unlatching of a door, but it stopped McLean and Arlie in their tracks. The cabin door opened, and a woman carrying a rifle stepped outside.

She was dressed in faded jeans, a navy T-shirt, and a flannel over-shirt. From where he stood, McLean could see she was tall and strong, with long, straight blond hair falling loosely over broad shoulders. He couldn't quite distinguish her features, but she was apparently looking or listening for something. She stood very still, rifle held low, as though she had heard something and gone outside to investigate. McLean guessed she'd heard him and Arlie, either their voices or the rustling of their footsteps. They were standing at a safe distance within the grove, but the clearing was a still, quiet place, and McLean surmised any loner out here would likely be keen to trespassers. Even a loner who drove a sleek black Mercedes-Benz ML500.

He wanted badly to take her picture, but he didn't dare move. He'd brought her face into sharper focus, and she looked pretty fierce. Surely a well-to-do, striking woman like her wouldn't shoot a couple of hapless passersby, he thought, but the longer he held her in his sight, the less he wanted to provoke her. He hoped Arlie saw things the same way.

They both stood painfully still, obscured by the shadows and ivy tangled about the poplars. After she had cast her eyes around the clearing, the woman deftly turned around and went back inside the cabin. McLean gently touched Arlie's forearm and led him away, at a faster clip than they'd been walking before.

"She was a nice-looking lady," Arlie panted as they scrambled for the boat launch, "but she had a scary edge to her, didn't you think?"

"Oh, she was just looking after herself," said McLean. "You know, an attractive woman alone in the woods like that, she's gonna be a little paranoid."

"I'm feeling a little paranoid myself right now," said Arlie.

"If you were thinking she was gonna shoot any trespassers," McLean said, "that wasn't paranoid. That's exactly what she was gonna do. I'd bet my ride back on it."

Minutes later they paddled, not quite as languidly as before, back toward the Apple Creek campground. They didn't talk much, and each pop and crack of the forest made them paddle a little faster.

Lombard arrived early at Wolf Branch Farm. She didn't look forward to dealing with Abel Wolf, but she had to find out as soon as possible what the name of his matchmaking agency was if she were going to get the information to Dana, who would be working at the office this afternoon.

Mashburn had been right: Abel was in a state. And his mother wasn't faring much better. "He's torn the house plum apart," she told Lombard. "I tried to get him to tell me what the hell was the matter, but that just made him blow up at me. He fretted so much I called the lawyer and put Abel on the phone. He just hollered and screamed at him too."

"Mashburn said he's lost something," said Lombard.

"That's right. Only he won't say what it is," said Mrs. Wolf. "Just that it's valuable. I thought he was talking about his computer equipment the police took, but he says that ain't it."

"Where is he now?"

Mrs. Wolf jerked her head. "Down in his bunker. He said he needed to be by himself for a while." Lombard started for the door, and Mrs. Wolf added, "I wouldn't go down there if I was you. He's touchy about people coming around his bunker."

"Gussie, he's gonna have to grow up someday," said Lombard.

She hopped down the porch steps and rounded the path to the back of the house and down the hill to the lean-to shielding Abel's sanctuary. She knew better than to try going inside, so she hollered from the top of the steps. "Abel! This is Loy Lombard. I want to talk to you."

"Go away!" he hollered, his voice slightly muffled in his subterranean confines. "I'm in a fretful state."

"So I heard. What's wrong?"

"Something of great value has been taken from me."

"Abel, I have to come down there."

"I'd rather you didn't," he said, but she went down the stairs and squatted on the bottom step. Abel was sitting forlornly in his wooden swivel chair. "I take it Mashburn reported our heated conversation of last night to you," he said dimly.

"Yeah. He said you were pretty upset about something."

Abel, whom Lombard had not yet seen smile, smirked. There

113

was something deeply unsettling and unnatural in it that made Lombard draw back slightly and avert her eyes. "I think you know what went missing, Ms. Lombard."

Lombard looked him in the eye very suddenly, as though offended. "Abel, I don't have time for this bullshit. You know good and well I haven't the slightest idea what you're talking about. Now what gives?"

"Only four people besides my mother and myself have entered our home since last Wednesday," he said. "Only four people could have removed items belonging to me. Naturally, I would guess that Lieutenant Church or Deputy Potter would have custody of any and all items removed since that time, since they executed a search of the premises and did in fact remove several of my possessions." He spoke in a measured tone, though not losing that awful self-satisfied smirk.

"What was it went missing, Abel?" Lombard asked.

He held his tongue for a moment, staring at her. "Clearly, they have it," he said at the last excruciating second. He looked off to one side. "I'll have to call them and offer an explanation."

Lombard tightened her jaw. She had to talk him out of it. There was no other way. Abel thought Church and Potter had taken the thumb, and he was going to call them and try to explain why he had had it in the first place. She couldn't let him do it. It would be a terrible blunder, would lead to his arrest, and she would be to blame.

"Abel," she said softly, "let's take a walk."

❖

Around noon Lombard's Pathfinder peeled into her parking space at the office on Haywood. The only other car in the lot was a blue Civic with a rainbow strip across the bottom of the back windshield. Well, well, well, Lombard thought. Her instincts were still sharp.

Dana was sitting at Retta's desk, fixated on her computer monitor, her fingers racing along the keypad. She was wearing a Walkman, and her hair was pulled back in a ponytail. Just out of curiosity, Lombard checked her fingers for any significant-looking rings but saw nothing.

Dana glanced up and gave a start. Lombard realized she'd been staring for a few seconds. "Hello," Lombard said.

Dana removed her earphones. "Hey, how're you? It's too nice of a day to be working on the weekend, unless you have to."

"I had to go see Abel this morning, to find out about the matchmaking outfit. Remember? You suggested it."

Dana nodded. "Yeah, I remember. So, you want me to work on that today?"

"Well, I haven't found out the name of it yet," Lombard said.

Dana gave a flat smile and nodded. "Hmm. Oh, well."

Lombard pulled a chair nearer the desk and sat down. "So you're building our Web site?"

"Mm-hmm. Working on it." Dana's eyes fell back on her monitor, and she went back to typing. "So. You went to Abel Wolf's but didn't find out about the agency."

"Nope. Abel's really mad at me right now. I think we may be fired, actually."

"Wow. What happened?"

"Well, I found something very unusual in his house when he wasn't looking and thought I should hang on to it in case the police spotted it and, you know, got the wrong idea. Or the right idea. Hell, at this point, I don't know what to think." She flung her left forearm onto the desk and leaned in a little. "Anyway, he noticed it missing and went nuts, and I pretended at first not to know anything. He was about to run his mouth to the police, so I confessed what I'd done. Of course, I told him I did it for his own protection, and I'd give it back as soon as the case was over, but he went ballistic. I guess stealing from your own client and then lying about it is pretty offensive, but I plead exigent circumstances. Anyway, I thought he'd kill me. If he'd had a gun on him at the time, he probably would have." She shrugged. "So I didn't get around to finding out about the matchmaking agency."

Dana's face brightened. She was just shy of smiling. "I don't know what to say."

"You don't have to say anything."

"I mean, I'm glad you're OK. I guess I'm just really flattered you confided all that in me. Maybe even a little surprised, since I'm so new."

Lombard grinned. "I didn't tell you everything." But she'd told Dana enough to make Lombard realize she trusted her on some level. She liked Dana an awful lot.

But that had nothing to do with business, she thought, and got up suddenly, pretending to have work to do in her office.

It was the twilight of a near-perfect Saturday, and for McLean the best part was yet to come. Sara had gone to stay all night with a friend, and Maggie was at a slumber party. Hannah had nibbled on fish sticks and mac 'n' cheese and was sprawled out on her parents' bed watching cartoons, where she always fell asleep by nightfall, to be carried off to bed later. Selena's mood improved once the older girls were out of the house, and she apparently forgave McLean for having spent an hour away from his family at the campground. Steaks were on the grill, alongside Selena's marinated veggie kebab. They had rented a movie, and his-and-hers TV trays were set up in the den. This was McLean's idea of a fabulous Saturday night: steaks, Jackie Chan, and virtually no kids.

The doorbell rang. McLean prayed it wasn't Mrs. Milliken bringing Maggie back home. Maggie had gotten over her homesickness, McLean thought, when she went to church camp in July. His mind raced as he advanced to the front door. Mrs. Milliken would have called for him to pick Maggie up, and if she had brought the girl back, she would have dropped her off, and Maggie wouldn't ring the front doorbell. She'd come in through the kitchen patio door. Or perhaps it wasn't Maggie at all but a police officer—Sara had, after all, gone to spend the night with that

Durbin girl, whose father owned a bar rumored to stock poker machines. His heart thumped as he swung the door open.

It was Lombard. "Sam, I hate to disturb you on a weekend night. I was on my way home, had something to tell you, but my cell phone's gone dead, and—"

"Come on in, Loy," he said.

"No, no," she insisted. "Let's go talk in the car. Something's come up. This won't take ten minutes."

"No, we'll talk out on the patio. I'm grilling."

"Oh, no. I've interrupted dinner. I thought you WASPs ate at, like, 5 or something." She followed him inside. "If I'd known you were cooking, I'd have brought some wine or dessert. Not that I have any intention of staying—I wouldn't dare—but hell, I should have called first. Did I mention my cell phone needs recharging?"

Lombard rarely came to McLean's house, and then only by invitation. He knew Lombard was very private and sensitive about other people's privacy, unless they were the subjects of investigation. She rattled on about how she wouldn't bother him and Selena for more than a few minutes—he'd never seen her act so nervous, and suspected she'd done something as uncharacteristic for her as to show up at somebody's house uninvited on a whim. McLean hadn't thought Lombard had any whims.

McLean sat Lombard down in a deck chair on the patio and resumed his steak sentry. He pretended not to notice the stony look on Selena's face when she offered Lombard a drink. Lombard declined any alcohol but agreed to a glass of iced tea. McLean privately, and a little shamefully, reflected that there was probably more than enough alcohol in Lombard's immediate future once she got home. But for now, he realized, she needed company. And he knew why: because she was lonely, and she drank when she was lonely, and she started drinking early unless there was something like work or friendship to distract her.

"Loy, you're going to stay for supper whether you like it or not," he said. "We always make more than enough." For steak and eggs tomorrow, though he censored that thought.

"Well, thank you," she said. "But like I said, I came here for a reason. Sorry I've been beating around the bush. I don't know how to say it: We're fired. I think."

He turned away from the grill. "Who fired us?"

"Abel Wolf. Of course, his mother hired us and only she can fire us. But I'd say she'll go along with Abel on this one." She gave McLean a sheepish look and averted her eyes. "OK. You were right. I shouldn't have taken that damned thumb." She told him about her morning at Wolf Branch Farm.

McLean forked the meat onto a platter and set it on the patio table. "Mashburn will know now."

Lombard nearly spat. "He would've pitched that thing in the French Broad River, is the only thing he would've done different."

"We're eating inside," McLean sighed, picking up the platter.

The TV trays were folded up, and the dining table was set. McLean persuaded Lombard to stay, and though she looked genuinely embarrassed, she finally accepted and sat down. Things weren't working out as McLean had planned, but Lombard was a different person when away from work—always up for a laugh even when she was feeling down. After a while they were having a pretty good time—even Selena, who had mellowed after a couple glasses of wine, seemed to be enjoying Lombard's company. So McLean decided to give an account of his canoe ride at Apple Creek campground.

He told the story like it was a joke. He described Arlie and how he'd persuaded the long-haired tree hugger to paddle him across. He told of how they'd bumbled around finding nothing of interest, when they spotted a cabin. Lombard and Selena both nearly fell out of their seats laughing when he told them about his heathen sixth sense intuiting the cabin was occupied before Arlie pointed out a Mercedes M-class SUV parked next to it. Then he came to the part where the big blond woman stepped outside wielding a high-powered rifle, and suddenly Lombard's smile vanished.

"A big blond woman?" she repeated. McLean nodded, chuckling through a mouthful of potatoes. "Good-looking woman?" Lombard asked.

McLean shrugged and reached for his glass of tea. "She looked pretty good from where I was hiding." He winked at Selena.

"Describe her." Lombard had left the social hour and gone back to work.

McLean wondered where he'd gone wrong. "Like I said, Loy, she was blond, tall, you know, big-boned. Kind of like you, buildwise, come to think of it. Real yellow hair, long, but not dumb blond–looking. She looked mean, smart. Like she knew how to handle that rifle. That's why me and Arlie didn't take any chances."

Lombard went into one of those curious trances that overtook her whenever she was vexed about something. After a minute she said, "That really bothers me."

"It bothers me too," said Selena. "Sam could've gotten shot."

Lombard arched her eyebrows and nodded. "He could have, if it's the same woman I'm thinking of. Only that's not what bothers me."

"Gee, thanks, Loy," said McLean.

"Oh, you know I don't mean that. You weren't going to get shot, because your instincts told you not to mess with her. What bothers me is she sounds exactly like a woman I met at Desmond Holliday's party, a woman who probably knew Natalie Wolf though she won't admit it, whose origin is Eastern European, and whose last known residence—according to Tyler Rhodes—was near Miami. And that cabin she's guarding is within a brief, quiet moonlit canoe ride of where Natalie's body got dumped—and just across the river from Wolf Branch Farm."

Lombard stood up and thanked them for their hospitality. "I'll call Mrs. Wolf tomorrow and try to talk her out of firing us. Things are getting much too interesting for me to let that happen."

The door closed behind Lombard, and McLean turned around and glanced through the archway to the dining room, where Selena was pouring herself another glass of wine. She raised the glass and said, "Here's to things getting too interesting."

CHAPTER 9

Gussie Wolf told Lombard she knew all about the thumb—though Abel hadn't said anything about it until after Lombard had left the farm on Friday—and no, of course she wasn't fired. "I told you he ain't right," the old lady said, "and yeah, he sure as hell wants you fired. Says you're deceitful, a poisoner."

"A poisoner?" Lombard bellowed. She was sitting in her office early on Sunday afternoon, talking to Mrs. Wolf on the phone. "Where did he get that idea?"

"He says women are historical poisoners. It's how they kill people, he says, and he says you have the black heart of Lucrezia Borgia, whoever the hell that is."

"That's a little over-the-top," said Lombard.

"So you know who he's talking about?"

"She was the bastard daughter of Pope Alexander VI, late 15th century, Spanish origins. She probably murdered at least one of her husbands by poisoning."

A long sigh poured into Mrs. Wolf's end of the phone line. "You two beat all."

"Mrs. Wolf, your son cut his dead wife's thumb off and hid it in your house. Doesn't that bother you?"

"Why, course it does! But I know how he is. He was always loitering around down at my brother's funeral parlor, still traipses over there from time to time. He's acted strange since Natalie's disappearance, that's a fact. And he grieved when she turned up dead. You better believe that. Cried like a baby. And I tell you something: It made me sick. That bitch stole $200,000 from him, worth a lot more than one lousy thumb. That's a fact, lady, I don't have to tell you twice."

Lombard got chills listening to Mrs. Wolf. The only time the fire left her voice was when she mentioned Natalie's name, and then it turned bitterly cold. "No, you don't have to tell me twice," she agreed. "Listen, I need some information, since I'm not fired. Do you know the name of the matchmaking agency Abel used to find Natalie?"

"I'll have to ask Abel."

"It's important that you do," said Lombard. "I don't think he'll be talking to me anytime soon."

"Probably not, but you're still on the case," Mrs. Wolf assured her. "Don't you worry about that one bit. I'll get that info from him pronto. We'll need all the damned help we can get now that he's run his mouth to Mike Church."

Lombard nearly dropped the receiver. "He did what?"

"Told on his thumb token, is what. Called Church at home early this morning."

"Why? My God! Why did he do that?" Lombard spluttered.

"I don't know. I told you he ain't—"

"Damn it, Gussie Wolf!" Lombard shouted. "This is way past him not being right. It's like suicide. You realize they'll arrest him as soon as they find…" She felt as though the flesh of her face had turned to wax. "Did he tell them where it is?"

"You'll have to ask him," said Mrs. Wolf.

Outside, an Asheville police cruiser drove past the window of Lombard's office. "I have a feeling that won't be necessary," said Lombard. She hung up and went out to the front lobby, where, sure enough, a young police officer was standing outside under the front-door awning.

When she opened the door, the policeman introduced himself as Officer Staley. He was wearing latex gloves and carrying a small vinyl zipper bag. He asked her if she was Loy Lombard and, finding out she was, said the police believed she was in possession of an important piece of evidence in the investigation of Natalie Wolf's murder. "I don't have a search warrant," he said, "but I was asked to track you down and request that you turn it over voluntarily."

"Mike Church sent you?" Lombard asked.

"Yes, ma'am. I thought, given the nature of the requested item, I might need backup, but he said that wouldn't be necessary."

Lombard sighed and motioned him inside. "He's right." He followed her into her office, where she unlocked a file drawer in her desk, reached into it, and produced the medicine jar. She handed it to him, though he stared at it for a moment before taking it. He unzipped his vinyl bag and slipped the jar inside, sealing it up.

"You're not crime lab, are you?" said Lombard. "You're a patrolman."

"Yes, ma'am," Staley said.

"Why didn't they send out somebody from the lab?"

Staley shrugged. "Well, it is Sunday, and there's nobody in the evidence lab. And, well, I hate to tell you this, Ms. Lombard..."

She stared at him. "What?" she snapped.

He took a deep breath. "You're under arrest."

"Oh, hell," she muttered, and sat down behind her desk. "Mike Church told you to arrest me, is that it?"

"Yes, ma'am."

"You don't have a warrant."

"Lieutenant Church theorizes I don't need one, as long as I saw you in possession of the evidence being concealed, and thereby also obstructing justice."

"Ah, he finally realizes his fantasy. And not to my surprise, doesn't have the balls to be here carrying it out himself."

Staley looked uncomfortable. "Ma'am, Lieutenant Church is off today. Otherwise—"

"Otherwise he would've had to dig up some other excuse not to be the one to try and haul me off."

"I'm sorry, ma'am, but you're under arrest."

"No, I'm not," she said wearily.

He looked perplexed. "Yes, ma'am, you are."

She leaned back in her chair and inspected her nails. "No, I'm not."

Staley's complexion darkened. "Ma'am, I know you were a decorated officer in Charlotte. I respect that." He sighed. "Lieutenant Church warned me about you."

"Warned you?" Lombard said in a surprised tone. "Am I dangerous?"

"Not exactly!" Staley put his hands on his hips and shook his head. "Look, you have to come with me."

"You and what army, big boy?" she grinned. She shoved her telephone over to him. "Call up that chickenshit lieutenant and tell him to get his ass over here if he wants to play rough." She felt kind of bad treating Staley this way, but it was Church driving her to it. She gave him a sympathetic look. "What would be worse for you? Calling him, or having to call extra men to help get me out of here?"

Staley flung his hands up in front of him. "You know what? Forget it," he said. "I didn't want to take you in anyway. If the lieutenant wants to bust you, then he can do it. I got what I came to get." He turned around and stomped out of her office.

"Be sure you seal that bag and take it straight to the lab," Lombard hollered. "Don't fuck it up like Mike Church would. And by all means, quote me!"

Mashburn looked very tired and very angry when he marched into Lombard's office early Monday morning. Lombard was just hearing a bit of bad news from Retta on a contract that was about to expire. It was one of their most dependable, the Blue Ridge Bus Depot, and the company now wanted to take bids again rather than automatically renew Lombard & McLean's services. She spotted Mashburn glowering at her from just inside the front door and offered him some coffee.

"This isn't a social call," Mashburn said. "I'm on my way to a bail hearing. Wanna guess whose?"

Lombard shook her head. "I don't have to. When did they arrest him?"

"Yesterday, before my flight left New Orleans."

"How was your trip?"

"Don't start with me, Loy," Mashburn snapped. "I was up half the night at county jail listening to Abel's garbage. I don't need your smart mouth on top of no sleep." Mashburn, apparently having reconsidered her offer, poured himself a cup of coffee. "He told me what you did, which you did right under my nose without telling me."

"We work independently, Sig. You're his lawyer. I'm his investigator."

"*His* investigator? Seems to me like you're doing a bang-up job for the prosecution." He sat down on the sofa. "Why did you turn that damned thing over to the police?"

"They knew about it. Abel told them."

"So what? You could have told them it was bullshit. For that matter, you could have told Abel—"

"He was going to the police if I didn't tell him the truth, Sig."

"He went to the police anyway!"

"I didn't know he'd do that. Why did he? He tell you?"

Mashburn slurped his coffee and said sullenly, "He tried to explain, but it didn't make any sense."

"What did he say?"

"He said he was tired of being robbed and wanted you held accountable for what you'd done."

Lombard and Retta traded glances, and Lombard leaned against the desk. "He knows they've traced the bullet to a rare gun exactly like one registered to him. He knows they found out about his theft warrant against Natalie—and the motive it showed. Why would he tell them he'd kept a body part of hers, and that I'd stolen it, just to get me held accountable?"

"I spelled all that out for him too. He said the truth will out. He expects to post bail today and get on with his life until the trial."

Lombard said, "Sounds like you've got your work cut out for you, Sig."

"No thanks to you," Mashburn grumbled. "Mrs. Wolf told me she wouldn't fire you. Why don't you do the noble thing and quit, then? You're less dangerous to us that way."

"What's that supposed to mean?"

"It means you still think like a cop. You just handed that evidence over like you were working for Mike Church."

"That's a lie." Lombard was livid. "You're right about me thinking like a cop, though. Sometimes it pays to. Did you ever think of that, counselor? It pays to know how to piece *facts* together, instead of bullshit fancy talk. That thumb wasn't evidence as long as they didn't know about it. I believe Abel took it from the funeral home. That's why I was hiding it, so the police wouldn't find it and get the wrong idea. But once the lunatic told the police, it became evidence, so I had to turn it over. That's the law."

Mashburn finished his coffee, set the mug on a side table cluttered with old magazines, and stood up. "That's Lombard's law, not any law I know. You twist lies and the truth in equal measure. I'm not even sure you know the difference."

"Ha! *I* twist lies and truth? Rich stuff coming from a greasy lawyer like you. Why did you even show up here today? Just to chew me out?"

"To insist that you quit this case."

"No deal. Next?"

Mashburn tightened his jaw. "All right, then. Just stay clear of me and my defense of this case. I should've known better than to think we could work together." He straightened his jacket and tie and started out the door. "If you ladies will excuse me, I have court business to attend to." He sneered at Lombard. "And a great big mess to clean up!"

"You wouldn't even have the blasted case if it weren't for me," she hollered as he sauntered out the door. "You should be kissing my ass!" She looked at Retta. "Can you believe that arrogant son of a bitch? After all I've done for him."

"Like what?" Retta yawned. "You mostly just make him mad."

"Everybody's mad at me," Lombard sulked. "My client, his lawyer, even Sam, I'm pretty sure."

"Sam ain't mad at you," said Retta.

"Yes, he is," said Lombard. "He wishes I hadn't taken the case. He thinks Abel killed Natalie. He wishes I'd leave well enough alone and focus on business. Once he finds out we're about to lose the bus depot contract, he'll blame me for it."

The door blew open again, and a short, pudgy fellow dressed in khakis and a polo shirt came inside. It took Lombard a moment to process his familiar face, and she sounded surprised when she said, "Mr. Coburn? What brings you here?" The horrifying thought crossed her mind that the Skinner Movables contract was somehow in jeopardy. Coburn had come to lay down some mighty blow in person, as punishment for the mental cruelty she'd served him over Natalie Wolf. But if he were trying to get out of the contract—Lombard's mind was racing as he walked over to her—he would have sent a lawyer, not come in person.

"May we speak in private, Ms. Lombard?" he asked like it was his First Holy Confession.

Lombard was relieved to hear the contract was safe after all. Coburn was merely scared out of his mind over the Natalie Wolf case.

He was sitting where her clients usually sat, in the same standard waiting-room chair Tyler Rhodes found so appalling. He had just told her he was now convinced the woman who had danced at his bachelor party was, in fact, the deceased Natalie Wolf. "I wasn't sure at first. It didn't look like her exactly. This girl was all tarted up. You know, heavy eye makeup, teased hair, lipstick." He nervously waved an index finger and rested it on his lips. "You know those collagen treatments? That's what her mouth looked like."

Lombard frowned. "I don't remember noticing that in her picture."

"Well, I don't know. Big lips. On the face, you know. She wore a lot of makeup. But I think it was her. She had that red hair, nice body." He sighed. "Russian accent." He nodded at Lombard. "I know it was a Russian accent. And she called herself Nadine."

"Nadine," Lombard echoed.

"Is that like an alias?"

"Probably wouldn't use her real name," said Lombard. "Mr. Coburn, why are you here telling me this? I thought you wanted to stay as far away from this case as possible."

"I do," he said. "But I'm afraid, Ms. Lombard." He glanced over his shoulder.

Lombard cocked her head. "We're in my office, Mr. Coburn. What are you looking at?"

He looked at her again, as though coming out of a fog. "Huh? Oh," he chuckled. "I was nervous about coming here, but I'm so paranoid right now, I thought it was safer than calling, the way phone lines can be tapped. And my company has a business contract with you, so I'd come here as a matter of course, and—"

"Absolutely," said Lombard. "You're our newest client. You can come here any time you like."

Coburn stared at his lap for a moment and seemed to be struggling with what to say or how to say it. "Ms. Lombard."

"Loy."

"Fine. Yes. Loy. I, uh, realize I got very emotional the last time we spoke." He chuckled again, cleared his throat, and looked earnestly at her. "I don't want you to think I'm crazy."

"You were very upset, understandably. I'm sorry I caused you any discomfort."

"Just let me spill my guts here," he snapped. His voice was suddenly hard. "Seth Agee is dead, and it wasn't an accident."

"How do you know?"

He studied her for a moment, as though sizing her up. "Agee came to Skinner Movables last year. He wasn't like the rest of the men in management. I'm in the Chamber of Commerce. I'm in the Rotary. I'm like everybody else. Agee wasn't." He cleared his throat again. "Agee was from Seattle. He got a job in D.C. after college working for a consulting firm. He liked hiking and canoeing, but he was a partyer too, and he was real up front about taking the job at Skinner because he liked the progressiveness of Asheville and the access to the outdoors. And it's a lot cheaper than D.C. So, Hendersonville being right next door to Asheville, he took the job Skinner offered him." Coburn rolled his shoulders and shook his head. "He didn't fit in. It was just convenience."

"He was your boy for finding fun things to do," Lombard guessed aloud.

"Right," said Coburn. "And fun ladies for doing them with. After you came to see me, I grilled him pretty hard. I knew he must have talked to you or your partner. He blew it off at first, telling me to lighten up. Then a few days later he suddenly started acting strangely. He said he'd found out some things that bothered him, and he said somebody was calling him at odd hours of the night, threatening him."

"Who?"

Coburn shook his head. "He didn't know, or at least he didn't say."

"Did he say what it was he'd found out?"

"No. He just acted nervous. Not scared, exactly, but nervous. Like a man under a lot of pressure, only there wasn't any pressure at work. His job was airtight as far as I was concerned. Yeah, I was pissed off at him for mentioning the party to Sam McLean, but he was always spouting off about what he called his party prowess. The day he died, he got a call at the office, and it made him want to go home sick."

Lombard felt a lump in her throat. "I think that may have been me, actually."

"No," Coburn said reflectively, "it wasn't. It was the voice."

"What kind of voice?"

"He didn't say. He just called it 'the voice.' " Coburn sighed. "That night, his car went into a ravine, and he was dead. I think he was run off the road."

"But there are no witnesses to corroborate you," Lombard said. "Mr. Coburn, did you know that Agee also told the police about that bachelor party? Only he told them more than he told Sam McLean, my partner."

"No," Coburn said, shaking his head. "I didn't know that."

"Well, he did. Did you know he was having an affair with Natalie Wolf?"

Coburn looked aghast. "What? Why? She was a whore!"

"I didn't say they were gonna run off and get married. In fact, I'm pretty sure it was a paid arrangement. But he left me with the distinct idea they'd rolled around in the sheets on more than one occasion. He said he'd been trying to contact her." Lombard watched for a reaction. Coburn only looked impatient to learn more. "I visited with Agee before he left work that day, just before his death. He acted very scared of something. He knew more than he was telling anybody."

"It's possible," said Coburn. "But what do I know? Why bother me?"

Lombard was silent for a few seconds. "What are you talking about?"

Coburn smiled. "I've been getting the same call, the same one Agee was getting, and I hope I can persuade you to provide a bodyguard."

"What does it say?" asked Lombard.

"It says, 'Leave it alone.'"

The first and last time McLean had seen Gussie Wolf, she'd been raising hell with her son and Lombard just after his identification of Natalie's body. He hadn't been terribly enthusiastic about meeting her, but Lombard thought it was time. Lombard had told Mrs. Wolf to find out the name of the matchmaking agency Abel had used to find a Russian wife, and Mrs. Wolf had promised to bring all the information she could find to the office on Tuesday night, when Dana Gabriel would be working.

McLean, Lombard, and Dana were sitting in the front lobby waiting for Mrs. Wolf, who would be arriving any minute. McLean checked his watch; it was after 6:30. "Why does she have to come in person?" he asked. "Why not just give us the name over the phone?"

Dana said, "She could have called it in, but when Loy told me she was old, I knew it would be easier for her to dig up all the papers she could find and just bring them. I'm interested in domain names and ways of tracing e-mails and Internet sites if I can find them. If she brings the computer printouts I asked for, I may be able to find what I'm looking for by following up with my own search."

McLean looked at Lombard. "Remind me why we're doing this again."

"To find out if there's any possible link between the matchmaking agency and a call-girl service, the one Agee used," said Lombard.

"Right," said McLean. "I take it you think there's an organized-crime angle."

"I don't think so yet," said Lombard, "but I think it's worth checking out."

"What if Mike Church and Deputy Potter took all that stuff in?"

"I have reason to believe they missed it," said Lombard. "My hunch is even if they got it, they won't know what to look for."

"And just getting it straight: Tony Coburn doesn't know the name of the escort service, and Seth Agee might have, but he's dead."

Lombard glared at McLean. "Yes. That's right," she said slowly.

"Just checking," McLean said, and glanced at his watch again.

Mrs. Wolf arrived a little late, breathing heavily as she lumbered into the office. She grunted slightly when Lombard greeted her, and set her big baby-blue purse on Retta's desk. She dug around in it for a few seconds and pulled out a crumpled manila envelope. "Who do I give this to?" she asked.

Dana said, "That would be me."

"Who're you?" Mrs. Wolf snapped.

Dana introduced herself before Lombard could open her mouth.

Mrs. Wolf looked at Lombard. "You didn't say anything about outsiders."

"Gussie, Dana is crackerjack at computer work, and this is my partner, Sam McLean. He's done a lot of work on this case."

Mrs. Wolf eyed McLean and shrugged. "Suits me then, I guess. Y'all are lucky you got jobs. Sig Mashburn tried like hell to get me to fire you."

"Why didn't you?" McLean asked, ignoring Lombard's scorching stare.

Mrs. Wolf looked sharply at him. "What did she say your name is?"

"Sam McLean."

She handed the envelope to Dana and buckled her purse. "Well, Sam McLean, I've got too much invested in that hellcat you work for already, is why I ain't fired y'all. I'm hoping you can track down that money, plus dig us out of this mess before that lawyer costs us too many more trips to the courthouse." She shot her index finger at Dana. "That there's all I could find when Abel wasn't looking. The cops took his file folders, but I found those papers in a book he keeps in his bedroom."

"Which book?" Lombard asked.

"Some French writer he's crazy about, been reading his stories since he was a kid. Guy Maupin Zant, or something like that."

"Guy de Maupassant," Lombard said under her breath.

Mrs. Wolf directed her finger at Lombard this time. "That's it. I know he's kept all his private papers stuffed in there for years. The cops didn't think to look there." She picked up her purse and headed back to the door. "I have to get back. Supper's late."

She was gone very quickly, and Lombard said, "What a weird place to stuff papers. What a weird man Abel is."

"Perhaps even a guilty man." McLean's voice had a sarcastic edge.

"It may look that way to you," Lombard said. "I worry about it too. But I think there's something else going on, whether he's involved or not. It's not as simple as it looks, Sam."

Dana sat quietly at Retta's desk, watching Lombard and McLean. He noticed her watching and smiled. She looked curious but not at all uncomfortable with the tension in the room. "What do you think, Dana?" McLean asked.

"Me?" Dana rolled her shoulders. "I don't know. I can't wait to check out what's in that envelope, though."

He stood up. "Well, Loy, if we're going to find out what's more to it, let's get going right away. Where did you say that good-looking blond woman is staying? Desmond Holliday's?"

CHAPTER 10

By midweek Abel Wolf was out of jail on bond, but if the press were to be believed, his conviction and imprisonment—if not death by lethal injection—were inevitable. Someone in the police department had seen fit to reveal the gruesome discovery of a human thumb said to have been in Abel's possession, and police had ordered DNA comparison to tissue samples taken and preserved by the forensics lab at the time of Natalie's autopsy.

The story broke headlines far past western North Carolina's borders. The tale of the ill-fated Russian bride in search of the American dream, yet fallen into the hands of an American psychopath, fascinated the morbid minds of an international public. The most famous tabloid headline read MURDERED RUSSIAN BEAUTY CASE HEATS UP; THUMB POINTS TO HUSBAND. Clumsy Abel Wolf, with his slack jaw, shifty eyes, and cheap, ill-fitting clothes, had become a world-class ogre.

The court of law was the only place in American society where a citizen could legally be marked for death or put in a cell to waste away forever. Courtrooms were places of destruction and rehabilitation; nobody who messed with the law—whether or not he or she did so voluntarily—came away unscathed. For victims, defendants, the guilty, the innocent, and the dead: There was no guarantee of justice, only the ever-present danger of injustice. In the law was a dark and ominous power unlike any other.

Most newsmen and -women didn't see it that way. For them the law was sport, and the courtroom its playing field. The lives caught up in the arena were numbers in the lineup of players primed for the public's entertainment. Abel was player number one; Mashburn his swaggering sports agent. And if Lombard hadn't deliberately avoided the spotlight by milling about in the sidelines, she might have found some renown too, in today's media climate probably less for being a private detective than for the sideshow appeal of being a lesbian PI.

Let the show go on, was Lombard's attitude. Let the hungry jackals gnaw on Natalie Wolf's disembodied thumb all they wanted; she was certain it meant nothing in the grand scheme of things. Dr. Fredericka Sanger had angrily insisted that all of Natalie Wolf's extremities had been intact at the time of her autopsy, and all her records proved it. Still, the police suggested it could have been missed—the body had been in a fairly advanced stage of decomposition, and Dr. Sanger's assistant had no memory of whether the thumb had been attached. The funeral home director to whom Lombard had spoken was understandably silent: No doubt he would prefer the public and the police not find out about his connection to Abel Wolf.

Everybody in law enforcement and the news media badly wanted Abel Wolf to be guilty, and if Lombard and McLean didn't act— or Mashburn didn't come through in the end—Abel would end up a convicted man. Lombard and McLean also knew: If the whole world thought Abel was guilty, then the real guilty party or parties would be starting to relax just about now.

Lombard and McLean had been sitting for nearly two hours in the parking lot of a flea market, across the highway from the turnoff to Holliday Lane, Desmond Holliday's private drive. They had taken the inconspicuous McLean family car—a tan Honda Pilot—for its tinted windows and unfamiliarity to those who might already be aware of what Lombard and McLean ordinarily drove. "How do you know if anybody's home?" McLean asked.

Lombard said, "I had one of our guards make a fake wrong turn in there an hour before we came out here. He told me there was a black Mercedes SUV." She squirmed a little. "Attila's there, but my hunch is she's not there for pleasure. It's probably more like a head-quarters for whatever she's up to." She cringed and leaned over the dashboard.

"What's wrong with you?" McLean asked.

"I have to pee. Bad," she said. "I've had to for a while."

"Well, go."

"What if she comes down?"

"We'll catch up. Just hurry. Get it over with."

Lombard got out and raced into the flea market. She tried the ladies' room door, but it was locked. A cashier told her she'd have to use a key, but she couldn't have a key if she weren't a customer. Lombard rushed back out to the car for her billfold—she had to pee in the worst way—but realized when she got there she'd left her billfold in the Pathfinder. McLean gave her his wallet. She tried to buy a packet of gum, but there wasn't any cash in McLean's wallet, and the cashier wouldn't take a credit card for purchases under $10. So Lombard grabbed a cheap-looking corn doll she figured McLean could give one of his kids and which ended up costing 20 bucks. Her bladder was about to explode, so she threw down his company credit card, but it had McLean's name on it and he had to sign for it. So she had to go get him, and he asked her why hadn't she just asked for cash—he carried cash separately on a money clip. Lombard crammed the doll into his hand and snatched up the keys to the bathroom.

She was in mid stream when the horn began to blow, loud and frantic. By the time she got out to the car, McLean was in the driver's seat with the engine running. She fell into the passenger's side just as the car began moving and shut the door as they sped onto the highway.

"She's probably a couple of miles up the road by now," he said.

"Did she wave and smile when you started laying on the horn?" Lombard said acidly.

"Listen, smart-ass, I waited till she was out of sight to honk."

"Floor it," Lombard ordered.

McLean plowed down the road at 80 miles per hour before the Mercedes came into view. He lay back behind by about ten car lengths and followed the Mercedes onto I-40. By the time they exited the interstate, he knew where they were going. "She's going to the cabin," he said. "How do we stay inconspicuous now?"

There was no way to be inconspicuous, so they merely slowed to a stop on the side of the road as the Mercedes turned onto Quarry Road, the evident turnoff to the old logging site where the cabin stood. Hours passed without any sign of Attila or her car. "What the hell is she doing up there?" Lombard said.

"I'm hungry," said McLean.

"Did you see a boat or a boathouse when you were up there?" she asked.

"No. But I didn't look for one." His stomach growled.

"I wish you had. I bet anything there's a boat up there, and she uses that SUV to put it in the water. Her car's got a trailer hitch, you know."

"Well, Loy, it's hard for me to guess what to look for when you haven't really offered a theory as to how this Attila woman is involved in the Wolf case."

Lombard said, "Attila knows something about Natalie Wolf's death, if she isn't directly involved in it." She glanced at McLean. "Sam, pretend for just a minute you think Abel is innocent. OK? Humor me." She frowned and went on. "Desmond Holliday has a checkered past. He's been in prison for drug-related crimes, so he's been connected in some way to organized crime. Attila, according to Tyler Rhodes, came up here from South Florida, where Holliday is from. She's got an accent—I think she's Hungarian. There are three primary facts about Natalie Wolf: She was from Eastern Europe, she married Abel a couple of years ago, and she got murdered less than two weeks ago. Two things we suspect: She was a prostitute of some kind, and she swindled Abel. If those last two things are true, she was working for somebody else, somebody in organized crime." She bit her lower lip. "Mm, mm, mm. Why, or what, is she hiding at that cabin? Why so close to Wolf Branch Farm? Why so close to where the body was dumped?" She nudged McLean. "And what about the fact that Attila arrived at Holliday's estate a day or two before Natalie's murder?"

McLean shrugged. "But that would have been several days after Natalie's disappearance. If she got here after the disappearance, she's not responsible for kidnapping." He shook his head. "Attila's arrival time helps her more than it hurts, the way I see it."

"Who said anything about kidnapping? Natalie swindled Abel, and Attila came to town to collect, and she wasn't happy for some reason." Lombard smacked McLean in the side of the head. "So she killed her. She hauled her off in a boat, dumped her on that camp-site next door to the farm, and made Abel look like a murderer." She looked out in the distance of the Quarry Road intersection. "If Dana is able to find a link between the matchmaking service Abel used and the escort service Seth Agee used, that will show me the marriage was a sham for some larger swindling enterprise. It'll give us the proof we need."

McLean stretched. "Yep. Giving him all the more reason to want to kill her when he found out about it."

Lombard smoldered quietly for a few seconds. "Well, Sam, let's just forget the whole thing. Put the car in drive, and let's go to Burger King. Fuck it. Let's have a Whopper and wait for Abel to fry."

"I wish you hadn't said that. I really am hungry."

Suddenly the Mercedes appeared at the mouth of Quarry Road. It turned onto the highway and sped past the spot where Lombard and McLean were bickering. McLean peeled out about 15 car lengths behind the Mercedes, with other traffic between them. "One thing's certain," McLean said as he whipped past cars and the speedometer passed the 75-mile-per-hour mark, "whatever that big blond is up to, she's in a hurry."

✠

Just one day, Lombard had promised McLean, and that would be the end of their amateurish stakeout of Attila the Blond. By 10 P.M. she was glad for her sake she'd made the promise. McLean was driving her insane. After hours of enduring his intermittent demands for food and sarcastic jabs about Abel, her mood had blackened.

She'd managed to get them some sandwiches around 4 that afternoon, and they had just finished a late supper he'd snagged for them as they sat waiting curbside along a corner near Pack Square. Across the plaza, past the fountain in the middle of the square, Attila was sitting in the café of a restaurant with a young blond woman.

Attila was looking expensively butch tonight, all leathered up in Burberry, Gucci, and René Lezard, from her jacket down her pants to her boots. Her hair was brushed back but not tied; it fell in one length to her shoulders. She was a blend of money, menace, and sex, and her swooning companion looked familiar to Lombard.

"I know who that girl is," Lombard mumbled.

"What? Who?" said McLean.

Lombard looked at him for the first time in an hour. "I recognize that girl sitting with Attila."

He grabbed the binoculars and looked. "She's a pretty girl." He handed them back to Lombard.

She sighed as she peered through the binoculars. The couple sat about a hundred feet from where Lombard and McLean were stationed in the Honda. Pack Square was bustling with activity; it was a pleasant moonlit Friday evening, just cool enough for a jacket in the light breeze. "Lucky bitch," she said.

"How does that work, anyway?" McLean asked. "Which one's the bitch?"

Lombard eyed McLean. "Stop being a pain in the ass, will you?" She raised her binoculars again and studied the café table. "I'm trying to figure out where I've seen that girl. I... Oh." Lombard smiled. "Oh, I know. She drove me back to the office that night Chris and I broke up. What a small town! She's friends with Dana, you know."

"The new girl?"

"Mm-hmm. Name's Stella. I'm not surprised Attila swept her up. She's a honey."

"Lemme see." McLean grabbed the binoculars. "*That* girl's a lesbian?"

"She sure as hell is," Lombard grinned. "The kind that can make you wish you were dead. Attila better watch out."

"If your theory about Attila's right, Stella's the one who'd better watch her back." He stared through the binoculars. "Hm. So she's friends with Dana? Is Dana—"

"Yeah."

"She tell you that?" He handed Lombard the binoculars.

"She didn't have to."

"You sure it's not just wishful thinking?" he asked.

Lombard smirked. "I know a cute dyke when I see one. But I have no designs on Dana, Sam. She's my employee. I'm her boss. I don't want to fuck every pretty girl I see."

"That's not what I heard back in Charlotte. So you think Dana's pretty?"

"Of course she's pretty."

"I don't really think so. She's stacked, but I don't know if I'd go as far as pretty. Cute, maybe, but—"

Lombard said, "She's not conventionally pretty, no. But she's very pretty, Sam."

"I guess I follow you. She's pretty in an odd sort of way. Maybe it's the glasses."

Lombard shook her head and raised the binoculars again. Attila and Stella had gotten up and were walking toward Patton Street. Lombard started the engine and followed them. "By the way," she said suddenly, "who made that crack about me in Charlotte?"

❖

"Dana," Lombard began the next morning, "I need a favor."

Dana looked out from behind the computer monitor on Retta's desk. She had the habit of raising her eyebrows and sucking her upper lip whenever Lombard spoke to her. "Yes, and then can I ask you for a favor?" she said. She scooted her chair back and stretched her lower back.

"Your back hurt?" Lombard asked.

"This chair kind of kills me," said Dana. "I wonder if you have a smaller one."

"I'll get you a new chair at Office Expo. Go pick one out this weekend."

Dana looked surprised. "Wow. In that case—not to push it or anything—what are the chances of having my own desk? It would be nice to have my own place to put my stuff." She pointed at her overstuffed backpack. "I keep everything in there for now."

"Your own desk, your own chair, you got it." Lombard fished around in her shoulder bag and pulled out a Lombard & McLean company credit card. She handed it to Dana. "That's our Office Expo account. Be reasonable."

Dana looked astounded. "Thanks!" She zipped the card up in a pocket of her backpack.

"I guess if you have your own desk, you'll want a computer."

Dana shook her head. "I have a laptop at home I've already hooked into your server, and that way I can work here and at home." She smiled. "So what sort of favor can I do for you, Loy?"

"You're friends with Stella the bartender, right?"

Dana looked thoroughly taken aback. "Sort of. Well, it's Stella Hines. And she prefers to be known as a drummer."

"She's a drummer?"

"Yeah, for an all-girl group called Tang. Ever heard of them?"

Lombard laughed. "No."

Dana said, "They're really good. They went to Athens a few years ago, but it didn't really work out for them. Nobody gave a shit about girl groups at the time. So now they just kind of do their music, you know, cut a CD every now and then. They've got a big regional following."

"Good for them," said Lombard. She leaned back in her seat. "Dana, there's a woman in town who I think knew Natalie Wolf, but I need to find out for sure. Her name is Attila. Ring a bell?"

"No."

"I saw Stella with her last night."

"Well, I'm not, like, really tight with Stella. We're friends as far as just the broader scene, if you follow me."

"You're both in the hip young lesbian scene."

Dana blushed. "Well, that's a little generalized."

"Would you be able to find out what she knows about Attila? Of course, I wouldn't come between friends. I'm not asking you to spy, but it borders on it."

"It's secret. I get it," said Dana. "I do know Stella, though not all that well. To be perfectly honest with you, Loy, she once dated my girlfriend."

Lombard's merry expression melted. "Oh. Well, I wouldn't want you to bother her if it would cause any—"

"As far as loyalty," said Dana, "I have none for Stella. She tried to be friendly with me when I started seeing Jane, her ex, but I realized pretty quick she was using me. So if I can help you and fuck with her at the same time, just tell me what you want."

In the meantime, Lombard would take matters into her own hands. Tyler Rhodes had been calling, leaving messages with nosy questions about how her investigation was going, but she hadn't called him back. She doubted he had anything useful or credible to tell her; he probably only wanted to get information out of her to sate some vain compulsion of his to tease Desmond Holliday. But now that Attila had become her focus, she thought it might be worthwhile to meet with Rhodes.

She went to Maddie's Bar, where she'd asked Rhodes to meet her and where she thought Stella might be working that night. She wound her way to a dark corner and stole an unoccupied seat somebody had claimed by tossing a jacket over the back. She lifted an arm of the garish orange suede jacket and thought she spotted its owner in a short, pudgy woman with teased hair, jiggling on the dance floor with two partners: Desmond Holliday and Tyler Rhodes.

A server came by and took her drink order. Lombard waited for her bourbon, annoyed at Rhodes for bringing company but amused by the sight of the men dancing. They seemed to thrill their beaming dance partner, who looked just like the sort of woman who would waste half her life in the pointless pursuit of a man like Holliday or Rhodes.

Lombard checked out the club for any sign of Stella. If she was working, it wasn't downstairs. She must be in the private lounge upstairs, then. Lombard doubted she could schmooze her way up there, and anyway, she couldn't do it inconspicuously. She glanced behind her in the direction of the stairs leading up to the lounge, studied the ready expression of the gentleman seated in front of it, and opted to stay right where she was. She turned around and barely raised an eyebrow at the statuesque blond who'd just sat opposite her at the table.

"Attila," said Lombard, "you're still in town."

Attila's hair was twisted in a chignon, and she was wearing a black satin minidress and black stockings. She glided from butch to femme with the quiet stealth of a cat. "I like it here," said Attila, lighting a black Sobranie cigarette. Shaking the flame out of her match, she added, "I might stay. Open a shop or something."

"Mm, yeah," said Lombard, "People who stay in Asheville seldom want to leave."

Attila almost smiled. Just then Holliday and Rhodes and their cheerful lady friend crowded around the table. When Holliday began entertaining Attila and the lady friend—a client of Holliday's named Carol—with one of his stories, Lombard nudged Rhodes. She said peevishly, "I thought we were going to meet alone."

He beamed. "Loy, I've missed you."

"Yes, I've missed you too. I've missed you so much, I can't believe you brought all these goobers with you to come between us."

"Now, Loy," Rhodes said in mock reproach, "I know you don't consider Attila a goober."

Lombard cut her eye across the table. Attila was coolly staring at her, but the music was loud, and Lombard could talk in Rhodes's ear without being overheard. Lombard shifted her chair to face away from Attila and leaned in toward Rhodes. "You knew we had to talk alone. What the hell's wrong with you?"

"They insisted on coming. I had dinner with Desi, which has lately become rather a habit. Attila was there, and that awful friend of Desi's was there, and they more or less invited themselves along when I begged an early departure."

"Well, it's no good tonight," said Lombard. "Not with them here. Come by my office Monday."

Attila suddenly shouted over the loud music and conversation. "Loy!" She stood up and towered over Lombard. "Come upstairs with me."

Suddenly and inexplicably, Attila was interested in Lombard. She wanted to know everything about her, and Lombard gave her what she considered the public records version of herself: New Orleans childhood, Italian Catholic roots, her world tour in the Navy, her police career in Charlotte. She left out the chapter covering her last, humiliating, and ruinous year in Charlotte, and fast-forwarded to the new life and business she'd launched in Asheville. She also left out any details of her personal life. She only told Attila enough to get Attila talking about herself. Lombard wanted to learn all she could about her, and she was vexed by Attila's apparent eagerness to talk.

"I grew up in Budapest," said Attila. "I was a competitive swimmer, so I got to travel a lot around the old Soviet bloc. I went to East Germany, Czechoslovakia, Poland, all over."

"Russia?" Lombard asked.

Attila sighed. "Yes, I was in Moscow and Leningrad—now St. Petersburg. I learned a lot, especially about language and travel. When the Iron Curtain came down, I already had a taste for world travel. So I went to Vienna first, then Paris. It was only a matter of time before I would come to America. I was 30 when I visited New York. There, I got a work visa and a job with a travel agency. I was transferred to Miami, and I've been there ever since."

"You're a travel agent," Lombard said flatly.

Attila pulled a card case out of her purse and withdrew a business card. She handed it to Lombard. BLUE SKY TRAVEL, INC. was embossed in forest-green on a pale-blue backdrop with doughy white clouds. "That's my name at the bottom. M. Attila, for Mari Attila."

"Mari Attila," Lombard repeated. "Rolls right off the tongue. You speak a lot of languages?"

"Hungarian, German, French, English…" Attila leaned back in her chair and crossed her legs. "And Russian. What about you?"

Lombard shrugged. "I never spoke a word of Italian till I lived in Italy in the Navy. I picked up quite a bit there. Not enough to impress anybody, I'm afraid."

"Americans don't think they need to learn anybody else's language."

"No, I guess not," Lombard agreed. She pocketed Attila's card. "So, Attila, did you bring me up here to trade life stories? Or did you have anything special in mind?"

Attila smiled. "I don't have many friends here other than Desi. I thought it would be interesting to talk to you."

"Aw, haven't you met any nice girls during your stay in Asheville?" Lombard asked.

Attila stared at Lombard for a moment. "I've been going out, as you know by seeing me at the café that afternoon. Why do you ask? Have you seen me out?"

Lombard sipped her drink. "No. I don't get out much myself."

Attila looked around the lounge. It was comfortable and dimly lit, with only a few well-heeled patrons enjoying each other's quiet company. "You should go out more often. I enjoy it more in this smaller town. It's not noisy and dirty like the bigger cities."

"So what sort of shop are you going to open up? A travel agency?" Lombard had finished her bourbon and waved at the bartender. Stella was nowhere in sight.

"I don't know yet," said Attila. "I'll have to check the possibility. My residency status is an issue, of course."

"Ah, of course," said Lombard. "That whole citizenship thing. Maybe you ought to bite the bullet and marry some old boy, then." She laughed, but Attila didn't.

She cut Lombard an icy glare and pursed her lips. "Sometimes," Attila said darkly, "it doesn't pay to do that."

Lombard arched her eyebrows. "Just ask Natalie Wolf, huh?"

"The famous dead woman," Attila said. "Desi's friend."

"Some friend. I haven't heard him lament her passing yet. He was all worried about her when I met him, yet there hasn't been one word about her since." Lombard watched Attila light a cigarette. "Has he said anything to you about her?" Lombard asked.

Attila blew smoke through her nose. "No."

Rhodes was standing over them all of a sudden. "There you are!" he cried. "I'm exhausted from charming that bouncer into letting me and Desi up here." Holliday and his friend Carol were laughing behind him. "Everybody sit down," Rhodes commanded cheerfully. "Bartender, a round for everybody in the room. Let's all get blind tonight!"

It was 4 A.M. when their party was politely asked to leave. Rhodes led the charge onto Broadway, everyone else stumbling behind him in a line. "We're like little baby quails," said Holliday. He slapped Rhodes in the ass. "Say, Mama Quail, where the hell's the car?"

"You mean Attila's car?" said Rhodes. "She's no quail, by the way. She's a fox."

"Mm-hmm," Holliday agreed. "A sly vixen."

Everyone stopped in back of the Mercedes, and Attila ordered them to get in.

"I'll get a cab home," Lombard said. She had no intention of either riding with them or passing out in her office again and risking another chance encounter with Dana; it didn't enter her bourbon-addled brain that Dana would be long gone at 4 A.M., because Lombard was too gassed to grasp any concept of hour or day. She usually maintained enough conscience, however drunk, to fend off humiliation.

"You're coming with me," Attila said, grabbing Lombard by the arm and shoving her into her Mercedes. Holliday and Rhodes climbed into the back.

They were a few miles past the city limits when Rhodes shouted, "Oh, we forgot Carol!"

"We didn't forget her," said Holliday. "I left that dreadful thing behind on purpose. I'm sure she'll be all right."

"Wait," Lombard said. "We're nowhere near my side of the county."

Attila said nothing. She didn't act drunk, though she had to be. She'd had more than any of them, and the more she'd guzzled, the more trancelike and seething she'd looked. She sped up Holliday Hill and screeched to a halt in front of the house. She grabbed Lombard's hand and locked eyes with her.

"Darling," Lombard said ruefully, "I'm way, way past it."

By the time she found herself halfway up the stairs to Attila's guest room, Lombard's memory of coming into the house was already foggy. Holliday and Rhodes were nowhere in sight or sound. "I'm blitzed, honey," Lombard mumbled. "Just lay me down to rest."

"Don't be a coward," said Attila, pulling Lombard's arm as she hurried up the steps. "I know you're fit for anything right now."

Lombard regretted that she was right, for the most part. Lombard was fit for anything but resisting the sexual advances of a beautiful, powerful woman. Had anybody ever successfully resisted anyone named Attila? The name itself was dominion.

Attila pushed her bedroom door open and gently shoved Lombard inside. "Sit down," she said, pushing Lombard into a plush purple chaise longue. Lombard leaned back, resting her head on the soft, low back of the chaise, and closed her eyes. She heard a faint zip and the muted thud of fabric falling to the floor. She sighed a little when she felt the cushions depress under Attila's weight, and opened her eyes. Attila was kneeling over Lombard, her knees on either side of Lombard's hips, her hair falling down about her shoulders. She was almost totally nude, swathed only in a camisole and the soft pink light of a bedside lamp. Lombard smiled at Attila's bosom, draped in indigo satin. She tugged at the hem and said, "Why so shy?" She cupped her hands over Attila's bare buttocks and pushed her closer. She rubbed her thighs and caressed the patch of dark pubic hair as Attila held herself up by gripping the back of the chaise.

When she climaxed, Attila drew back quickly, falling backward onto the chaise, her legs splayed out over the sides. Lombard leaned over her and moved her hands underneath the camisole. Attila abruptly slapped Lombard's face and pushed her back.

"Honey, just say no," Lombard mumbled, rubbing her jaw. She gave Attila a wounded look, but the sight of Attila's bosom—hot and sticky under her sweaty camisole—and the glistening spot between her legs displaced any hurt pride. She wanted to fuck her so badly it sobered her up.

Attila smiled. "It's in that drawer." She pointed at a bureau behind her. "Third one down. Hurry."

After a few awkward moments of search and assembly, Lombard lay bosom-to-bosom on top of Attila, moving on top of her in the slow, undulating rhythm she'd learned—and made more frequent use of—as a younger woman. She thought vaguely how she'd always liked gadgets and wondered why she'd lost interest in them. Some old girlfriend, she guessed, one of those nature-or-nothing types. Attila might be sinister, but at least she liked having a good time in bed.

Suddenly Lombard was alight in a jolting sensation in her groin. Oh, life! She buried her face in Attila's neck and gripped the brass bars of the headboard till her knuckles were white. Attila arched her back, pressed her thighs against Lombard's hips, grabbed the flesh of her shoulder blades, and bit her ear. Lombard cried out, on the border of agony and bliss, "Easy!" She glared at Attila, who was smiling like a new bride.

Lombard pulled out and fell on her back, grimacing as she worked the straps loose. As she leaned over to throw the rig on the floor, she noticed a newspaper laid out on an ottoman. The headline was a few days old: MURDERED RUSSIAN BEAUTY CASE HEATS UP. Lombard felt dizzy and passed out.

CHAPTER ► 11 ►

It was the worst hangover. An ordinarily bad hangover any tough, grown-up partyer worth her salt could handle with something approaching dignity. There would be the splitting headache, the roiling nausea, the telltale cotton mouth—nothing gallons of water, an overdose of ibuprofen, and hours of sleep couldn't cure. But this was the one Lombard couldn't stand: The Hangover of Shame. The guilty hangover, that which transcends—or more accurately, sinks below—common physical wretchedness, grips the conscience, and strips its victim down to the base fears and insecurities of childhood. Lombard thought about going to Mass, and, in a momentary lapse of agnosticism, swore to God and the Blessed Virgin she would make her confession as soon as her brain jelled back into place, and she would never make so indecent a spectacle of herself again.

She was too sick to go to Mass, and besides, there was no way home until after noon. Attila was still out cold by the time Lombard was able to slide out of bed and collect her clothes off the floor, sweating and retching through the ordeal of just getting dressed. She crept downstairs and called a cab on her cell phone but realized Holliday's address was occluded in the part of her brain where lucid thought was only just beginning to awaken. She was a wreck, but her luck was still with her: The cook, a plump, pleasant woman who seemed used to the task, called up a valet to take Lombard back to her car.

By Monday morning she wanted nothing more than the peace and stability of the humble, ugly offices of Lombard & McLean. Retta would have coffee ready; McLean would amble in a little late as was his habit; some of the guards would be clocking in and lounging about with their coffee mugs, shooting the breeze and calling for Lombard's opinion on this or that current event. In short, she would be home with the only family she had or wanted. And it would take her mind off things like the weekend's debauchery.

If only she could shake thoughts of Attila. The woman had stripped her of every warp and woof of her sexual being. Lombard had thought her wild days lay years behind her. She enjoyed some of those memories the way a wiser woman entering middle age might find amusement in reflections on the reckless forays of youth. She'd made some mistakes, like everybody, done some wild things she regretted, some she didn't regret; on the whole, the old days held fond and passionate memories she would enjoy to her dying day.

But Lombard's sensibilities had become more rigid over the years. She believed people of a certain age ought to behave in a certain way. What was acceptable at 25 was merely excusable at 30, distasteful at 35, and pathetic at going on 43. It was bad enough she'd fucked a woman she barely knew and cared nothing about; but carrying on like that with a murder suspect, particularly *her* murder suspect, was grotesque. Lombard was, stripped to the bare bones, an essentially moral woman with a weakness for breaking her own rules.

She'd forgotten all about having asked Rhodes to come to her office. She'd wanted information on Attila when she'd agreed to meet him on Saturday night, but the intervening and unexpected romp with the subject of her investigation had quieted any intention of discussing Attila with Rhodes anytime soon. She needed a break first, but Rhodes apparently did not, and he hadn't forgotten their appointment. She was startled at the sight of him when she walked into the office, and she was doubly surprised to see him standing beside the apple of her eye, Dana. Yet there they were, in the front lobby of her office on Monday morning, with Retta brooding behind her cheap, metal desk with its outdated computer monitor, and that wouldn't have mattered one wit were it not for the fact that Rhodes and Dana were chatting over a beautiful new walnut writing table and black leather swivel chair, newly installed.

"Loy!" Rhodes said brightly. "So good to see you. You're looking well."

Lombard knew she looked far from well, and she only vaguely acknowledged Dana, who wasn't supposed to be working on Mondays or any other morning. "Hello, Dana. Rhodes, come with me."

Once her door had closed behind him, she said, "What's with the fancy furniture?"

"Oh, don't tell me you don't remember."

"What are you talking about?"

Rhodes smiled. "Surely you haven't forgotten our appointment."

"Right." Lombard shook her head. "But what's with the furniture?"

"Oh, you know. The other night, when we were all really lit, I started teasing you about your awful office furniture. And you told me if I was so high-and-mighty, then why didn't I cough up a new desk and chair for an employee of yours who needed it? And I said, "Oh, she must be a cute girl," and you said I was damned straight she was a cute girl, and you mentioned her name. Dana, with one *n*. I think Attila was a little jealous."

Lombard blushed. Yes, she remembered now. "I was drunk. I always say things I don't mean when I'm tanked. I didn't mean for you to interfere, though I appreciate the obvious whatever. Now, please take that stuff back."

"Of course I won't. I could tell you really liked her. You went on and on about the pretty librarian from Pack Memorial, how she would by God have her own desk and chair. We all started laughing when Desi called her the 'lipstick librarian.' So I had my people deliver the desk and chair first thing this morning, and I asked for Dana with one *n* over at the library to check it out and tell me what she thinks. That's why she's here."

"That's over the line! I won't have it. Now, take that stuff back."

There was a knock on the door. Dana slowly opened it when Lombard gave the go-ahead. She peered inside and said, "I have to get back to the library. I just wanted to thank Tyler and say it's nice to have met you." She looked at Lombard. "Loy, I gave Retta your credit card. I went to Office Expo yesterday and ordered some stuff, but Retta said we can cancel it. I thought I'd ask you first, though."

Lombard sat down at her desk. "It's OK, Dana. I'm glad you like it."

After Dana had gone, Lombard said, "I can't afford walnut tables and leather chairs."

"It's gratis," he said. "It's just me being playful. And it's also a way of thanking you for being such a sport this weekend."

Lombard leaned forward and rested her forehead in her palms. "I don't want to talk about that."

Rhodes sat down. "I thought you wanted to talk about Attila."

"No." Lombard looked up. "I've reconsidered."

"Do you like her?" He sounded surprised. "I thought that was just a—"

"It was, and that's it. Let it rest." She blew out a deep breath. "Dear God, I've complicated things miserably."

Rhodes said softly, "Loy, I know I can be a glib bastard, but I like to think of myself as a friend of yours, whether you want to believe that or not. I want to help you. And, well, that's why I brought the furniture. It's my kind of salve for nerves I may have helped to fray just a bit."

Lombard looked crossly at him. "What do you mean?"

"I know you were drunk and things got out of hand. It happens to the best of us." He shrugged and grinned. "And to the worst of us. If you want information about Attila, I may be able to help. Sometimes, girlfriend, you just have to trust people."

Trust Tyler Rhodes? Lombard told Rhodes that if he could be trusted, then he could talk to McLean about Attila, from whom she wanted to distance herself as much as possible. And so on Tuesday, McLean went to Rhodes's office on Lombard's behalf. He didn't know about her one-night stand; Lombard rarely made any reference to her sex life. The poor guy had come a long way accepting homosexuality as a fact of life, and he'd gone to great lengths to empathize with his friend Lombard. But the wild side of it was outside his reach.

Rhodes was not as understanding, and in fact relished raking uptight straight people—men in particular—over the red-hot coals of gay reality. He had a way of strapping them up, pinning their eyelids open, and throwing the switch on the bright light of truth.

"All I know about Attila," he told McLean as they sat in Rhodes's office, "is what I've learned from Desi. She never talks when I'm around. Frankly, she's the weirdest, most off-putting woman I've ever met, and I try to stay away from her."

Lombard had already filled McLean in on what Attila had told her. He was more interested in what she was doing in Asheville now. "Desmond Holliday and Attila must be pretty close friends. She's been at his house over two weeks, hasn't she?"

"I don't think they're friends," said Rhodes. "And it's technically my house."

"What?"

"How do you think Desi affords a home like that, staffed with servants, on a smattering of wealthy clientele in western North

Carolina and east Tennessee? He built the house on my land, but I paid for it. I lease it to him, and I provide the staff." Rhodes frowned. "And I don't like Attila one wit."

"That was generous of you, building the house for him," said McLean.

"I'm a nice guy! And I was thrilled when I met Desi. So nice to have somebody like him in town. Eventually we began an affair, and I helped him with the house, which was, of course, a smart investment on my part as well."

"But you don't live with him."

"Hell no. I have my own house in town. I dislike country life. I grew up on an estate outside of Greensboro and got my fill of it young. Anyway, I don't live with him, though we occasionally hook up for old times' sake. He is tremendously charming, not to mention agile."

McLean cleared his throat. "Why is it you don't like Attila? Is she getting between you and Desi somehow?"

"Somehow? I would say yes. Though not in terms of relationship. Hardly that. She just oozes dark power. She's a fucking wet blanket. I can't stand her! Even after Desi hooked her up with that girlfriend."

"What girlfriend?"

"Some cute blond bartender Desi got to know in the gay community. He's all into that scene." Rhodes rolled his eyes. "Anyway, Attila wanted a woman to have fun with, so he hooked them up. She's been shaking that little hottie down for over a week now, almost every night. She's insatiable." He bit one of his nails and slyly eyed McLean. "And she likes variety, if this weekend is any indication of her appetite."

McLean shrugged. "What do you mean?"

"Well, it's the soft blond hottie one night, and your strapping butch business partner the next. She'll ramp it up for Sig Mashburn before this is all over with."

McLean was speechless. He stared at Rhodes for a moment. "What? Loy? When?" He frowned at Rhodes. "Wait. You're kidding."

Rhodes clamped his mouth shut. His complexion paled a little.

"You're not kidding," said McLean.

"I thought you knew," Rhodes said rapidly.

"Knew what?"

"Nothing."

"Don't bullshit me, Tyler! Loy slept with Attila?"

"I thought you two were close," Rhodes sputtered. "I thought you shared everything, after all you've been through together."

"We're not that close," said McLean, his voice edged with a mix of disgust and disappointment. "What's happening to her?"

"She was drunk, Sam."

"Yeah," McLean said, "that's Loy, all right." Although she'd never sunk to sleeping with suspects when they'd been real cops, he thought. But she hadn't been a drunk in those days.

"Please don't tell her I told you. She's very embarrassed by the whole thing, Sam."

"She should be." McLean shook his head. "Look, I'm not here to discuss Loy's private problems. You know good and well I came here to talk about Attila. Now, what do you know for a fact? If she and Desi aren't friends, then what's she doing here?"

"I think it's about business. Unorthodox business. That's why Desi's so tight-lipped and nervous all the time. Listen, I like Desi. I want to help him. I want that scary bitch off Holliday Hill as soon as possible."

"It's your house," McLean said. "Why don't you tell her to leave?"

Rhodes said, "That's easier said than done. I may own the house, but it's Desi's home for now, and I wouldn't dream of telling him how to run his household. For another thing, Attila scares me."

"You might have good reason to be afraid of her," said McLean. "Loy and I want to know if Attila has a connection to Natalie Wolf."

"I wish I knew." Rhodes looked troubled. "But if I did, I wouldn't know what to do."

"You'd go to the police."

"Of course I wouldn't! Sam, I'd have to know Desi was in the clear before I ratted out Attila. He'd kill himself before he went back to jail. I won't be responsible for that."

McLean sighed. "I have a feeling you know a lot more than you're telling, Tyler. As usual." He added, "Though sometimes you tell more than you should."

"Fair enough, but I'm not playing around. I swear. All I know for certain is that Desi is scared shitless of Attila. And it's starting to scare me."

❖

That evening Dana had news. "I've pinged the domain name and gotten an IP address," she said.

Lombard looked bewildered. "What do you mean?" she asked.

"The domain name Mrs. Wolf brought." Dana shook her head a little irritably. "The Web site for Russian brides? You wanted me to see if I could locate its origins."

"Right," said Lombard. "What's a ping and an IP?"

Dana smiled. "A little Internet primer might help to explain this. OK. IP stands for "Internet Protocol," which allows computers to talk to each other. There's a set of numbers assigned by the American Registry for Internet Numbers, or ARIN. In order to register a Web site, you have to give ARIN a physical address." She clicked her mouse and waved Lombard closer in. "Look. I've logged on to an IP2LL site, which stands for Internet Protocol to Longitude/Latitude. It's a tool for finding the physical origin of a Web server or site. The smaller the ISP, or Internet service provider, the better your chances of isolating a site to a specific geographic location. I'd say it's about 70% accurate with smaller Web sites."

"So what are we waiting for?" said Lombard. "Ping the whatty-acallit."

"Domain name. It's www.occidental-love.com," she said. "Let me show you its IP address." She clicked her mouse. "Bring up the command prompt and type in the domain name," she said, typing, "and I get the numbers." She clicked on the IP2LL screen. "Now, I type the numbers here, *et voilà!*" She turned around and pushed her eyeglasses up the bridge of her nose. "P.O. Box 477Y-2X, Miami Beach, Florida. Registered to N. Gromyko."

"Well, how about that?" Lombard said.

"It's almost scary," said McLean, eyeing Lombard.

"No, it's laughably simple. The Internet is a lot scarier than that," Dana grinned.

"How do we connect it to that escort service?" asked Lombard.

"Assuming they can be connected," McLean added.

"They've got to be connected," said Lombard. "Agee said it was a Miami-based escort service. That's it! They're connected."

Dana said, "Find out the escort domain name, if one exists, and I may even be able to tell you who owns it."

"Can't you do that off the bride site?" asked McLean. "I mean, if they use the same ISP, then—"

"It's possible," said Dana, "but it's a lot easier with the actual Web address." She studied the perplexed looks of her employers and sighed. "Look, I have a friend who's employed full-time just to find domain names like that. It can be done, but it's tedious and costly in terms of time, and often unsuccessful. You normally go to ARIN.net and search the ISPs using a swipe handle, but it's all quite a process. So it would be well worth your while to find somebody who knows the escort service domain name."

A flat, stony smile crossed Lombard's face. "Well, I guess it's time to crack down on Tony Coburn. I've been letting him slide long enough." She looked at McLean. "Sam, you want to be good cop or bad cop?"

Dana was glad to help, and she hadn't forgotten her other promise: to find out what Stella knew about the blond woman with the weird name. Attila the Blond, Lombard referred to her without smiling, yet Dana could tell it was her new boss's peculiar, wry way of cutting up, and Dana found it funny. Lombard almost never smiled at her, never acted very friendly at all, really. But Dana sensed Lombard's confidence in her, and she was eager to find information for her about Attila.

"So what's she like?" Stella asked. They were sitting in the café of a vegan restaurant sipping on veggie juice blends, and they were talking about Dana's new part-time job.

"She's strange," Dana said. "It's like, she looks really butch, but she doesn't play that up at all. She acts like a strict aunt or something. Never smiles at me. I was on pins and needles around her at first. I totally thought she didn't like me."

"What makes you think she does now?"

Dana shrugged. "She got me a new desk and chair, for one thing."

Stella cackled. "Oh, my God. She has a crush on you."

"No!" Dana said. "That's not it. I'm way too dorky for somebody like her."

"And too young," Stella added, evidently letting pass Dana's assessment of herself as a dork.

"Not really," said Dana. "She's around 40. I'm 31. Same general ballpark."

"That's not the same ballpark, Dana. That's a span." Stella pursed her lips around her juice straw. "Besides, I've seen her drink, and you couldn't keep up. Trust me."

Dana winced. "Why are we discussing this? I have a girlfriend."

"So do I," Stella beamed.

"Really? Who?"

Stella shook her head. "You'll tell Jane."

"Of course I'll tell Jane. You want me to tell Jane."

"Yeah, right!" said Stella. "I consider you a friend, Dana. It has nothing to do with Jane. It's obvious she prefers brains to beauty, which is cool with me."

Dana clenched a fist under the table and smiled. "Come on, who are you with?"

Stella giggled like a schoolgirl in love. "OK, there is somebody. She's European. Very sophisticated."

"Who is she?"

"Her name is Mari. Gorgeous, cool, sexy, intelligent." Stella leaned back in her seat and bit her lower lip with a dreamy look in her eyes. "I've only been seeing her for a little over a week, and she is kind of just visiting. So maybe *girlfriend* isn't the right word." Stella tightened her shoulders and gave a tiny squeal. "Oh, she's so good in bed!" She thumped her feet on the ground and laughed. "Oh, come *on*, Dana! You're blushing."

"It's a little more information than I needed," Dana said primly, "but I'm dying to know more." She leaned over the table and rested her chin in her palms.

"No way! You'll tell Jane."

"You want me to tell Jane, but I probably won't. She'll sulk if I do."

"No, she won't," Stella said indifferently. "She obviously isn't jealous of what I do if she dumped me for a brainiac with a big nose and glasses."

Dana breathed deeply and considered charging Lombard overtime for having to put up with Stella's petty shots. "You're forgetting. Jane didn't even know me when you broke up."

"Oh, I'm kidding. You have bigger tits. So whatever."

"Look, if you're going to resort to catty swipes at me, I'm not interested."

"I'm teasing! Relax, will you?"

"I'm intrigued," Dana said with mock eagerness. "A foreign lover? So what does she do? What does she look like?"

"I don't know her line. She's pretty quiet; we don't talk much. But she's spectacular. She's really tall and cut, you know. She looks like a blond barbarian. And she has the coolest fucking tattoo I've ever seen in my life: a big blue scorpion, half a foot long down her spine." Stella tensed her shoulders. "She made me swear I'd never tell anybody about it, but how could I not? Is that cool or what?"

✥

It was Wednesday night, hump night to working stiffs, though even management types like Tony Coburn didn't mind mixing with blue-collar men in small towns like Hendersonville. It was probably the only escape for a man strapped to a new, impetuous marriage by his own poor judgment. The bodyguard Lombard had assigned Coburn told her he was a regular at the Front Porch Tavern in Hendersonville every Wednesday. She and McLean arrived in the parking lot of the bar around 6:45, enough time for Coburn to have gotten on a buzz.

McLean had been quiet and sullen the whole drive to Hendersonville. "What's wrong, Sam?" Lombard finally asked. "You haven't said two words. Come on, maybe a beer will loosen you up."

"I don't want a beer," he said.

Lombard smirked. "What are you gonna do? Wait in the car?"

"Yup."

She could tell something was wrong. "What gives, Sam?"

McLean stared out the windshield for a moment. "Do me a favor, Loy. Don't drink while you're in there conducting business."

Lombard bristled. "Oh. I see. Tell you what, if I promise not to drink, will you condescend to join me inside?"

"No," he said. "I'll wait here until you get Coburn outside, and over to the plant like we planned."

"What's the matter with you?" Lombard demanded. "You're acting weird."

"*You're* acting weird!" McLean shouted all of a sudden, glaring at Lombard. "You're an alcoholic, Loy. You can't control yourself."

Lombard's heart sank. "Where the hell did that come from?"

"From my talk with Rhodes."

Her eyes widened, and her lips parted in the realization that Rhodes had outed her romp with Attila. "That wicked bastard. Oh, my God. How dare he?"

"He didn't mean to tell on you," McLean said. "He thought we shared things like that."

"Of course we never talk about things like that," said Lombard.

She was humiliated; she had to steel herself not to cry. She sat stone quiet for a minute or so and worked up her temper. "Anyway, it's none of your business either. You and Rhodes are so good at gossip. You ought to start your own goddamn quilting circle."

McLean's tone lightened. "You're right. It's none of my business. But I'm butting in because I don't want to see you make any more mistakes on account of booze. I never minded before, because you've always handled yourself. But with every setback, with every pound of pressure at work or at home, you take a little extra to drink. You went too far this past weekend." Lombard grabbed the door latch, and McLean added, "Wait. I don't mean to lecture. I'm just saying it was a wake-up call, Loy. You have to stop. I'll do anything to help, but you have to quit. God only knows how far you'll go when you don't have bourbon to block your every move forward."

Lombard stared straight ahead. Tears crashed over her cheeks, and she quickly turned her head and wiped them away. "I have to talk to Coburn," she said. "You can wait here if you want to." She got out of the car, slammed the door, and trudged through spitting rain to the front-door awning of the tavern. "God knows I could really use a drink now," she said under her breath.

Lombard felt not the least bit out of place in a tavern occupied by a couple dozen men in flannel shirts and jeans. She'd cut through crowds like this by herself countless times as a kid, catching up with her father after school as a little girl, leading him home by the hand when he'd been so blind drunk he could barely walk. In those days she had read quietly in a corner of the bar nearly every night, imagining herself as the hero of her novel. And at some point in the evening Joe Lombard had come to her, plaintive and weary, promising her a big wedding someday for being such a good daughter. And she'd gotten him home, and she'd made him eat something she cooked, and she'd put him to bed with his rosary. And when she was

15, he'd gone to bed after a bender, and died a few weeks later after a doctor's diagnosis of cirrhosis of the liver.

Something in Coburn's ruined expression turned her thoughts to her old man; he had that same hopeless look, that gaze of defeat. And she regarded Coburn as she had her father, with a mixture of pity and contempt, like the blend of sorrow and relief his death had brought her.

"Mr. Coburn, how are you?" she asked, shaking his hand.

Coburn's nose and cheeks were shiny and red, his eyes moist and good-humored. He was a happy drinker, just like old Joe, Lombard thought again, a lot easier to deal with than a crying or mean drunk. "Hey, there, Miss Lombard, what can I do for you? Can I buy you a beer?"

"I don't have time," Lombard said pleasantly, glancing at her watch.

Coburn asked, "What's the rush?"

"Something's come up," she said. "It's kind of important that we talk about it tonight."

"Well, talk away," he said brightly.

"At your office."

"Office? Why there?"

"Mr. Coburn, are you still getting those phone calls?"

He frowned. Lombard said, "I don't want to frighten you, but I should tell you I got a couple of calls like the one you described to me in my office. I may be able to figure out where they're coming from. Mr. Coburn, do you know anything about computers?"

Ten minutes later Lombard, McLean, and Coburn were in Seth Agee's old office at the Skinner Movables plant. "How many people work here after business hours?" Lombard asked as Coburn switched on Agee's computer.

"Just the guards," Coburn said dimly.

"Did Agee ever work late?"

"I don't know. I guess so."

"Any address book?" Lombard looked pointedly at Coburn. "Friends and family, that kind of thing?"

"Not here," said Coburn. "We shipped his personal items to his folks out in Washington State. I don't remember any address book, though. It was all stuff like mugs and posters and whatnot."

"Who combed through his house?"

Coburn shrugged. "I don't know. I don't even know where he lived."

"I take it nobody's been hired to replace him yet," said McLean.

Coburn sighed, shuddering a bit. "I've had too much on my mind to take care of that yet. We're working on it." The computer screen was ablaze in the screen-saver image of a setting South Pacific sun. Coburn chuckled. "He always talked up going to Fiji."

Lombard asked him to let her sit in Agee's chair. She sat down, put on her reading glasses, and unfolded the notepaper on which Dana had written instructions for opening what she called "cookies," or Web addresses encoded in a computer's hard drive.

"We should have brought Dana," said McLean.

"I can do it," Lombard said.

"So you've been getting those phone calls?" Coburn asked Lombard. "My caller ID didn't pick up anything. Do you think it's a hoax? I mean, I'd just starting sleeping again. I only got two of them and they stopped, and I thought it must be a prank. But if you're getting them, and Agee got them, it's no coincidence. It's something strange." By now Coburn was wringing his hands. "My God, will I ever know peace again?"

"Stop whining," Lombard snapped. "Sorry. I've got to concentrate." She furrowed her brow as she examined the scroll of domain names. "Jeez, did he ever work? There must be hundreds!"

"Thousands," said Coburn. "It was his job."

"*What* was his job?"

"Marketing. He was assistant manager in charge of marketing. He used the Internet all the time. He was very talented at finding things, my bad luck."

Lombard scrolled down the list of domain names, reading each one carefully for anything that smacked of vice. Her eyes locked on one particular line. "Mr. Coburn, Agee told me the dancer he hired had a distinctive tattoo. Do you remember it?"

"It was a scorpion. A stinging, deadly, paralyzing scorpion."

"Well, look here, boys," she said, highlighting the Web address. "www.scorpio-social.net. Provocative name, huh?" She clicked on it but got an error page. "It looks like somebody's seen fit to take it down." She stared at Dana's instructions again and flipped the notepaper over, where more instructions appeared on the back. She followed them and keenly watched the screen. When she saw the address and name, she was beside herself. "Sam! Sam Sam Sam! Look." She clapped her hands together and kissed them. "P.O. Box 477Y-2X, Miami Beach, Florida," she said. "Registered to N. Gromyko."

Lombard and McLean were headed back to Asheville. Lombard said nothing for most of the drive when suddenly she pulled into a strip mall parking lot.

"I want to get two things straight. One, I know I'm a drunk, and I have to do something about it. I want to quit, and I'm going to work on that. It's not going to be easy." She drew a deep breath. "But that's personal, and what I have to say next is professional. It's all I care about right now."

"OK." He faced her and braced himself for the summation he knew was coming.

"Attila's behind Natalie's murder," she began. "Natalie was working for her, as a prostitute probably, maybe a more sophisticated kind than we're used to seeing. The escort service and the so-called matchmaking service are one and the same. Natalie operated for both of them, obviously. She married Abel Wolf in the guise of a mail-order bride, and she made money for the escort service by dancing and/or sexing it up with Agee and Coburn and probably other parties around the region we'll never know about. Agee was the go-to man for the Chamber of Commerce, and if I'm to believe what he told me, he'd fooled around with Natalie—or Nadine, her pro name—more than once. He might have known too much, which explains why he was scared shitless the day I ran into him, and died later that night." Lombard spoke rapidly as a theory emerged in her head and spilled out of her mouth. "Abel is innocent, thank God. He was set up—twice, in fact. He was set up by Natalie, who found a mountain of cash to rob in his bunker. Meanwhile, living out on that farm with a couple of isolated freaks like the Wolfs gave her a safe cover for the operation she and Attila were working together."

"Why North Carolina?" McLean asked.

"I think that relates to Holliday. He either brought them here, or they found him here, and for some reason, they stayed."

"What about the fact that Abel met Natalie in Russia?"

Lombard shrugged. "If this is connected to organized crime, international operations are commonplace, especially with Russians. Attila said she was a kind of travel agent, tongue in cheek, to say the least." Lombard suddenly began laughing. "Oh, it's just too clever."

"What?"

Lombard was smiling joyfully. "I just love a clever woman. Oh, the wicked ones are so interesting."

"What are you talking about?" McLean cried insistently.

"What's the easiest way for a foreign woman to immigrate to America?"

"Marry a citizen."

"So Abel did go to Russia, where he'd been matched to Natalia Godunova, whom he liked—and how could he not?—and brought back here to marry. So she's got a safe cover and a job to do. He talked about her *excursions*, remember? Didn't know what she was up to. And we know she had dealings with Desmond Holliday, and we know Attila still does. Something weird's going on."

"Why not just smuggle her in? Why go to all that trouble with Abel?"

"Sam, she *was* smuggled in, through a sham marriage."

"So why did Attila kill her?"

"I don't know. I can't know everything all at once."

McLean shook his head. "And how do you explain the Luger?"

"Natalie probably stole that too, and ended up on the wrong side of it when she somehow crossed Attila."

McLean sighed. "I don't know, Loy."

"Hey, we've got some good leads here," Lombard said confidently. "You've seen Attila at the cabin within a short distance of where Natalie's body was dumped. They both were well-acquainted with Holliday, so we can surmise they knew each other. The gun supposedly used to kill Natalie wasn't at Abel's house, or in his bunker. It could have been stolen along with his cash when Natalie left him, and later used to kill her." She patted him on the knee. "There's the opportunity. We just need to find out the motive."

CHAPTER 12

"So who's N. Gromyko?" Sig Mashburn asked.

"That, we don't know," said McLean. He and Lombard were sitting in Mashburn's office, where McLean had just outlined their theory of the Wolf case.

Mashburn looked at Lombard. "You're awfully quiet. You sick or something?"

Lombard pursed her lips and shook her head. McLean said, "She didn't want us to tell you any of this yet."

"Why not?" Mashburn asked, still looking at Lombard. "He's my client too."

"Don't ask her. She's madder than hell," said McLean. "I'll tell you why. This is all confidential. We can't prove anything yet. So you can't discuss it with anybody."

"I'll discuss it with my client," said Mashburn.

McLean had hoped he could talk Mashburn out of telling Abel about any of their theory until they were able to prove it. But he'd insisted to Lombard that not telling Mashburn could jeopardize Abel's case. "Do you have to tell him?"

"I *told* you he would have to tell him," Lombard blurted out. "You never listen to me. You're gonna get us all whacked."

167

Mashburn chuckled. "It all sounds pretty far-fetched." Lombard turned crimson, and Mashburn added, "But I'll run it by Abel and see what he says. And I guess I'll need to run out and talk to this Holliday fellow."

"You do just that, Mashburn," said Lombard. "It'll be the last interview you ever have. Do me a favor and don't mention my name. You can take all the credit for this one."

Mashburn rolled his eyes and giggled. "My, my, my. Loy's afraid."

"It isn't time yet to confront them," Lombard said. "Let me do the investigative work, counselor. You stick to lawyering."

Mashburn looked surprised. "Is that a vote of confidence?"

"No. It's a nice way of saying mind your own fucking business."

"Loy!" McLean snapped.

"You insisted on telling him," Lombard said, "and I reserved the right to raise hell about it. And that's what I'm doing."

"Well, I think you're overreacting," said Mashburn, pressing a button on his phone. He asked his secretary to call Skinner Movables and get Tony Coburn on the line. He smiled at Lombard and McLean. "I'll follow up with this Coburn fellow and find out what I can."

Mashburn then rang up Abel's number and, after a short wait, began speaking cheerfully, apparently to Mrs. Wolf. He told her he had news for her and Abel, and he would pay them a visit that afternoon.

McLean felt Lombard's glare on him, literally. His right cheek was burning slightly. "Loy," he murmured without looking at her, "it was the right thing to do. It's Abel's case, not ours."

"We have a duty to protect him," Lombard whispered, "and his case. This blows the lid off. Mashburn doesn't believe us. I knew he wouldn't. Now he's going to tell Abel, who, experience shows, can't keep his mouth shut. Then he'll tell Coburn, who will probably not only never speak to us again but will find some way to get out of our contract over this. And then he'll call on Holliday, the riskiest link of all. Attila will know, and if she doesn't kill somebody else over it, she'll run, vanish, be gone. And so will Abel's case."

"What are you two mumbling about?" Mashburn asked, hanging up the phone.

"Oh, just about how you're fixing to screw everything up and put people's lives on the line," Lombard said with mock cheer. "That kind of thing."

Mashburn said, "You should know that I like your theory. It'll sound great in court, and I have every intention of using it."

"But you don't believe it," said McLean.

"He's not paid to believe anything," Lombard said. "He makes up crazier shit than this every day for his other rich, spoiled clients."

Mashburn laughed. "She's right." Suddenly a feminine voice rose from the telephone speaker. A secretary asked Mashburn to pick up. Still grinning, he pressed the receiver against his ear. "What's the secret, Cindy?" His lips closed around his smile, and gradually the smile faded. He looked at McLean. Mashburn's eyes were grave, then a little worried. He hung up the phone. "Coburn didn't report to the office today," he said. He cleared his throat and added, "His secretary says there was a break-in last night. Computers were stolen, and the office main server was gutted. It's pandemonium over there, but nobody knows where to find Coburn. He's missing."

Lombard said, "And he was your best witness."

Mashburn said, "Didn't you have a guard contract out there?"

Lombard suddenly went pale. "Oh, my God. Sam, who was on duty last night?"

"Whoever it was got off at 3 A.M.," said McLean. "Skinner wouldn't pay for two shifts because our rates go higher. The place was unguarded after 3."

Dana worked on Thursday nights and had waited until then to fill Lombard in on what she had learned from Stella the night before. "I would have called earlier today, but I basically got nothing for you," she explained.

"Tell me what you got, then," Lombard said distractedly, lounging on the lobby sofa.

Dana was sitting at her pretty walnut desk. "Are you OK, Loy?"

"Occasionally," said Lombard. "What did Stella tell you?"

"Well, other than the standard peppering of snide, insulting barbs, she did talk about her affair with Attila."

"What snide barbs? I thought you two were friends."

"I told you we're not friends. She dated my ex. She haunts me occasionally, like the demented spirit of Max de Winter's dead wife in *Rebecca*."

"Yeah, but you put up with it," said Lombard. "You'll get over that shit by the time you're 40, if you have any sense at all."

"What shit?"

"The idea of being palsy-walsy with the ex, yours or hers. There's hostility there whether you're willing to acknowledge it or not."

"I think I made it clear we're not friends," said Dana. "We're civil, because Jane wants it that way. And frankly, I think that's the mature way to act."

"No, it isn't. It's the fake way to act. Honey, when it's over, it's over."

"Well, you can't just shut them out if they want to be friends."

"Sure you can. You must."

"Jeez, that's so bitter. Sometimes it doesn't work out, for lots of reasons. You move on in peace. It's just a part of growing."

Lombard sighed. "You can't possibly believe that and know what passion is."

"I know passion," Dana said defensively.

"Not if you buy into that bullshit. When somebody leaves you, or if you leave them—it doesn't make any difference—and there was real passion between you, the only way to survive is to leave all the way. *Arrivederci*."

Dana was quiet for a moment. "I think you have abandonment issues."

Lombard sat up slowly and yawned. "What are you, a shrink?"

"My father is a psychology professor. But I'm just guessing."

Lombard studied Dana for a few seconds. "What did Stella tell you?"

Dana gave Lombard a detailed account of their conversation, mentioning in passing Stella's description of her lover's tattoo.

Lombard smiled. She hadn't noticed a tattoo during her night with Attila, who had kept on her camisole and refused to turn over even once. "A scorpion? Did she say what color?"

"I don't remember. I don't think so."

"Didn't I tell you Natalie had a tattoo like that?"

Dana shook her head. "No, you didn't mention it. I don't think that's been in the papers, has it?"

"Not yet," Lombard said. "It will come out at trial, since that's how Abel identified her body." She rubbed the back of her neck. "So, did she say what part of Attila's body it was on?"

"It was big. I think on her back," said Dana. "Why?"

"Just curious." Lombard wondered if Attila had meant to conceal the tattoo from her. She must have, if Stella had seen it. If that were so, then Attila might be on to her.

The next day Lombard and McLean had lunch together at their usual diner. There was no sign of Coburn yet, who had been missing, officially, for more than 24 hours. Given the nature of the burglary of Skinner Movables, an investigation into his disappearance—and possible connection to the burglary—was under way, and in the news. Lombard had already read the newspaper account, which made no connection of Coburn's disappearance to the Wolf case. She quietly ate her BLT while McLean reviewed the newspaper article for the first time.

"What do you think?" she asked as he folded the paper.

"I think he's dead."

"So do I," said Lombard. "Poor thing. He was so scared. What I meant was, do you think he was being watched? You know, it's strange the way he vanished right after we got into those computer files."

"I don't know," said McLean, his mouth full. "Anyway, we'll have to talk to the police about our part."

"We don't have a part," said Lombard. "Our guard, Bill Kelly, said he got off at 3 A.M. without incident. He watched the last employee drive off at midnight, in fact."

"That's just it," said McLean. "We can narrow the time frame from 3 to 6 A.M., when the next company shift starts. Our guards only work from 5 P.M. to 3 A.M."

"Oh, I've already sent that information to the police," said Lombard. "I had Bill Kelly go downtown and give them a report."

McLean reached for his Diet Coke. "You didn't tell me that."

"It was routine. Do you tell me your every move?"

"Most of the time, yeah," he said.

"Nuh-unh. You told Mashburn all that stuff without me wanting you to."

"I consulted you first. We disagreed, but you gave in only because some little part of you knew I was right. I didn't go behind your back and tell him."

"Sam! I didn't go behind your back. I sent Bill downtown to tell his story, and you would have done the same thing without telling me. What's the big deal? It's like filling out an incident report, not like when we used to figure out what parts of our file we'd take to the DA."

"Whatever," McLean said. "I think you might need some security."

"Why do I need security?"

"You got those same weird phone calls Agee and Coburn got."

"So?" Lombard shrugged.

"Loy, whoever was calling Agee and Coburn was calling you."

"Well, I don't get those calls anymore."

"That's because you were warned," he said, "but you ignored the warning."

Lombard stared at him for a moment. "Are you fucking with me, Sam?"

"No, I'm not. I think you should stay with me and Selena for a few days."

"Certainly not. If I'm in danger, that would put your whole family at risk." She frowned at her plate, having lost her appetite. "This is stupid. This is just stupid bullshit. I'm not in danger." She looked up. "I'm not in danger, Sam. Let's change the subject."

"OK," he said. "So Dana's friend is dating Attila, and Attila has the blue scorpion tattoo. What else did Dana say?"

"That was it."

"That was it? Didn't you tell her about all that stuff we found out at Agee's old office?"

"No."

"Why not?"

Lombard threw her napkin on her plate. "Because I don't want her to get any deeper into this. I think she's helped enough with the case, and she should concentrate on our Web site. We hired her to bring in business, not get mixed up in this sleazy crap-ass side gig of ours."

McLean narrowed his eyes at Lombard. "You like her."

Lombard waved him off. "Eat your gravy."

For the first time ever, Lombard was nervous about being alone. Other than two fairly brief attempts at domestic partnership, she'd lived alone her whole adult life. She was physically strong, she had guns, and she was a good shot. She had always been confident about living by herself, but she knew she would not rest easily tonight.

McLean was right. She'd gotten the warning phone calls from somebody who knew she had too much information. Agee and Coburn had defied the warnings; Agee was dead, and Coburn was missing. Lombard had defied them too. She lounged in her bathtub, listening to a slow drip from the faucet into the hot, steamy bathwater, thinking it over. Whoever called was no doubt the killer, and she thought it was probably Attila. But then it occurred to her that Holliday could have a hand in all this somehow. Whoever the killer was, it was clear the warnings were meant to shut people up. The killer had wanted to avoid murder. Lombard knew she was dealing with a professional, because the pros thought like that: kill only as a last resort.

This killer was smart. The faint criminal side of Lombard strangely admired her, or him. Lombard had always hated the sloppy killers when she was a cop: the messy, compulsive rapists and robbers; the gangster morons who rode around shooting people like they were riding in an arcade. Catching people like that had been contemptibly simple detective work, most of the time. The only complexity had been getting them to confess, and even that was tediously easy in many cases.

Whoever had killed Agee had done so out of necessity, and had staged the murder to look like an accident by running him off the road. The police were now looking into that angle, but Lombard was ahead of them. She also believed Coburn's body wouldn't be found unless the killer had a purpose in allowing its discovery. Natalie's body had been dumped where it would be found, but the killer had hedged his or her bets on Abel Wolf's being the prime suspect. The need to throw suspicion off of Holliday, perhaps, was why Natalie's body had been dumped on land adjacent to Wolf Branch Farm. Wicked motives, to be certain, and deserving of swift, merciless judgment, but they were the clean, logical motives of a killer who knew what she or he was doing.

If silencing Agee and Coburn had motivated their eliminations, what about Natalie's murder? Why had she disappeared more than a week before the time of her death? If Attila were the killer, why was she still hanging around Asheville? Why wouldn't she have skipped town the instant she felled Natalie? If it were Holliday, what was Attila's connection? And for that matter, why was Rhodes hanging around with them? And what had Lombard done to get the attention of the anonymous caller? Lombard didn't know where the answers lay, but she knew where to start looking for them: on the night she first heard the warning voice, Tuesday, the 13th of September.

Lombard leaned forward in the tub and pulled the rubber stop out of the drain. She drew her knees up to her chin and hugged her calves as the line of warm water descended along her flesh. Two things had happened on each of the days she received the phone calls: She had spied the boat launch, and Dana had been made privy to information about the case.

Unless Attila was keeping constant watch from her cabin retreat—which was impossible—the boat launch investigations hadn't precipitated the calls. Maybe Dana hadn't kept her mouth shut. Maybe she and Stella were better friends than Lombard knew and details of the case had slipped to Attila through Stella's contacts with Dana. She stared at the last bit of bathwater spiraling down the drain. She'd thought Dana smarter and more trustworthy than to do something like jeopardize her case. But more disturbing to Lombard than that: Dana would have put herself in danger.

Lombard spent Saturday morning in her office writing a memo for Abel's file and cross-referencing all the information she and McLean had obtained up to that point. She read a newspaper article about the missing Coburn, which gave biographical information about his personal life and career, and read more like an obituary than the backdrop of a pending police investigation. She browsed the Internet for any trace of the Web sites Abel or Agee had used to their ruin in finding Natalie Wolf, but both sites had been obliterated. Then, on a whim, she typed "N. Gromyko" into a search-engine field. Narrowing the field to English, there were a couple dozen hits but nothing useful to Lombard.

Dana arrived at work around 10 o'clock, though she didn't bother Lombard, and Lombard didn't want to be bothered. At 1 o'clock Dana appeared at Lombard's open door. "I brought some sandwiches," she said, raising a lunch bag slightly. "Are you hungry?"

"I'll run out and get something," Lombard said.

"I made these mini sandwiches." Dana walked in uninvited, set her bag on the desk, and pulled out sandwich squares wrapped in wax paper. "I cut off the crust and quarter them. I always make a lot of them to nibble on through the day. But I made too many. Here, do you like tuna salad?"

Lombard shrugged. "I like everything. Even crust."

Dana grinned. "I've got pesto too, and goat cheese."

"Tuna, then," said Lombard.

"Is it OK if I eat with you?"

Lombard was unwrapping a sandwich. "Sure," she said quietly.

Dana sat down. After a moment she asked, "Can I ask you a personal question?"

Lombard's mouth was full, and she gave Dana a wary look. "I can't stop you from asking."

"Do you go out much?"

"You mean at night?"

"Yeah, like go to the movies, plays, clubs."

"Rarely. I don't like modern movies, and theater gets on my nerves. I don't mind hearing some jazz or blues once in a while."

Dana chuckled. "You must stay home a lot."

Lombard shrugged. "I used to go out a lot, when I was younger, around your age. I'll be 43 in November. At this point in my life, there's no place like home."

Dana smiled sheepishly. "Then, I don't suppose I could talk you into meeting me and my girlfriend out tonight?"

"Certainly not, but thanks." Lombard crumpled up the used wax paper and threw it into her wastebasket. "Speaking of girlfriends and exes, I have a personal question for you. How much have you told your friend Stella about Abel Wolf's case?"

Dana frowned. "I haven't told her anything."

"What about your girlfriend? You go home at night and tell her about your work? And does she see much of Stella?"

"I don't live with my girlfriend, first of all." Dana snipped. "And I told you I'd never reveal any confidences. Not to anybody, including Jane." She added offhandedly, "Besides, I've only been going out with her for a few months."

"I don't necessarily mean that you've flagrantly discussed details of the case," Lombard explained. "You know, when you're not used to this kind of work, you might just casually let something slip about what you've done that day, thinking that by swearing everybody to secrecy they'll keep their mouths shut. When in fact nobody ever keeps their mouth shut. That's one of those things people never seem to learn: If you want to keep a secret, don't tell it."

"Do you think I'm an idiot?" Dana asked incredulously.

"I think you're smart as a whip. But do you keep your mouth shut when it needs to be?" Lombard rolled her eyes when Dana got up to leave. "Sit down, Dana."

"This just sounds very accusatory to me," said Dana.

"Will you sit down?" Lombard waited until Dana was back in her chair. "All right. I just want to emphasize how secretive we have to be about this Wolf case. You can't say *any*thing to *any*body, for any reason." She put her reading glasses on, picked up a document from Abel's file, and added dismissively, "And by the way, you can't be involved in the Wolf case anymore."

"Why not?"

"Because your work on the case is over. You're doing a good job on our new Web site. Keep it up." Lombard returned her attention to the file and waited for Dana to leave.

"That's bullshit," said Dana, frozen in her seat.

Lombard jerked her head up, eyebrows raised. "What did you say?"

"I said that's bullshit. There's more that needs to be done. I know it. You just don't trust me, and I haven't given you a reason not to."

"You haven't given me a reason *to* trust you, either," said Lombard. "I brought you in because I needed you, even though I didn't have a clue how reliable you were. I have found that you are reliable, and thank you very much, but now keeping you in is too risky. And that, my dear, is that."

Dana's eyes welled up, and she burst up out of her chair and stormed out.

"Oh, for God's sake," Lombard grumbled. She got up and went to Dana's desk in the lobby. Dana's face was beet-red and puffy, as though she were about to explode into tears. "You're not gonna cry, are you?" Lombard said.

"No," Dana sobbed.

"Good. Because something else is on my mind, and I have to tell you."

"What is it?"

"I don't want you hanging around that Stella character any-more."

All the color left Dana's face, and her eyes dried up. "Are you kidding?

"No, I'm serious."

Dana's tone was measured and stern. "Loy, I love working here. I respect you and Sam and Retta. I am very disappointed that you just threw me out of the case, and I'm probably going to cry about it." Her voice began shaking again, and the tears came back into her eyes. "But don't tell me how to run my personal life just because you don't trust me or my friends." She took off her eyeglasses and cried piteously.

"What did I say to get you this upset?" Lombard asked bewilderedly. Good God, she thought, it was like she'd just broken off a romance with the girl or something. "It was a practical decision. It's not personal!" But Lombard knew, as the words were leaving her mouth, it was all personal. She wanted Dana out of harm's way, and she wanted her far away from Stella, and the reach of Attila.

Perhaps, Lombard thought later, she should have taken up Dana's offer of spending an evening out, even if it had to be as third wheel to a couple of hipsters in low-slung jeans, surrounded by even younger Lilith Fair types in some godforsaken, arty coffeehouse. Of course, Lombard had turned Dana down without giving her a chance to say where exactly they would be going out, so maybe it wouldn't have been a coffeehouse. Maybe it would have been worse—like the time she had let a date drag her to a Buddhist chant recital. Or maybe it would have been all right, and they would have planned on going to a bar with a good rhythm and blues band.

Lombard had automatically turned Dana down because she didn't want to meet her girlfriend. She didn't want to see how much younger and more attractive than Lombard she was, or how much more even-tempered and good-natured. Dana's girlfriend was probably healthier too, and better educated. Lombard was already jealous, and she didn't even know what the girl looked like. But it was just as well, because Lombard couldn't fake cordiality with someone whose girlfriend she'd already imagined naked about half a dozen times.

On the other hand, she would at least have avoided being home alone, which had been all right with Lombard until the past couple of nights. Friday night she'd barely slept. Every faint creak of old wood in her house, or whistle of wind through the trees outside, had stirred her. Her cat's footsteps had made her heart race. She'd been meaning for a long time to have an alarm put in but had always felt well-secured by the presence of a Glock semiautomatic she kept in her bedside table.

To calm her nerves, she'd put away her copy of Kingsley Amis's *The Russian Girl* and poured a drink. She was presently doing a bang-up job of looking at the glass as more than half full. She was watching Hunter Lyle anchor the 11 o'clock news when the phone rang. Without checking the caller ID box, she snatched up the phone and braced herself for another creepy warning.

"Yeah?" she said uncertainly and a little menacingly.

After a slight pause, a man spoke in polished, even tones. "Is this Loy Lombard?" Lombard said it was, and he told her he was Desmond Holliday.

Lombard got up off the sofa and asked him what he wanted as she checked the caller ID box, which indicated the caller was anonymous.

"I know it's very late," he said, "but Tyler told me you stay up late and it would be all right, under the circumstances, to get in touch with you."

"How would he know my sleep habits?" she asked, plopping back onto the sofa. "He's never talked to me late at night."

"Loy, I assure you I wouldn't bother you were it not an emergency of sorts."

"Of what sorts?"

"Well, I'm very nervous and unable to sleep, and you may be able to calm my nerves." Holliday chuckled as might one who was a little embarrassed. "Like I said, Tyler told me—well, you see, I called him first. And he said you might know the answer to this, so please forgive me for disturbing you like this, Loy."

Lombard took a drink and sighed, eyeing the TV screen and Hunter Lyle's muted broadcast. Lombard wanted to hear what Holliday had to say, but she couldn't tear her eyes away from the perfect artifice of Lyle's expressive delivery of whatever local news she was blabbing about. "Spill your guts, Holliday," she said.

"Please call me Desi. As you know, Natalie Wolf was a very dear friend of mine, a lovely young lady."

"Mm-hmm."

"Well, her death came as a severe blow."

"Really?" said Lombard. "I guess you'd had time to get over it by the night we all met out at Maddie's Bar. You didn't say a word to me about it then, and you seemed to be having a hell of a good time."

"I was drunk before I even got there," Holliday said defensively. "I've been terribly upset about it. Too upset even to visit her grave site."

"She was cremated."

Holliday was silent on his end for a few seconds. Then he said, "I don't like discussing this over the phone. May I come to your house and talk to you in person?"

Lombard was crunching an ice cube. "Right now?"

"Yes."

"Hell no! I'm buzzed and ready for bed. Got my fuzzy slippers on and everything. You can come over tomorrow morning, though."

"I understand," he said. "Thank you. Well, how do I get there?"

Lombard stopped crunching. She swallowed and said, "I'll be at the office in the morning. Meet me there at 10. Tyler knows where it is. Call him for directions." They hung up, and Lombard was embarrassed, crimson with shame over how unnerved she felt. She'd held back giving him directions to her house because some weak part of her was afraid of Holliday. How she would have ridiculed anybody for her fear of an interior decorator! But she'd been right about one thing: She was buzzed and ready for bed. So ready, she sank slowly down the cushions as her eyelids grew heavier, narrowing the babbling flaming-red head of Hunter Lyle to an iridescent band of orange, white, and blue light. As she drifted off, she heard the thud of the remote control box as it slipped from her fingers to the floor.

She mistook another thud for the same thing a few hours later. She'd been running away from a redhead who appeared to her alternately in her dream as Hunter Lyle or Natalie Wolf, chasing her through a series of doors she slammed on one, only to fall under the pursuit of the other. Her mind began to dawn into consciousness as one of the dream doors slammed again, and her waking mind took it for the remote box as her eyes opened onto the darkness of her living room.

She was flat on her back, her right foot planted on the floor, her right knee leaning awkwardly in its blue pajama pant leg against the coffee table. The TV screen was a blank radiating red, the channel having lost its cable signal after the station had signed off. She fumbled for the remote box to click off the TV, and that's when she realized she'd been out for hours, and the remote had slipped hours ago, and the thud she was certain she'd just heard had come from somewhere else.

She rose up sharply despite a dull, lingering buzz of alcohol. Adrenaline was a good antidote for it, and when Lombard felt the cool draft coming from the direction of the kitchen, she lost her buzz entirely. She could hear the wind chimes on her screened-in porch as though they were hanging inside the house. The back door was open.

If only she were in bed, so near the gun! But whoever was inside could be anywhere between the back door and where she sat feeling as though all the blood in her body were draining into her legs. As deftly and quietly as she could, she moved over to the fireplace and, gritting her teeth and tensing her shoulders nearly into spasms in an effort to make no sound, loosened the poker from the andirons. She stood listening for any noise at all, wanting to start for her bedroom and that gun she so dearly needed now.

The floor in the dining room creaked in the steady rhythm of cautious footsteps. She'd turned off the TV, but in the merest light conducted through a window from a distant streetlamp outside, she made out the silhouette of what she could only be certain was a human being. Lombard was crouched next to the fireplace, her eyes strained on the shadowy form that seemed to be advancing in the opposite direction, nearer a door leading from her living room into a hallway, at the rear of which her bedroom was situated. So it was impossible for Lombard to get to her gun now, with the intruder so inconveniently placed between them.

Lombard wanted to surprise her intruder by bludgeoning him or her to a pulp, but any surprise would likely be on her if the burglar had a gun to outmatch her iron-age tool. As soon as the black form crept into the hallway, Lombard's fuzzy slippers slid along the hardwood floor into the dining room and raced along the kitchen floor tiles to the back door—whose deadbolt lock had apparently not been in place, the door having been kicked open against the inert knob lock—and out the screened-in porch to the backyard, where she hid behind a tree and noticed the offender had somehow put out her backyard lantern.

October had just begun, and it was cool at night, though at least this was a clear night, and Lombard was wishing now she had a neighbor's house to run to. But her only neighbors were the vast poplars, pines, and oaks of the woods behind her house, and they would make a good-enough hiding place tonight, she hoped. There was nothing else she could do but hide and wait, and watch, trying hard to stay awake.

By the time McLean arrived at Lombard's house around 7 on Sunday morning, the police had just left. Lombard told him she'd waited for a while before venturing out of the woods behind her house and following the lights of road lamps to the Go Station convenience market a mile down the road. She told him that when she'd arrived there in her blue flannel jammies and by-then filthy green fuzzy slippers at about 4 A.M., the concerned cashier had called the cops before she'd had a chance to ask for the phone. Lombard had been in the bathroom when the sheriff's deputy arrived, and Lombard told him what had happened.

"For a minute, I was sure he was going to call out the boys with the straitjackets," she chuckled as they sat at her kitchen table, sipping coffee. "But when he saw the house, he called for backup instead." Her smile fell, and her eyes seemed to look out toward the living room, which the intruder—or intruders—had turned into chaos.

It seemed to McLean that the rooms that had been ransacked— the living room, the guest bedroom where Lombard kept a computer and file cabinet, and her bedroom—had been violated more out of rage than any apparent purpose in searching them. Nothing had been taken, and the only upheaval had been to contents of drawers emptied, furniture turned upside down, or lamps knocked over. One of Lombard's antique lamps, given to her by her deceased Aunt Anna Mae, had been broken to pieces. The intruder hadn't known about Lombard's aunt, but the lamp had had the sentimental look of an heirloom—it was ugly and cheap, clearly valuable to its owner for some reason other than its material worth. It had been smashed out of frustration, the only means available at the time to hurt or warn Lombard. Lombard told McLean she'd been upset at first, but when she'd realized her cat was OK—he'd scrambled outside before she had, probably—she'd been relieved.

One thing was clear to McLean. "You're staying with me and Selena," he told Lombard.

"No, I'm not. I have a man coming out here tomorrow to put in an alarm system. That guard we've got out at the raillery—Alton what's-his-name—his brother-in-law has a security alarm business. I've heard Alton talk about it, so I called him before his shift was over at 6. So that'll be done tomorrow." Lombard took a deep drink of coffee. "I'll be fine. Now that I'm pissed off, I'm not scared anymore. I want to get my hands on that son of a bitch as soon as possible."

"What son of a bitch?" McLean asked.

"Desmond Holliday. He called me not three hours before the break-in, wanting to know where I lived. He made it obvious, but if it had worked out, I wouldn't be alive right now to tell on him."

McLean listened as Lombard reviewed her conversation with Holliday the night before and described what had happened when she realized the house had been broken into. When she was finished, he said, "Loy, if Holliday had the balls to call you up, ask for your address and directions, get them somehow when you failed to give them out, and then come out here, break into your house, and ransack the place when he realized you'd slipped away, that tells me a few things. Number one, he's one determined son of a gun. Number two, he's a tough, mean son of a gun."

"I'm meaner," she said.

"I don't doubt that." McLean smiled. "Look, all I'm saying is, don't go out there without somebody to back you up. Now, did you tell the deputies about him?"

Lombard frowned. "Of course not. Why would I do that?"

McLean gave her a look of disbelief. "Uh, because he's the most likely suspect in a burglary, Inspector? And if he is, he might come back? Loy, you're staying with us tonight."

"No, I'm not, sugar. Thanks all the same. And I'm not telling the cops about Holliday till I've had a crack at him. If the cops start paying attention to him, I'll never get anything out of him."

"What makes you think you can get something out of him now, Loy?" McLean nearly shouted. "If you think he came here trying to kill you last night—and by the way, I think whoever it was clearly wanted to hurt you—you can't possibly think he'll talk!" He watched Lombard hunker down a bit as she brought her coffee mug to her lips, giving him an almost childish, lowering look as he scolded her. He eased his tone. "Loy, pack your things. Just one night, until the alarm gets put in tomorrow, and then you can come back home."

She looked pale and withered, exactly like somebody who had been frightened nearly out of her wits, had spent too long in the elements, and who'd gotten no sleep to speak of. She sniffed. "OK. One night. But as soon as I get a shower, you come with me to talk to Holliday."

CHAPTER 13

Desmond Holliday seemed puzzled when he opened his front door and discovered Lombard and McLean looking not at all like friendly callers. "What bad form," he said. "We have an appointment at your office. I don't appreciate surprise visitors."

"I don't either," said Lombard. "But I like to return favors."

"What do you mean?"

"Let's talk about it inside," she said, pulling her jacket open to reveal a shoulder harness with a handgun holstered in it.

Holliday nervously eyed the gun and asked them both to follow him, but McLean stayed outside on the porch while Lombard accompanied Holliday to a sunroom near his kitchen.

"I don't see the need for coming here armed," said Holliday.

"At the moment, I do," Lombard said once they'd sat down. "But maybe I'll feel better when you tell me where you were at 2 or 3 o'clock this morning."

"Here, asleep," he said, glancing again at her gun. "Would you like some hot tea?"

"No. Listen to me. I know you're lying. Not four hours after you called me wanting to know where I live, you broke into my house intent on killing me. I know it, Sam knows it, and every cop in

Asheville knows it, since I told them the whole story the minute the sheriff's deputies came to my place before the crack of dawn. So you can drop the act, Holliday, and tell me what's going on."

"The police?" he said. "You told them *what*?"

"You heard me. You broke into my house. I saw you. I managed to escape before you figured out where I was. I hid in the woods until I could get my wits up to find my way to a store and call the police."

"What? That's preposterous! Why in God's name would you assume *I*, of all people, would do something like that?"

Holliday was clearly appalled by her accusation, and Lombard believed him. "Maybe it wasn't you, but you know who it was," she said. "You need to be straight with me, Holliday; this has gone too far."

"Yes, it has," he said. "And so I'll tell you Attila's the whole reason I called you last night. You remember. I told you I had an emergency. I was afraid and wanted to talk to you about it in person. I needed to talk to you about Attila, Ms. Lombard. I wondered if you knew where she was."

Lombard cocked her head. "Don't give me that. How the hell would I know where she is?"

"I thought you were lovers," he said.

Lombard sank back in her chair. "Jesus, is it all over town?" she muttered. "For the record, we aren't lovers. What happened between her and me was a drunken fluke. I'd give anything if it hadn't. So don't mention it again. Please."

"My lips are sealed."

"Unseal them for the moment," she said, "and tell me about Attila."

"I haven't seen Attila since the last night she spent here, last Tuesday. After that, she disappeared. On Thursday, when she still hadn't come back, I checked her room. She'd cleared out. Her leaving like that made me nervous."

"Why?"

"She didn't tell me she was leaving. She didn't say a thing."

"Not like her to leave somebody who owes her a debt before collecting, huh? Come on, admit it: You're afraid of her. You owed her something, didn't you? And you think she killed Natalie."

Holliday narrowed his eyes. "Natalie," he said, as though to himself.

"Yes, Natalie. Your good friend, Mrs. Abel Wolf."

Holliday looked away. "Natalie. No, I don't know what happened to her. I had nothing to do with that. Look, if I tell you everything, you'll help me, right? I've done nothing wrong. There's no reason the police should suspect me of a thing."

"I'll clear your name with the police, if you come clean with the facts," Lombard promised with the sincere look of a Sister of Mercy.

"I came to North Carolina with nothing," he said. "I'd gone from having it all in Miami to losing it all when I went to prison. I know Tyler's told you about that. He's got a big mouth." Holliday drew a deep breath. "Anyway, it was all over for me by the time I got out of prison. I ended up here, partly because it held promise for me, and partly because it's a good place to hide. And I was hiding."

"From what?"

"From people like Attila. Before my house of cards collapsed in Miami, I'd borrowed money from some shady people. A few quick business deals with some of my associates and paying them back would be simple. But by the time I got out of prison, most of those shady people were dead or otherwise out of the picture. One of the dead guys was a Hungarian pimp named Attila Hunyadi, who ran rackets all along the East Coast. He came to Miami in its heyday, back in the mid '80s. That's when I met him. I didn't know then he had a sister."

"Named Mari."

"That's right. She got out of Hungary after the collapse of communism in the early '90s. She apparently changed her name to Attila in her brother's honor, after he'd been gutted—quite literally, I'm afraid—by some Colombian gangsters he'd had the bad taste to rip off."

"And Mari Attila assumed her brother's debts," Lombard guessed aloud.

"As well as his collection claims," Holliday added miserably. "Attila rose in the ranks of organized crime by her associations with Russians. She speaks fluent Russian and has traveled extensively there. Still, she keeps count of old scores, and she wasted no time in tracking me down after I'd been released from house arrest in Atlanta and settled here, where I thought nobody would ever find me. Only she didn't come at me directly. She sent out feelers."

Lombard was smiling vaguely, in marvel of Attila's mastery of intimidation. "She deployed Natalie against you."

Holliday smirked. "Something like that. Natalie did show up at my studio door wearing a wedding ring, telling me about how she was a Russian immigrant wife who'd married a local boy. I saw her as a potential client, and had no idea she could be connected to Attila. She looked a little wise to be some hick's wife, but I figured times over in Russia were desperate enough for even a girl as seemingly worldly as I suspected Natalie was to be showing up in Buncombe County."

"So she eventually blackmailed you. How? Threatened to kill you? When did you find out she was working for Attila?"

Holliday frowned. "I don't remember." He stammered a bit and said, "She just dropped the bomb one day in my studio, told me she was a friend of Attila's and that I owed them. Demanded 50 grand or else. I had owed Attila's brother a lot more than that. I knew it was going to be a long, hard row to hoe, as they say around here."

"You thought you'd gotten off scot-free," Lombard said.

"I was wrong," he said.

"So she was siphoning money out of you all this time, and ripping off Abel on the side, and operating as a hooker for good measure?" Lombard guessed aloud.

"I don't know about all that," he said uncomfortably. "I guess you could call Attila and Natalie a pair of whole-hoggers."

"So why did Attila kill Natalie?"

"I don't know, and I won't speculate. The police think Abel Wolf did it, and that's fine with me."

"So you'll let an innocent man fry to shield a woman who would no sooner look at you as kill you?"

"I have no choice. She'd kill me, and you too if you're not careful. Anyway, without me, you've got no proof."

Lombard didn't dare tell him about the Web site connection. "Why did you call me last night?"

"I told you why. I thought you might have talked to her, that you might be able to help me. You were right when you said I'm afraid of her. Obviously for good reason, if she broke into your house to kill you. And I know I'm not off the hook."

"There's more to it than that. You're not telling me everything; you're leaving out something important." Lombard stood up. "You still haven't explained why you called the police and led them to believe Abel should be a suspect. Maybe Natalie made you do it? She ripped him off and planned on getting out. You aided her, out of fear or a forgiven debt, by calling the police's attention to Abel. You even wanted me to believe Abel had killed her, so you fed me that bullshit about her complaints that he was an abusive husband. Then Attila came to town, and Natalie was murdered, and you freaked out."

"I don't know!" he shouted. "I can't tell you. Please go, Ms. Lombard. Just go."

"Or were you helping Attila set Abel up? You reported Natalie missing before her death. In fact, her body hadn't yet been discovered when you tried to persuade me, that night at your party, that her husband had done something to hurt her." She rubbed her forehead. "Something doesn't *fit*," she told herself. "So who were you backing up? Natalie or Attila?"

"If I could help," he said slowly, "I would. But I can't risk my life for that man, and I will not go back to prison." He closed his eyes. "Look, I don't feel well."

Lombard wasn't feeling so well either. She hadn't gotten any real sleep, and she felt weak from what she thought was overwork. "We're all pretty tired, Holliday."

She thought she could have drawn more out of Holliday if only she had the strength, but she was nearly delirious from exhaustion. And she now realized she had a fever. She left, promising Holliday another visit, but agreeing, for the time being, to do her best to keep at bay the police she'd never called in the first place. She knew she sounded disoriented, and by the time she met McLean outside, she had to lean against him to get to the car. McLean asked her what was wrong once they were on the road.

"I just need sleep," she said thinly as they drove away from Holliday Hill. She was quiet for a few minutes before saying, "Holliday is lying as much as he's telling the truth, and it's all so transparent. It was really annoying busywork, interrogating him." She wiped sweat from her brow. "Something doesn't *fit*, Sam."

"Sleep on it," McLean suggested.

"Tyler Rhodes is an ace liar," Lombard mumbled. "One of the best I've ever met. Holliday sucks at lying. He's so obvious." She looked at McLean. "You just can't respect a bad liar, you know?"

Lombard collapsed in bed while the McLeans put her house back in order. It wasn't like Lombard to let people rummage through her things, even when they wanted to help; had she been feeling well, she would have run them off and done it all herself. But she was too sick even to protest, and by the time they were finished, she couldn't go home with them.

McLean called guards to stand watch over Lombard's house that night, and the next morning the promised alarm system was installed. Lombard wasn't even able to get out of bed and learn how to use it properly; the guards had to come back again that night, and she fretted vaguely in her delirium about the cost of overtime, and when her aching and fever-induced nausea seemed to have turned her blood to boiling syrup, she hollered to the guards to get out and let Attila come and finish her off. She'd never felt that sick in her life.

By Tuesday she'd lost track of time. She was unaware that McLean and Retta had been taking turns checking on her, and that Retta had tried unsuccessfully to get her to eat something the day before. She hadn't heard McLean shouting at her about getting to a doctor and promising to drag her to the hospital himself if she hadn't shown signs of improvement by evening.

The first thing Lombard noticed on Tuesday afternoon—other than the novelty of being lucid for the first time in a day and a half—was that her bed linens were moist and reeking. Horrified, she thought she'd urinated on herself. "Oh, my God!" she cried.

Dana suddenly appeared at her bedside. "Well," she said, "you look like hell warmed-over."

Lombard was wild-eyed. Her hair was soaked, and she was sweating all over. "How long have you been standing there?"

"In this spot? Seconds. But I've been here all day. Sam asked me to keep an eye on you, so this morning I called in family leave at the library. You're family, so it isn't a lie." Dana smiled.

Lombard felt dazed and embarrassed. "I need to clean up."

"I'll run a cool bath for you," said Dana.

"I've got to pee."

"I don't need every detail." Dana helped Lombard up and led her to the bathroom. "Your fever's broken, is all. That's why you kind of smell. You didn't think you'd had an accident, did you?"

"Of course not. Leave me alone." Lombard woozily closed the bathroom door and stopped the bathtub drain under cool running water.

Twenty minutes later Dana knocked on the door as Lombard stewed in lukewarm bathwater, staring at the ceiling and breathing through her mouth. "I've changed your sheets. You're all fresh and clean now. Come on."

After she'd thrown on her robe and walked weakly into the hallway, Lombard noticed how warm the house was. Dana had put on one of the jazz records in Lombard's collection, and something aromatic was simmering in the kitchen. And Romeo had curled up on Dana's bright green backpack, thrown in a corner of Lombard's bedroom.

Lombard climbed under the covers, the sheets crisp and cool and scented with her favorite lilac fabric softener. Her hair was damp from her bath, and she was weak and woozy. But she felt good in a weird, sickly way. Dana drew a blanket over her and smiled, a slightly crooked, sweet smile that made the freckles on her nose darken. She was very pretty, thought Lombard, and McLean was a macho fool not to see it, but what the hell did he know?

"You're not leaving now, are you?" Lombard asked softly.

"No," said Dana. She sat on the edge of the bed and patted Lombard hands. "I've made you a pot of soup. You hungry?"

"I could eat."

"I'll fix you right up." Dana hopped off the bed and headed through the door.

"You're a sweet angel," Lombard mumbled. "I could look at you all night."

Dana stopped at the door. "Huh? What was that?"

Lombard hesitated. "I said, be an angel and call Retta for me. Tell her I'll be back tomorrow. And find out if Sam's talked to Sig Mashburn or Mike Church yet."

McLean was talking to Mashburn and Church at that very moment, in fact. They were sitting in McLean's office and had just heard his full account of what had happened at Lombard's house in the early-morning hours of the previous Sunday. McLean had spoken to Mashburn earlier by phone, asking him to sit in on the discussion with Church on Abel's behalf. Mashburn had agreed only on the condition that he would be allowed to close the conversation if he thought it in the best interests of Abel Wolf's case. McLean had thought that reasonable enough.

"But why don't you think Holliday is behind the burglary?" Church asked. "He'd called her right before it happened."

McLean said, "Loy seemed satisfied he wasn't, though she thinks he's in deeper than he'll admit."

"How can she tell?" Mashburn asked.

McLean smiled. "She can spot a liar."

Church harrumphed. "Takes one to know one. Where is she, anyway?"

"She's working at home today," McLean said.

"So who broke into her house?" Mashburn asked.

"We don't know," McLean further lied.

"But you think it's related to the break-in at Skinner Movables, and Tony Coburn's disappearance." Mashburn gave Church a patronizing smile. "Sam and I went over most of this by phone this morning. Got to protect Abel, you know."

"What the hell does he have to do with any of this?" Church asked. "Sam, I thought you said you had info on the Wolf case. So far we've been yammering about burglaries. Look, this is how I see it. Loy's been sticking her nose in where it don't belong ever since the Wolfs got y'all involved in this. The mere fact that one of your clients had the bad luck to be a crime victim—"

"Homicide," McLean said.

Church held up his hands impatiently, "Lemme finish, will you? We don't know if he's a homicide victim. So far, what I know about Coburn is that he had damned good reason to fake his own death and skip town. He was bankrupt. His ex-wife is the most vindictive goddamned woman alive—she had him in court even after their divorce, alleging nonpayment of alimony and child support. He's tied down to a new wife with a baby on the way. And Skinner Movables, I've heard," Church added, giving McLean a wilting look, "is sinking. He was also facing job loss. He had plenty of reason to vanish."

"What about Seth Agee?" Mashburn asked.

"So what?" Church snapped. "He had a car wreck. What possible link could there be between these men's deaths and Natalie Wolf's?"

"Two men in the same company die violently within weeks of each other—" Mashburn began but was interrupted.

"One died in a violent accident," Church shouted. "The other one is missing. Even if they're both dead, and they were both killed, it's more likely they were killed by an irate former employee. We think an ex-employee or employees may be behind the burglary of the plant, in fact. There was a strike last year at Skinner, and in the past year there have been dozens of layoffs. That's why Skinner hired guards even while they were strapped financially. Threats by former employees made them sensitive about security. But in any case, there's no proof whatsoever of foul play." He scowled at McLean. "Now, as I asked earlier, what the hell does any of this have to do with Abel Wolf, who murdered his wife?"

"Allegedly," Mashburn offered primly.

McLean said, "Mike, don't you remember talking to me about a phone call you got from Agee? You were wondering if you should call the feds in." Suddenly Mashburn cleared his throat. McLean looked at him: "What?"

"Nothing," Mashburn grinned. "Just get a little nervous when you say, 'feds.' "

"Yeah, well, no point in calling them," said Church. "I got a little excited about the Russian connection, but it turned out to be a routine wife-killing. I didn't look far into it, but if the Russian stripper was also Abel's wife, there was even more reason to kill her."

"And why didn't you look any further into it?" asked McLean.

Church shrugged. "I no sooner got that call than Agee was dead." He abruptly drew silent and looked down at his knees. "Anyway, I didn't think much of it."

"He died on September 13th," said McLean. "When did you speak to him?"

"When did I tell you about talking to him?" Church asked.

"It was the night Loy went to Desmond Holliday's party, which was the Saturday before, on the 10th. Remember? You were pissed off that she was going."

"No, I wasn't," said Church.

"Yes, you were. But that's not the issue," said McLean. "The issue is, you got a call from Agee about a Russian stripper he'd hired, and a few days later he was dead. And a few weeks after that, his boss goes missing and a whole computer system has been ripped out of a company office." McLean leaned forward. "And do you remember how he said he found that stripper?"

Church's eyes cut to Mashburn, who was beaming at McLean. Church said, "The Internet. He found her on his company computer."

"Now, when did he tell you that?" McLean asked again.

"The day before I met you at that cantina. So it was four days before he had the wreck," said Church. He shook his head. "I still don't see how this relates to Abel Wolf." He grabbed his jacket and added, "Or any damned break-in at Loy's house, for that matter. If you're trying to save Abel Wolf, you're gonna have to give me better than that." Church abruptly got up and left.

Mashburn waited until after Church had gone to slap McLean on the back. "Boy, that was one hell of a show."

"What are you talking about?" McLean asked.

"If I could work a witness as well as you just worked Church, I'd be undefeated in court. You have the gift, Sam." He patted McLean again and pointed upward. "You do indeed."

"Well, I hope I didn't go too far."

"Too far? You made him do all the talking. You didn't give him a damned thing more than a reasonable doubt as to Abel's guilt that will live in his mind through the rest of this case. You were brilliant. Now, who did the break-in? You can tell me."

"I don't really know," McLean said.

"I see." Mashburn looked disappointed. "Well, when Loy says it's OK to fill in her client's lawyer, y'all call me."

Mashburn had been gone for several minutes, but the sting of his last remark was still fresh as McLean sat at his desk feeling like an underappreciated servant. Mashburn had rightly guessed that Lombard was the last word on how much information she and McLean shared with Abel's lawyer. McLean knew that if the tables were turned and he were lying in his sickbed with Lombard left to pitch her theory to Church, she wouldn't have given a thought to

McLean's assent. And yet he'd negotiated the whole meeting on pins and needles of what Lombard would have approved of. And he'd done a good job he was proud of, and she hadn't even been around to see it.

"Sam?" Retta was speaking to him on his telephone intercom. "Are you OK?"

"Huh? Why?" he asked.

"Mashburn's been gone 15 minutes. I thought by now you would be out here telling me about the meeting. And Loy's had Dana call twice already. She wants you to call her back."

"You call her back," he said. "I'm going home."

Dana had spent the night in the guest bedroom of Lombard's house without asking, and Lombard hadn't minded a bit. The guard was gone, and Dana had learned how to set the house alarm until Lombard felt well enough to fool with it. Dana walked into the kitchen around 8 A.M. on Wednesday, in time to find Lombard slumped at the kitchen table, clutching a coffee mug with one hand and her forehead with the other. "This flu is crueler than the worst hangover," she said weakly. "When will it end?"

Dana touched Lombard's brow. "You're warm again. Jeez, you're in no shape for work today."

They argued for a few minutes about Lombard's fitness for work, Lombard telling Dana she had to find out what McLean had done on the Wolf case. She'd been livid at McLean's failure to return her phone calls yesterday afternoon but had slept through so much of the ensuing evening that, by the time she'd awakened, it had been too late to call McLean at home. And he hadn't even bothered to call and check on her, she sulkily observed. She was determined to get showered and dressed for work, but as soon as she entered the bathroom, she bent over the toilet and threw up her coffee. She was so unnerved by the unexpected downturn of her condition, she let Dana pat her face clean and tuck her back into bed. Dana promised her an ice rub later if Lombard cooperated and rested.

And so Lombard spent another full day in bed, only this time alone, as Dana went to work at the library. She alternately watched her bedroom TV and called the office, ultimately succeeding in contacting McLean and finding out about Mike Church's position. "So he won't budge?" she said. "Stubbornness and stupidity make the solving of a case impossible. He's hopeless."

McLean said, "Well, as you requested, I made no mention of Attila to him, or Mashburn even."

"Good."

"He did make some interesting points, though."

"Like what?"

McLean summarized Church's theories on possible ex-employee motives for the plant burglary, and Church's skepticism of any connection in Agee's and Coburn's very different and not clearly suspicious fates. "And to be fair," he added, "without any knowledge of Attila and the representations Holliday made to you about her, his take on the situation isn't unreasonable."

Lombard said, "I suppose not." She coughed into a rag and fell back on her pillow. "What else is going on without me?" she asked.

"Uh, Gussie Wolf called today. She wants a meeting. Says she doesn't trust Mashburn, and he won't talk to her because he says she's not his client, Abel is. And then she went on for about ten minutes on how it was her money bankrolling him, and she called him a son of a bitch."

Lombard chuckled. "What about Abel? How is he?"

"Still crazy as a shithouse rat, I imagine. Mrs. Wolf didn't mention him."

"Anything else I need to know about? The guards OK? Do you mean to tell me you all don't really need me anymore? And I can just stay home and goof off while you do all the work?"

There was another pause on McLean's end, followed by a long sigh. "Mashburn wants to talk to you ASAP."

"Why can't you talk to him?"

"He sees you as the boss, I guess. Says he wants to talk to you about who you think broke into your house. I think he believes—or wants to believe—our theory of a connection between the Skinner guys and Natalie Wolf. He wants you to clue him in."

Lombard reflected for a moment. "OK. I'll do it."

"You mean you're going to?" McLean sounded surprised.

"Yes," she said, yawning. "Sam, call Mashburn up and tell him I'll have that information for him by tonight, if things go the way I want them to."

As soon as she hung up, Lombard called Dana at the library. She told her it was extremely important that she contact Stella right away. She told Dana she was sorry she'd been so abrupt in dismissing her from the Wolf case; that Dana could get back into it in the time it took her to arrange for Stella to come to Lombard's house that night.

She got off the phone and nestled in her pillows for a long nap. The noonday sun was just rising over a hillside behind her house, and light dazzled her bedroom as she drifted off to dream about an ice rub and the execution of a strategy. Lombard had a sinking feeling Holliday had been wrong in assuming only he had intimate knowledge of Attila's relationship with Natalie.

Lombard remembered that Desmond Holliday had hooked up Stella and Attila. If Stella had known Holliday well enough for him to have fixed her up with Attila, then Stella might very well have had some connection to Natalie Wolf, if at least a passing acquaintance. Lombard would have bet on it.

CHAPTER 14

Misty Coburn told McLean the same thing she'd told the police: Her husband had come home late on the evening of Wednesday, September 28th. They never talked much, so he had said little to her that night. But he drank when he was upset. "I could tell when he got home that he'd been drinking," she said. "And he always goes to the tavern on Wednesday nights."

McLean looked askance. Misty didn't know he and Lombard had met Coburn at the tavern on the night of his disappearance. But if Coburn had gone home late, he must have returned to the tavern after leaving the plant, where Lombard had examined Agee's computer files. "Did you see your husband leave again that night, after he got home?"

Misty nodded and rested her hands on her swollen belly. She was seven months' pregnant. "Yeah. Like I told the police, Tony stayed downstairs drinking. He just sat by himself and stared at the TV. I didn't like the way he was drinking, so I went up to bed. I was asleep for a while. Then I heard the phone ring—"

"When?"

"It was about 3. It was real late. It woke me up. Tony wasn't even in bed yet, so I got up and snuck downstairs and heard him on the phone. Oh, Lord, he was just so drunk. He was talking to somebody, but I didn't hear what they said, and I didn't dare get on the line. So anyway, he staggered out in the hallway and saw me standing on the stairs, and he said, 'I gotta get it over with sometime, don't I?' Or something like that, and he took off out the door."

"Mrs. Coburn, did Tony ever say anything at all to you about getting strange phone calls or messages?"

Misty shook her head. "No."

"Did you notice him acting strangely before that night? Like something was on his mind?"

"Sure. Something's always on Tony's mind. He's keyed up a lot."

"Misty, I know you're worried. But I have to ask, do you have any idea where he is? Any clue what's happened to him?"

"Well, the police think all this has to do with the strike last year and layoffs. Maybe one of the strikers or somebody that got laid off called him up that night. Maybe they know where he's at now." Her voice trailed off to a mumble. "I don't know."

"Did Tony ever mention a fellow named Seth Agee?"

Misty's mouth hung open, and she stared off to one side for a while, as though trying hard to think. "Seth Agee," she said, shaking her head slowly. "No. Uh-unh. Ain't never heard of him."

The more Misty talked, the more McLean couldn't help but wonder what the former Mrs. Coburn was like. It was obvious what Coburn had seen in Misty despite the fact he'd been married to somebody else: Misty wasn't exactly pretty, but she was cute and sexy in the guileless way that drove men to distraction and made straight women hate her guts. She was petite and voluptuous, alluring even at nearly full term. McLean's wife was pretty and had plenty of sex appeal for her husband, but she didn't ooze sexuality the way a woman like Misty did just by sitting with mute, bovine serenity during an interview. An insecure man with lots to prove would have no chance resisting a woman like her. Poor Tony Coburn, thought McLean.

"Mrs. Coburn—"

"Call me Misty," she said. "I get nervous when people call me Mrs. Coburn. It reminds me of that other one, you know, the ex."

"Well," McLean coughed, "Misty, Seth Agee was an employee of Skinner Movables—"

"Do you think he knows something about where Tony is?" she asked.

McLean paused. "No. No, I don't. Look, Mrs. Coburn—I mean, Misty—I think the police are doing a good job trying to find Tony. But I want to help. If Tony had an address book or a date book, that might help me."

"I think he kept stuff like that at his office. Besides, the police got most of his records that he kept here. And most of that other kind of stuff? His ex-wife has that kind of thing, only she called up here one night screaming about how she burned up all his papers. Even his high school yearbook." Misty shook her head. "She's a mean old so-and-so." Suddenly, she beamed. "Oh, hang on! Just a minute." She stood up unsteadily and left the room, her sandals clacking down the parquet floor of the hall. After a couple of minutes, the clacking resumed, and Misty reappeared holding a photo album.

"What's that?" McLean asked.

"It's got pictures in it," she said. "It was a wedding gift from some of the boys he knows. And they took all these crazy pictures from his bachelor party. I know it ain't nothing, but it's all I've got."

McLean resisted licking his lips as Misty handed him this golden piece of evidence. Lombard would have kissed it and danced around the room, he thought, and probably would have kissed Misty as well. He calmly asked Misty if he could borrow the album for a few days, and she shrugged. "I don't care," she said.

McLean had just taken the photo album in his hands when his cell phone buzzed.

"We've got a body," said Church. "Come on out to Skinner Movables. Tell them I said you could cross the yellow tape."

"That feels nice," said Lombard, stretched out on her belly, naked but for a towel draped across her ass, every pore of her skin bumping up as a smooth sponge of icy cold soapy water glided across her flesh.

"Stella should be here any minute," said Dana, sticking a thermometer in Lombard's mouth. "Are you tired yet?"

"I'm peaceful," Lombard mumbled, careful not to dislodge her thermometer. "You tell me when you're tired. I could let you go on and on."

"You've had enough bathing. You're totally broken out in goose bumps." Dana pulled a sheet over Lombard.

"But I still feel warm," said Lombard. The phone rang. "Don't get that."

Dana ignored the phone and waited for the minute to pass before taking out Lombard's thermometer. She read it just after the last ring. "The house is very warm, but your fever's gone way down. Time for your jammies."

"Damn."

"Don't you have an answering machine? I didn't hear one."

"I have voice mail."

Dana glanced at the caller ID box as she pulled Lombard's terry-cloth robe out of a laundry basket of clothes she'd just washed and dried. She pitched the robe over Lombard's body. "Put that on. Whose number is 500-1290?"

"That's Sam's cell." Lombard modestly rose in her bed, drawing the robe around her. She'd made Dana look the other way when she lay down and covered her backside with the towel. "I'll need to call him back."

Just then, the doorbell rang. Dana was facing Lombard and glanced over her shoulder in the direction of the living room. "That'll be Stella." She looked at Lombard, sitting with hunched shoulders and a runny nose on the edge of her bed, clutching her robe at the chest. She abruptly leaned in and kissed Lombard's cheek. Then she pulled an orange bandanna from her hip pocket and handed it to her. "Wipe your nose. I'll get the door."

Stella Hines looked ill at ease despite the smile on her face. "Cool house. Hard to find, though. I had to turn around," she said, standing near the front door with her hands in her duster pockets, glancing curiously around the room for a moment before spotting Lombard in the door of the hallway.

"So what's the emergency?" Stella asked. "Dana said you had to talk to me in private."

Lombard said, "You know I'm investigating a murder, right?"

Stella shook her head. "No, but that sounds pretty cool."

Lombard suggested they all sit down. She took the armchair and looked at Stella, sitting apprehensively next to Dana on the sofa. "Stella, how could you not know I'm investigating the Natalie Wolf case? It's been in the news."

"I don't watch a lot of news. But yeah, I've heard about the missing Russian woman that big, gross man killed."

"Well, his name is Abel Wolf, and I'm working for him."

"Sounds like you've got your work cut out for you. I heard he got caught with, like, her thumb. That is so wrong. How can you work for somebody like that?"

"It hasn't been easy." Lombard pulled a tissue out of the Kleenex box and blew her nose. "Listen, do you mean to tell me you've never met Natalie Wolf?"

"No. Why would I have?" Stella looked bewilderedly at Dana. "What's up, Dana? I have to be at work in an hour."

Lombard studied Stella's features for a moment, deciding she was an extremely pretty, milky-complexioned, blond gay party girl who was telling the truth. "How did you come to know Mari Attila?"

Stella's eyes narrowed, and she pitched Dana a cold look. "Bitch. What did you tell her that for? That was totally supposed to be a secret. Guess you wouldn't like Jane to know how much time you've been spending out here, would you?"

Dana said, "Stella, Loy already saw you with Attila before I told her anything."

"Her name is Mari," said Stella. "*I* call her Mari. Only Desi calls her Attila." She abruptly shut her mouth and pouted.

"Well, that leads nicely into my next question," said Lombard.

"Which involves how you met Ms. Attila, presumably through Desi Holliday, correct?"

"What are you, a cop?" Stella's lips were pursed in consternation. "I don't have to take this shit, you know. I could just get up and leave."

"But you won't," said Dana.

Stella rolled her eyes at Dana. "Excuse me? I am *so* not getting this," she said. "I just came out here for the scoop on your new…" She raised her hands up and made quotation symbols. "…*friend*. I didn't expect to be sitting under a magnifying glass."

The young women began lobbing curses at each other, and Lombard followed their banter impatiently. Clearly, something was going on between them that she wasn't in on. "Will you two shut up?" she shouted, and the two girls sank into their shoulders a bit. "Now, I know you don't have to take any shit off me, Stella. You can get up and head straight out that door if you want. And I'll get dressed and mosey on down to Maddie's Bar and hound your cute little ass in front of your boss about your connection to Desi Holliday and his cabal of criminal associates. Is that what you want?"

"No," Stella sniffed. "OK, look. I've bartended a few of Desi's parties, and that's it. I moonlight a little, and I get business through some gay guys I know." She looked at Lombard. "Like Tyler Rhodes, for example. So anyway, it had been awhile since I'd last seen Desi, and he came by my work one night and we were just kind of shooting the shit, right? And he asked me if I was available, and I said I was. And he said he had a guest in from Florida who was looking to hook up with a girl, so I said I would meet her and, you know, hang out. It never hurts to check somebody out." She looked down at her knees. "Anyway, it's not supposed to. I really liked her."

Lombard noticed a tear trickle down Stella's cheek. "You haven't heard from her in a little while, I take it?"

Stella shook her head, and her lower lip trembled. She took a deep, shuddering breath and began crying.

"Dear God, honey, don't tell me you fell in love with her," Lombard said softly.

"She was nice to me." Stella buried her face in Dana's shoulder and sobbed. "And she was so cool and sophisticated. Not like all these fucking small-town losers in their mullets and biker rags and their stupid, P-town rainbow T-shirts and Indigo Girls goddamn stupid Lilith Fair conventional lesbian bullshit!" she wailed. "I'm moving to Canada!"

Lombard said, "Hell's bells, since you put it that way, I might go with you."

Stella's sobbing suddenly turned to chuckling. She pulled away from Dana and collected herself. She wiped her eyes with tissue Lombard handed her and said, "So what about Mari Attila? Should I be glad she left without so much as a word to me?"

"Have you tried calling her?" Lombard asked.

"I called her at Desi's, but he told me she was gone, and he was really shitty about it. He told me not to call back, even when I reminded him that I was still willing to bartend for him if he needed me." She blew her nose. "Bitch. She probably ran off with that skanky whore Nadine."

Lombard felt as though her eyeballs had tripled in size and were bulging out of her head. "What did you say?"

There was suddenly a loud rapping at the door, accompanied by an obnoxious laying-on of the doorbell. "Open up," a man thundered. "It's the feds!"

"Damn Mashburn," Lombard grumbled. "What's he doing here? Dana, honey, will you fend him off for just a minute? Now, Stella, who is Nadine?"

Dana went to the door and stepped outside with Mashburn while Lombard patted Stella's hand and repeated, "This Nadine, who is she?"

"She's another foreign whore friend of Desi's, but I haven't seen her in a long time."

"OK, now, Stella, it's important that you tell me everything: when you met her; how; when you last saw her. But first, what did she look like?"

"She's got red hair and dark eyes. She's pretty."

"So you've met her."

"Not exactly. I was bartending at the same time she was at some of Desi's parties. I only remember her because she was kind of foxy and had an accent, and you remember shit like that in Asheville. This was before I'd met Mari."

"And she went by the name of Nadine? Not Natalie?"

"Yes, Nadine." Stella smiled. "Oh, I see where you're going with this. Do you think Nadine was really Natalie? Why? Just because they both had red hair and accents?"

"No," said Lombard. "They shared more than that. They both knew Desi. He's admitted to me that he knew Natalie Wolf, and I've seen a picture of them posing together at a party, probably one you were bartending. Of course, Abel Wolf knew nothing about their association, which makes me wonder exactly what it was. I have a feeling it had nothing to do with home decorating or personal improvement."

Stella's lips parted. "Huh. That's no coincidence."

"So, when is the last time you saw Nadine or Natalie, whatever her name was?"

"Oh, it was way before all this murder news started."

"Do you know if Mari knew Nadine?"

"She knew Nadine, according to Desi. When he was hooking us up, he mentioned that Mari and Nadine had worked together."

The door opened, and Mashburn walked inside with Dana, who said, "Couldn't talk him into leaving. Sorry."

"She said you were having a little family crisis," said Mashburn. "Listen, I came over because Sam told me you'd have information for me on Abel's case."

"You could've just called me up, but you might as well stick around," said Lombard. "And how did you know where I live?"

"I don't discuss case details over the phone. You never know who the hell's listening these days. And Sam told me how to get out here. By the way, they found Tony Coburn's body, out in the woods in back of Skinner Movables. Bullet through his brain, pistol next to his body."

"Suicide, then?" said Lombard.

"Looks like it," he said. "And God knows he had reason. Skinner was about to fold, he'd be out of a job—"

"Yeah, yeah, and his wife was pregnant and the ex had him in court. Very neat." Lombard blew out a deep breath and leaned forward to grab a tissue.

"Look at you in your robe, with all these purdy girls rubbing your back for you. Ain't you just Asheville's very own Hugh Hefner?" Mashburn chuckled.

Lombard blew her nose. "I was just thinking the same thing." She introduced Mashburn to Stella and Dana, and told him that Stella could positively link Mari Attila to Natalie Wolf. "Only Stella knew her as Nadine," she said, "and Holliday told Stella the two women had worked together. How about that?"

The next night Lombard was feeling well enough to go out. At around 10 P.M. she and McLean sat down at Maddie's Bar and ordered a couple of drinks. Lombard asked the server if Stella was working downstairs tonight, and the server told her Stella was working a private party upstairs. Lombard said it was urgent she see her immediately.

Stella was furious when she saw Lombard. She marched over to her table and snapped, "You told me you wouldn't bother me anymore, Loy."

"I'm sorry, honey. Have you met my partner, Sam McLean?"

Stella flashed a quick, insincere smile at him. "What is it now?"

"I want you to look at a couple of pictures," said Lombard, "and tell me if you recognize the woman in them. Now, will you sit down? This won't take a minute."

Stella sat next to Lombard, who laid a single photograph down on the table. It was the same picture of Desmond Holliday and Natalie Wolf she had shown to Tony Coburn.

"That's Nadine," said Stella, pointing at the figure of Natalie.

"Very good," said Lombard. "Sam, bring out the good stuff."

McLean plopped a small photo album down on the table. "I'd prefer not to look at them again," he said.

"What is it?" Stella asked hesitantly. She began slowly flipping through the sleeves of photographs. Lombard alternated looking at Stella's face and the photographs as Stella examined each one. They were, for the most part, depictions of drunken guys laughing and striking stupid poses, and Coburn was in most of them. Stella giggled when she saw the picture of Coburn being tethered to a mock ball and chain. She flipped to the next picture, and her smile faded. She slammed the album shut. "Big deal. So what?"

Lombard opened the album back to the photograph that had upset Stella. It was a rear shot of a redhaired woman, squatting on the floor with her hands on her hips, leaning to one side as though swaying. It had probably been some kind of dance. She was also scantily dressed, wearing only—by that point, for discarded clothes could be seen on the floor nearby—a thong and bustier. She was all white flesh and red hair, though one could just make out some of her profile and the rise of her right breast in its scarlet bustier cup. And winding up the ridge of her back was a smashing blue scorpion tattoo.

"That tattoo look familiar, sugar?" Lombard asked.

"Yeah," Stella said dimly. "Dana filled you in on all of it, huh? I'm so pissed at her. Really surprised. I thought she could be trusted."

"Oh, come on, Stella. How close are you two, really? You were bragging to her about your sex life, and that's not the same thing as confiding."

Stella pursed her lips and looked away. "Can I get back to work now, before I'm missed? Please?"

"By all means, and thanks."

Stella paused after getting up and grinned maliciously. "Tell Dana I said thanks for the bag of weed." Lombard glared at her, and Stella added, "Well, I didn't drive halfway to Hendersonville for the company, you know."

Lombard was quiet for a moment after Stella had gone. "What a little bitch," she said, "trying to get Dana in trouble."

"You drug-test the guards," McLean reminded her. "Maybe you should drug-test Dana."

"Stella's lying," said Lombard. "It's written all over her."

"No, it isn't," said McLean. "You're just cutting Dana some slack because you like her. If Stella were talking about one of the guards—"

"She isn't talking about a guard," Lombard interrupted. "I test the guards because they're bonded and insured by us, and our clients' security depends on clear heads and ready bodies. Dana is a part-time computer geek. I don't drug-test Retta either."

"Nobody's ever accused Retta of using," said McLean.

Lombard gave an exasperated sigh. "And if some airheaded twit like Stella ever said so, I'd need a little more proof," she said. "Stella's jealous of Dana. It's as plain as day." The more she talked, the rosier her complexion got. "That's a low-down thing to do, trying to get Dana in hot water at work."

She pointed at the photo album. "Now, back to business. Some of those sleeves are empty. What do you figure happened to the pictures that were in them? You think Misty took them out?"

"Who knows?" said McLean. "I'd say Coburn had more reason to, if they were embarrassing. Anyway, this one picture is enough for us to go on."

"I can't wait to show them to Gussie and Abel," said Lombard. She reached for her belt when she felt her cell phone vibrate. "Maybe this is Gussie. Not like her not to call me in this many days. Hello?"

"You should have listened to me," said the caller. "I'm a fair woman, and I tried to warn you. I even tried to kill you, but you're too slippery."

Lombard gave McLean an astonished look. "Attila? What do you want?"

"I can't take responsibility for anyone, Loy. Not even for Dana. You got too close to the fire without getting singed, so now she'll have to burn for you. It's my parting shot, but I'll let Abel have the credit. I wanted you to know that."

"Attila, is that you? Where are you?" Lombard shouted so abrasively, patrons from all around the club looked at her.

"Loy, calm down," McLean said. "What's happened? Who was that?"

Lombard's heart was pounding; she felt like her blood was turning to ice. "Dana went into the office tonight, after she left my house. She said she had catching-up to do."

"Good God, you look like you've seen the gates of hell, Loy." McLean stood up and took her outside. "Get some air. Is Dana all right?"

"No. No, she isn't." Lombard began walking toward Haywood.

"Loy, the car's this way!" McLean shouted after her.

Lombard was running. "We have to go to the office!" She'd gotten about a block when McLean drove up beside her.

"Get in the car, Loy. We'll get there faster if we drive."

As soon as McLean's car screeched into the parking lot of their office, Lombard sprang out. Dana's car was parked near the door, which was unlocked. "Not a good sign," she muttered. "She always locks up safe and sound." They went inside, and Lombard called out for her.

McLean withdrew his pistol and quietly looked around the office. Lombard hadn't told him what she'd heard on the phone; there hadn't been time. Dana was nowhere inside. Lombard called her house, but there was no answer.

"Maybe she's at her girlfriend's," said Lombard. "If I weren't so damned vain, I would have asked her name, her last name, so I could look it up. It's Jane something."

McLean said, "Her car's here, Loy. But she isn't, and the door's unlocked. She's not with her girlfriend."

Lombard put her hands over her temples and breathed deeply. She'd never in her life been so afraid for another person. "Sam, we've got to find her. We've got to go and find out where she is."

"I'm calling Mike Church," said McLean.

"Good idea," Lombard said weakly. "Mike will help us."

CHAPTER 15

Mike Church ventured deeper into the countryside across-river from Wolf Branch Farm. "Are you sure you remember how to get there?"

"Yes," said Lombard.

"Loy, I'm not saying I believe your theory. Yet. But I do want to know why this is the first I've heard of it."

"I wasn't sure until tonight."

"I think you've been sure for a while."

"Look," said Lombard, "I had to sort things out first. I've been sick. The minute I got a solid lead, I was going to tell you. I've already told Mashburn, so you were next. I had to run it by the lawyer first."

"So what does this Dana have to do with anything?"

"She's fucking with me."

"Who? Dana?"

"No! Attila. I'm beginning to think she's just a common psychopath." Lombard shook her head. "No, there's more to it than that. I can't think right now, Mike."

"And you think that fag decorator knows something? Is that why Sam's headed out there?"

Lombard wasn't paying attention. "What does she *want*?" she asked.

"Money."

"I can't believe I don't know even that much."

"So are we gonna find her up here at the cabin?"

"I don't know," said Lombard. "But if we don't, there'll be something, some kind of lead." She glanced over her shoulder at the road behind them, and the stream of headlights following. "Those are backup units, right? We'll need them if she's there, that's for certain."

"You bet I called in backup," said McLean. "The last time I went out snooping around in somebody's cabin, I took a bullet."

Lombard remembered that. Church had been shot while working the Slade case with her and McLean. He'd gone to a remote cabin not unlike the one they were driving to now, and he'd confronted a killer by himself. Church might be a lazy, bigoted ass, she thought, but he wasn't a coward. That much, she had to give him.

Desmond Holliday was climbing out a side window of his house when McLean spotted him. Deputy Hugh Potter and another deputy named Buck were positioned at the front door and back door, respectively. Holliday didn't see McLean at first. He had just hopped off the windowsill and dusted off his trousers when McLean approached him. Holliday smiled ebulliently. "Hello, there. Lovely evening, isn't it?"

"Desmond Holliday, I presume?" McLean grinned.

"I've waited my whole life for just the right man to say that."

"Let's go inside," said McLean. "Using the front door, if you don't mind."

Dana was afraid, but she silently swore that if she survived the night, she would give Attila credit for at least having been a gracious captor. So far, however, Dana hadn't uttered a word. And as mild-mannered and gentle as Attila had been so far, she was some-how terrifying.

When Dana had looked out the front glass door of the office on hearing the knock, she had seen a tall, severe-looking woman in a long, belted black leather coat and boots, aiming a gun straight at her. She'd unlocked the door and done everything she was told since. This included giving out Lombard's cell number when a phone call to Lombard's house had apparently gone unanswered. Dana had heard everything Attila had said to Lombard as they sped somewhere in the Mercedes SUV, and her stomach had shrunken with every word.

She had no idea where she was now. She'd been blindfolded the minute she climbed into the SUV at gunpoint, and Attila hadn't removed the blindfold till they arrived wherever she was now. Attila had tied her hands behind her back too, and once they'd arrived in this room, she'd asked Dana if the binding was too tight. "I have to leave on the straps," Attila explained as she tied Dana's feet to a chair. "I don't mind if you see the room, but I can't let you roam."

So frightened she could hardly speak, Dana said, "I'm sorry to ask, but I have to go to the bathroom."

Attila frowned at the straps she'd just tied. Then she began to unloosen them. "Women," she grumbled.

They drove off the main road, along the quarry trail, and then came to a fork. "We should have brought Sam," said Church.

"Sam's never driven up here," said Lombard. "He paddled over from the campground upriver. His guess once we got off the main road would be as good as mine." She deliberated for a moment. "Take the right."

Church radioed two of the three cruisers behind him to take the left.

"We've only got one backup unit? What good will that do us if the cabin is this way?" Lombard asked.

"It's only one woman," said Church.

Lombard shook her head. "You make it sound so easy."

They parked the car and walked under the moonlight. There were only a few clouds tonight, and the trees had lost most of their leaves.

The driveway was empty, but Lombard suspected Attila could have parked in the woods. Under the cover of night her black SUV would be impossible to spot. Their path led to the side of the cabin, where a door faced them; from the cabin's other side, which faced the river, McLean had spotted Attila. Lombard doubted she could kick in the front door, and she was certain Church couldn't. The two young officers from the cruiser that had followed her and Church were young, fit, and eager to break down doors, however, so Lombard had them cover both of the doors to the cabin.

"When I give the signal," she whispered, "kick them in."

"What signal?" Church asked.

"My middle finger!" she snapped. "Just kick the doors down when I say so!"

The front door of Holliday's house was locked, and he didn't have a key with him. "If you'll let me climb back in through the window," he offered, "I can open the door from inside."

"I don't trust you," said McLean. "No offense."

"None taken, I'm sure," said Holliday. "Say, aren't you Sam McLean, the guy who escorted Loy Lombard here on Sunday? I've heard so much about you."

"Open the door, please," said McLean.

Holliday chuckled and glanced nervously at the officers surrounding him. "I'd rather not wake my guest. Why don't you just haul me off to the station house and interrogate me under a hot lightbulb?"

McLean shook his head. "Nope. We'll do all that inside the house, here. Now, you can open that door, like a gentleman, or we can open it like a passel of good ole rednecks. You pick."

Dana walked obediently back to the chair in which she had been sitting as soon as she was finished in the bathroom, which was more like a narrow closet. She still couldn't guess where she was. The room was cramped and dimly lit, and Attila hadn't let her turn on the bathroom light or even shut the door. She'd kept her eye on her the whole time, and Dana had struggled not to cry in humiliation.

In spite of the circumstances, though, Attila was treating her fairly decently. Once she had tied her up again, she asked if she wanted any water. When Dana said no, otherwise she might have to pee again, Attila had chuckled and promised her she could go to the bathroom whenever she asked. She was just beginning to wonder if Attila were really capable of killing anybody when Attila let her know just how dangerous she was.

She was sitting in a chair a few feet from Dana, though her face was shadowed in the dim lamplight. "I like you, Dana," she said. "You're very polite, a well-mannered young lady. But I will kill you if you try to escape. So don't."

"I won't," Dana promised.

"You're afraid," said Attila. "I don't blame you."

"Where are we?" Dana asked.

Attila leaned slightly into the light and betrayed a smile. Cradling the gun in her lap, she asked, "You don't know where you are?"

Dana shook her head. "Why would I?"

Attila said, "Ignorance is bliss."

Something in Attila's condescending tone pissed Dana off. It was that quick. She was terrified; then she was bold. "So," said Dana, "I hear you dated Stella Hines."

Attila looked surprised. "You know Stella?"

"She dated my girlfriend," said Dana.

Attila looked pensive. "You, your girlfriend, Stella, me, and…"

"Who?"

Attila squinted. "Never mind."

"The Asheville daisy chain," said Dana. "You sleep with two women, you'll be linked to the whole town."

Attila sighed. "Mind your own business, darling. My private life is neither here nor there as far as your survival is concerned."

"Just used her and dumped her like yesterday's trash," she said in a suddenly loud voice. "Like she was nothing, nothing at all. Well, that's a fine way for a sleek, world-class lesbian such as yourself to treat a nice, innocent young person. I'm sure you're very proud of yourself. Who wouldn't be?"

Attila looked very hostile. "Shut your mouth," she commanded.

Dana was certain she was going to die. But if she couldn't fight, by God, she could kvetch. "Such a butch!" she shouted. "If you'll untie me, I'll shake for you."

"I said, shut up!" Attila bellowed, and her voice practically laid Dana's ears flat against her head. Attila stood up and moved closer to her—all six feet, if Dana had to guess—her shadow imposing itself over her like a dark cloud under the moon. And just as Attila pulled a roll of electrical tape from her coat pocket, there was a rapping at the door.

"Don't knock, you goddamned fool!" Lombard hissed when she heard either Church or the officer who was with him bang on the front door.

"It's a knock-and-announce, isn't it?" the young officer asked. "It's procedure."

Lombard shouted from her position at the side door. "Now!" She slapped her assisting officer on his ass. "Move!"

The doors were kicked in simultaneously, and four nervous, shouting bodies spilled into the house all at once. As Lombard had ordered, the officers fanned out in prescribed directions, covering the house.

After every square inch of the tiny cabin had been trod over, and the lights were on, one thing was clear. Dana wasn't here, and neither was Attila. Lombard sat down on an old steamer trunk and ran her fingers through her hair. "I thought we'd find them hiding here," she said. "I hoped, anyway."

Church gave a deep sigh and patted her on the shoulder. "We'll find them."

Lombard looked up and searched her surroundings with moist, reddening eyes. "Yeah," she said in a weary rasp. She buried her head in her hands. "Where would she take her? Maybe she really is at Holliday's, and Sam will find her. Damn it, she only knows one or two places in Asheville not open to the public." Lombard fended off an urge to break something. She abruptly looked up at Church. "Mike, let's get moving." She stood up and charged outside. She told the other officers to search the surrounding landscape with flashlights until dogs could be called in. Then she remembered the orange bandanna Dana had give her, and which Lombard had put in her jacket pocket before leaving earlier that evening for Maddie's Bar. She gave it to the officers in the hope that if Dana were somewhere in the woods, a dog could pick her scent up off the cloth.

"You'll never get the door open," said Holliday. "This door was salvaged from a 15th-century church, bombed by the commies in the Spanish Civil War. I imported it. Besides, there's someone inside who can open it."

"Who?" McLean asked.

Holliday pressed a doorbell key. "Open the door, damn it," he muttered, as though to himself.

McLean knocked on the door. "Open up! Or we'll bust this pretty door off its hinges!" After a few silent seconds, McLean turned to the deputies. "OK, Potter, dust your boots off."

Suddenly the door swung open, and Tyler Rhodes stood before them in a crimson robe of what looked like liquid velvet and an impossibly bright white smile. He was holding a martini. "Come in. I know it's an ungodly hour, but the ice shaker is still full."

Attila had thrown off the light switch as soon as the knocking had started. There was no light at all from any source; Dana could open her eyes and see no more than when they were shut. And even if Attila's leather-gloved hand weren't covering her mouth, she wouldn't have dared utter a word. For in Attila's other hand was a gun, its muzzle pressed hard against Dana's right temple.

The furious thumping at the door was coming from above; Dana thought they'd descended steps when they'd arrived, though she couldn't be certain since in her blindfold and wrist straps she'd had no depth perception or bearings of any kind. Then she heard a voice, and she was certain they were underneath its speaker.

"Abel! Unlock the door this minute. You heard me!"

So this was the bunker she'd heard Lombard talk about. Dana thought it must be. She didn't know what to wish for. Perhaps Mrs. Wolf could save her. On the other hand, maybe she was in on it somehow. And if Mrs. Wolf weren't in cahoots with Attila, it could be worse for Dana should she open that door.

Attila's stillness and soft, hot breath on her neck told Dana there was no likely arrangement between the two women, though she couldn't imagine what purpose Attila could have had in bringing her here. She heard Attila whisper something to herself in a foreign language—she guessed Hungarian—then Attila spoke to her.

"Silence is golden, Dana," she whispered. "Let's hope the lady of the house goes back to bed." Then Attila lapsed into her native tongue, and to Dana it sounded like cursing.

Church let Lombard take the wheel. "Where are we going?" he asked as they peeled out onto the highway.

"Call Sam's cell phone," she said. "Use my phone. Find out if he's at Holliday's and what's going on."

Church tried McLean's number and waited for several seconds. "No answer," he said. "He must be tied up."

"Hopefully he has everything under control there."

"Isn't that where we're going?"

"Nope."

Church stared at Lombard's profile for a moment, barely visible in the scant light of the dashboard. "Well," he asked, "would it be too much to clue me in on where exactly it is we're going?"

"No," she said. "We're going to Wolf Branch Farm."

"You think Dana is at Wolf Branch Farm?"

"No, I think Dana is temping as a fry cook at Big Boy, and I'm just paying a social visit to the Wolfs at this hour of the morning."

"You don't have to be such a damned smart-ass, Loy," Church grumbled. "You've been saying all along you don't think Abel Wolf has anything to do with this. I think it odd at the eleventh hour we should be closing in on him, considering all that other shit you've been trying to sell me."

Lombard said calmly, "I don't think Abel has anything to do with it."

"Then why the hell are we closing in on him to save Dana?" Church shouted.

"I'll tell you when we get there. It's one of my hunches."

"Damn your hunches! I want to know what's going on."

"Tony Coburn didn't commit suicide, Mike."

Church drew a deep breath and balled his hands into tight fists. He was entirely frustrated by Lombard's evasiveness. "What are you talking about now?"

"You saw his body, right?"

"Yeah, right. So?"

"And he was wearing gloves, wasn't he? Gun on the right side?"

"Yeah." Church jerked his head. "How did you know that? Did Sam tell you that?"

"No. I guessed it."

"No great guess," he said. "It was cold the night he vanished. He would've been wearing gloves."

"I'm curious about a suicidal man who's fussy about keeping his hands warm before he blows his own brains out," Lombard said.

"Well, people are weird. Anyway, so what if he wore gloves?"

"He was left-handed." Lombard smiled at Church. "I've seen him use it."

"So what are you saying?"

"You know what I'm saying. His murderer shot him to death, execution-style, wearing gloves. Then she fitted those gloves on his hands to show powder marks."

Church gazed out the windshield. "I'm not convinced yet. I don't know why the hell we're going to the Wolf farm, but if Dana is there, and she's come in harm's way, as far as I'm concerned that makes Abel Wolf all the more suspect." He scowled at Lombard. "And Coburn ain't got squat to do with any of it! Even if he didn't do himself in, it wasn't some crazed Hungarian she-bitch after him. If it was anybody, it was one of those disgruntled ex-employees."

McLean, Holliday, and the two deputies followed Rhodes into the billiard room, furnished with felt-top card tables and a mahogany wet bar. "We haven't got time for a sit-down chat," McLean said. "What were you running away from, Mr. Holliday?"

"He was running away?" said Rhodes with a surprised look. "Where?"

" 'Running' may not be the right word," said McLean. "He wasn't all the way out the window when I spotted him, to be fair."

"I had no idea who was at the door," Holliday said sullenly.

"Who did you think it was?" McLean asked.

Holliday averted his eyes. "Tyler," he said after a moment, "would you make me one of those?"

"Hell no," said Rhodes. "Not if you were diving out of here in the midst of a home invasion without so much as warning me about it."

"Where were you?" McLean asked Rhodes.

"I was asleep, in the guest bedroom," said Rhodes, "and unaware of danger."

"I wasn't thinking clearly," said Holliday. "I was in a panic. If I'd known it was the police, I would have opened the door. I'm relieved it's you!"

"You still haven't answered my question," said McLean. "Who did you think it was?"

"I didn't know!" Holliday glanced at Rhodes, who looked uncharacteristically angry. "I was asleep, dead asleep, and I heard pounding at the door." He brushed back his thinning hair and sighed.

"Of course, *she* wouldn't have knocked first," said Rhodes, "not if it was who Desi was afraid of. She would have crept right inside without warning."

"Mari Attila, right?" said McLean.

Holliday looked down. "I've done nothing wrong," he said. "All I've done since I got out of prison is try to live right and do the right thing." He looked at McLean. "I never wanted any harm to come to anybody."

McLean cut his eye over to Rhodes, who caught McLean's glance and raised his martini glass to his lips. "Don't look at me, Sam. I'm just along for the ride."

Dana's hands were now tied to the armrests of Abel Wolf's old wooden swivel desk chair, and her feet were tethered to its stem. Her mouth was covered with electrical tape, and she was blindfolded. Her anger having subsided and been supplanted by a much starker fear than any she had ever known, she strained her ears for any sense of where Attila was or what she was doing. So far since she'd been bound up, she'd heard nothing other than occasional signs of movement to suggest Attila was still inside. Of course, she knew Attila still had to be present, since the door hadn't opened. Gussie

Wolf had long since retreated, probably back home and to bed.

She wondered what Attila was doing. Dana didn't move or twitch, out of the one thing she still clung to—her pride. She didn't want Attila to know how frightened she was, and she tried to make herself angry again by imagining that Attila was watching her like the cruel menace she was. But it wasn't enough. Dana's certainty that she was about to die rose in her like water in a sinking ship, pushing out hope with each passing second.

Suddenly a tinny, synthetic flourish of music startled Dana. She gasped through her nose and reflexively threw her head upright. Somehow, in her troubled, fear-addled mind, she recognized the single bar of music as it repeated itself twice. It was from Wagner's *Ride of the Valkyries*, programmed, evidently, into Attila's cell phone. Dana couldn't believe it: Even her cell phone was scary.

"*Da?*" said Attila. There were a few seconds of silence, followed by a firmer, more resolute "*Da,*" which Dana recognized as the Russian word for *yes*. To keep herself from shaking, she tried to think of all the other Russian words she'd learned during her stint as a reference librarian and from her Russian-born maternal grandmother.

"Goodbye, Dana," Attila said suddenly. The next sound Dana heard was of Attila's boots clomping up the steps, and of a door opening. After a few seconds, the door slammed shut, and there was a blunt hitching sound.

Dana struggled against her bindings, writhing around in her chair with more force than she'd known she had. Her mind was a blur of panic and raw fear, and sweat broke out all over her. She had no sense of time or space, only a primal urge to free herself that soon burned itself out. Overwhelmed, she grew faint, and with no light to go out or sound to go off, she drifted into unconsciousness.

Mrs. Wolf glowered at Lombard and Church as they passed by her when she opened the front door. "What do you want at this hour?" she hollered at them.

"Where's Abel?" Lombard asked.

"Paris!" Mrs. Wolf yelled. "Where the hell do you think he is? He's in bed."

"Get him up. We have an emergency."

"What for?"

Lombard told her they had to go down to his bunker, but there wasn't time to explain why.

Mrs. Wolf looked pensive. "Hmm. What's going on down there?"

Impatiently, Lombard started up the stairs to find Abel. Mrs. Wolf followed her. "All right. I'll get him up." She turned on a hallway light and knocked on a bedroom door. "I thought Abel was down there earlier," she said.

"Why?" asked Lombard.

"I have trouble sleeping sometimes. I went down to the kitchen to warm up some milk, and I thought I heard the bunker door slam. I thought, What on earth is Abel doing down there at this hour? I was so sure I'd heard it, I didn't even check his room. I went straight down there and thumped on that door but didn't get an answer. So I come back up here and checked his room, and there he was fast asleep, so I figured I'd imagined it." She banged on the door. "Get up, Abel! Something's going on down at the bunker!"

"It's just a chance," said Lombard.

"Naw, something's going on down there," said Mrs. Wolf. "I thought I was crazy, hearing things. In the clear of night on this lonesome old farm, I can hear noises half a mile away. That bunker door makes a noise when it slams shut, the way it falls down on that concrete. I heard it."

Lombard's face froze on Mrs. Wolf for a moment. Then she banged on Abel's door. "Abel! Get up. This is Loy Lombard. Hurry up!"

"You know the idea of going back to prison distresses me," said Holliday matter-of-factly. He was sitting on a burgundy leather sofa in his billiard room.

McLean was sitting at a card table with Rhodes. The deputies were examining the rack of pool cues. "Mr. Holliday," said McLean, "Dana Gabriel works for me and Loy. She was kidnapped tonight. I think you know by whom and why."

Holliday looked shocked. "No," he said, though it sounded less like denial than an exclamation of horror. "I don't know anything about a kidnapping. If I did, I'd tell you. And I have no idea where Attila is right now. I hoped she'd gone for good." He stood up and went to the bar and poured himself a drink. "She'll have been in town a month tomorrow, if she's still here. She arrived on a Thursday, and I'd never met her. I'd known her brother, you see. I've told your partner all this." He sat back down on the sofa. "I'd owed her brother money. That was true. She used Natalie to blackmail me. That was true too. She came here to pick up Natalie and leave the country for good. Things were getting too hot for her in Miami, and I don't mean in the literal sense. Her connections were adding up for the feds, and she had to get out."

"So why is she still sticking around here?"

Holliday frowned. "I can't say."

"Damn it, Holliday!" McLean shouted. "This girl is in trouble. If something happens to her, and you've withheld information, I'll see to it you go back to that prison you dread so much, only it'll be state!"

"I know nothing that can save that young lady," Holliday said thoughtfully. "If I did, I'd go back to prison to help her."

"Oh, *do* get off your cross, Desi," Rhodes wailed. "You most certainly would *not* go to prison for anybody or anything."

McLean glared at Rhodes. "So what do you know?"

Rhodes said, "I have steered clear of *Le Bête Attila* from the moment I laid eyes on her and saw Desi's reaction. I knew there was something there I wanted no part of, and I've had no part of it, and that is that." He took a sip of martini. "However, being as I was vaguely acquainted with Miss Natalie, when she went missing, I advised your business concern of her connection to Desi."

"Behind my back," Holliday added. "I called the police about it.

And when Loy Lombard showed up here asking questions, I gave her answers."

"No, you didn't," said Rhodes.

"Why don't you just shut up, Tyler?" Holliday shouted.

McLean stayed on Rhodes. "Come on, Tyler. What about you and Natalie?"

"There was never any me and Natalie," said Rhodes. "I only saw her at a few of Desi's parties, just like I've told Loy."

"Tyler, you're mistaken," said Holliday. "Natalie never came to my parties."

"Yes, she did," said Rhodes. "I distinctly remember the Russian redhead. She came as Nadine. I seem to recall that's how she introduced herself."

Holliday stood up. "Look, I've had enough. My nerves are shot."

"What are you so jittery about all of a sudden?" said Rhodes. "I know for a fact she came to your parties from the picture of you and her that I gave Loy."

"Picture?" Holliday's voice was shaking. "You gave them her picture? Why did you do that?" he shouted.

"Don't get in a state about it," said Rhodes. "It's just a photograph."

"Just a photograph?" Holliday spluttered, spit flying out of his mouth, his eyes wide around. "Just a photograph!" he repeated. "You idiot! What have you done?"

"Obviously something you disapprove of," said Rhodes.

"I think I'll have another look at that picture," said McLean. He looked for the deputies, who were by now in the middle of an all-out game of pool. "Having fun, boys?"

Lombard was sitting with Abel in the backseat of a sheriff's cruiser. Headlights illuminated the off-road path leading to the bunker, and the cruiser rose and bumped along the grassy hillside with as much grace as Crown Vic custom shocks would allow.

"Stop here," Lombard told the two officers in front. "I heard something." She scrambled out of the cruiser as soon as it stopped and listened in the cool night air. There was a buzzing sound in the distance, like that of a motorboat.

One of the officers said, "Look, up there." He pointed in the dark distance, where a faint light moved north in the vicinity of the water of the river, into which the creek of Wolf Branch Farm flowed. "Must be a boat."

"At this time of night?" Lombard mumbled. She turned her attention to the bunker door, visible in the headlights of the cruiser. "All right, Abel. Unlock it." Lombard leaned back against the hood of the cruiser.

Abel leaned over the door and threw back the wooden hitch. As he stuck his key in the lock, Church and Mrs. Wolf arrived in an ATV she used to drive around her property. The lock popped, and Abel pulled the hasp off the metal staple. When he opened the door, Lombard looked at Church. "You go in," she said. "I don't think I could stand finding her."

Mrs. Wolf said, "Abel, go down there and help that boy." Abel did as he was told.

"Loy!" Church shouted a few seconds later. "Hurry down here."

Lombard quickly went down the steps into the bunker. Church was kneeling next to the chair, using a pocketknife to cut through the cords around Dana's wrists and ankles. "She's breathing," he said. Dana was leaning backward, her head rolled to one side on her shoulder, the electrical tape dangling off her chin. "Hold her up," said Church.

As Lombard held Dana, she heard Abel puttering around back in the tiny room where the police had found his guns a few weeks before. The thought of asking him what he was doing vanished as soon as it entered her mind; she was too worried about Dana. The cords were loosened, and she pulled Dana up off the chair. Church helped carry her up the steps, and they laid Dana on the cool grass outside the bunker. Church told one of the officers to call for an ambulance, and Lombard sat next to Dana, pulling frizzy strands of hair away from of her eyes. She brushed her fingertips along Dana's cheek and smiled when Dana sneezed. Dana's eyes opened, and Lombard said, "We just need one good frost to kill the rest of that ragweed."

"Oh, dear!" Abel cried as he huffed up the steps. "Oh, dear! Everybody clear out!" he thundered. "Everybody! Clear!" He grabbed his mother's hand and pulled her away from the bunker, as Lombard lifted Dana onto her feet and dragged her in a spontaneous reaction to Abel's startling commands. Church and the other two officers followed up hill.

"What's going on?" Church cried.

"My device!" Abel cried. "My device is active!" No sooner had he spoken than a light flashed in the open bunker, and there was an earsplitting crack and roar.

"Down!" somebody shouted, and everybody fell down to the ground not 50 feet from the bunker. Splinters of wood and metal fanned out in the yellow-orange glow of the explosion, falling in a hard spray upon the prone bodies of Lombard's party. As if by instinct, everyone rose simultaneously and scampered farther up hill. By now, Dana was back on her feet and running. The fireball of the bunker poured out onto the police cruiser and Mrs. Wolf's ATV, igniting a second explosion.

After they had all scuttled uphill and watched in unbelieving wonder at the fire roaring below, Lombard got some of her own fire back. "Mike," she seethed, "don't tell me you boys searched that bunker for guns and didn't notice a bomb!"

Deputy Potter spoke up. "I remember this crazy little gadget box, come to think of it." He nudged Church. "Hey, remember? You thought it was a short-wave radio."

"Shut up," Church grumbled.

CHAPTER 16

Lombard was waiting in the lobby of the hospital emergency room where Dana was being examined. She couldn't stop thinking how she would never have forgiven herself had Dana died in the explosion. Perhaps that was why Attila had targeted Dana. It was the only way she could get even with Lombard for making things difficult for her. She knew Lombard was fond of Dana, the way Lombard had gone on about her that night at Maddie's Bar. Rhodes had probably brought it up again around Holliday and Attila. It was even possible Stella had run her mouth. People in small towns talked.

They were all lucky to be alive, but nobody was as grateful to be alive as Dana, whose eyes were red and puffy when she came out of the examining room, where she'd been treated for shock. She told Lombard she'd cried a lot but had managed to give an account of her abduction to the police as well as a description of Attila, who was now, for the first time, the subject of an official investigation.

McLean picked them up, and during the ride to Dana's home, Lombard played out in her mind the likely outcome had Attila pulled it off. For one thing, the case against Abel would have intensified. He was already convicted of Natalie Wolf's death in the minds of the police and the public. Abel had been portrayed as a dangerous loner: One of his own investigators' assistants would have been seemed like easy prey for somebody like him. And more than anything, Dana's violent death would have shaken Lombard to her foundations.

Even now, Abel wasn't in the clear. He would likely face federal charges for manufacturing explosive devices. And Church hadn't given up on the idea that Abel was connected in some way to Natalie's murder. In his view, Attila's attempt on Dana's life didn't absolve Abel from suspicion.

When McLean pulled up to Dana's address, Lombard asked him to wait and followed Dana to her half of a brick duplex. Dana chattered nervously as they went inside, telling Lombard her parents had helped her buy the house, that she'd had three sets of tenants in the adjacent apartment, and had learned never to lease to her friends. "So there's a couple there now—a guy and a girl—but the girl is the one who can fix things, which is totally convenient," Dana giggled. "They get a cut on their rent every month. There's always something that needs doing. I hope they never leave."

Lombard stood awkwardly at arm's length, hands in her hip pockets, as Dana hung her jacket in the closet of an oak staircase rising up from the foyer. "Are you afraid to stay by yourself?" Lombard asked.

"I'm fine. My tenants are right next door." Dana drew closer to Lombard. "Did you want to stay with me?"

Lombard averted her eyes to the floor. "Well, I suppose it would be the least I could do after all you put up with while I was sick. But I was going to suggest calling a friend over." She gave Dana a quick glance before impulsively leaning forward and kissing her. She meant it to be a small, sweet kiss, but Dana pulled her closer and wrapped her arms around Lombard's neck and drew her in for a long, sexy smooch. Lombard scooped Dana up and kissed her cheek. "You're not so upset you'd quit your job, are you?"

"No."

Lombard pulled away. "I think somebody should come over and stay with you. I would, but I can't trust myself."

Dana chuckled. "Then I wish you *would* stay!"

Lombard smiled pensively. "What would Jane think of that? Besides, we work together." She shook her head. "I shouldn't have done that...kissed you, I mean."

Dana frowned. "But it's already out there, isn't it? This is the thing, Loy. Something about being kidnapped and rescued and nearly blown to bits—suddenly you don't mind telling it like it is, what's really in your heart. So I just kissed my boss, which most people would say is stupid. And my boss thinks staying over would be a bad idea, probably because I'm all emotional and vulnerable, and you aren't going to take advantage of me like that. And besides, there's the age-old taboo about fooling around with employees. Bad idea, always wrong."

Lombard put her hands back in her pockets and rocked a little on her feet. "Dana, honey, I—"

"I'm not finished. So the acceptable thing to do is to call my girlfriend with whom I'm almost certainly going to break up because I'm in love with my boss who really, really isn't ready for that so soon after the end of a not so good relationship with somebody else." Dana leaned against the banister of the staircase. "Oops. Broke the other taboo. It was officially too soon to tell you that. Well, romance with rules isn't romance. That would be sexual politics, in which I no longer participate. And what was it you were saying about passion, I seem to recall?"

Lombard rubbed her forehead. She was tired and still a little weak. "I was so certain things couldn't get more complicated..."

"I guess I've put you in a spot," Dana smiled. "We either have to be coworkers and lovers, or just passing friends. 'Cause I'll have to quit if you don't want me."

"Whoa!" Lombard squeezed Dana's hand and kissed it. "Let's not make any sudden moves, OK? You have to give me a little time." Outside, McLean tooted his car horn. She said, "Though passion isn't the kind of thing you plan for." The horn sounded again. Lombard opened the door and hollered, "Go home, Sam! I'm gonna spend the night here." The car didn't move for a few seconds, but Lombard watched until McLean drove away. "I hate to think what he's muttering," she said to herself. She turned to Dana. "I'm sleeping on the couch. Just so you feel safe."

"You don't have to stay, Loy. I'll be OK."

Lombard shrugged. "I want to stay."

Lombard awoke in exactly the same position in which she'd fallen asleep. She hadn't dreamed, and she was still groggy. Dana's living room was gray-dark at 10:30 A.M. She rose quickly and threw the quilt off the futon when she saw the time, opening the wooden blinds of Dana's front picture window to the bleak autumn rain outside. She thought that would be good for the fire at Wolf Branch Farm.

Dana was still asleep, she surmised. Dana's room was upstairs, where Lombard hadn't ventured even when Dana had told her she could sleep on a twin bed in the spare room. Lombard knew herself well enough to realize she would have ended up in Dana's bed, and it was simply too soon for that, rules or no rules. Lombard wasn't looking after the interests of a vulnerable young girl: Dana was 31 years old, a grown, mature woman with her own house and responsibilities. Lombard was looking after herself and her heart, which she wasn't ready to give to anybody just yet, especially to a woman who could innocently destroy it.

She was annoyed at having overslept, but she was oddly proud of herself. It was unlike her to resist the opportunity for sex with a pretty woman who had come on to her. And she hadn't had a drink since the night of the break-in at her house. That had been five days and four nights ago. Of course, she'd been sick, and she'd been preoccupied. But four sober nights—that was a milestone.

She crept around Dana's kitchen, looking for coffee. There had to be coffee; Dana had a coffeemaker and a coffee grinder on her kitchen countertop. Lombard finally found a pretty orange-and-yellow tin full of fragrant coffee. She got the pot started and called the office.

Retta was apparently out, because McLean picked up the phone, much to Lombard's unease. "Well, well," he said. "Did you get plenty of rest?"

"Yes, I did," she snipped. "I went right to sleep after you left, and I just got up. Sorry I'll be late getting in. What have I missed?"

"I've heard from Mashburn. The ATF is after Abel Wolf."

"Great," Lombard muttered. "Hasn't anybody been looking for Attila?"

"The usual APB, but Abel admitted the bomb belonged to him."

"But Attila set the timer! She tried to kill Dana. Abel did nothing wrong."

"He possessed explosives. That's illegal. Plus, they probably think Abel knows something. You have to admit he's a suspicious character, Loy. He took his own wife's thumb off her corpse and kept it as a souvenir. He kept antique guns—one of which was used to kill her. He made a bomb by his own admission. Even if the police also suspect Attila at this point, it's perfectly reasonable to consider the possibility she and Abel might have been in cahoots. How else would she have access to his bunker?"

"You know good and well how," said Lombard. "Natalie took his money, his gun, and her copy of a key. Surely the police have factored in Coburn and Agee. Abel had nothing to do with them. Attila did, through Natalie, who was her whore and maybe her lover before she did something to piss Attila off and get herself killed."

"You can't explain why Attila would want them dead, though. Yeah, they knew something. But what? Loy, the fact is, Abel is still in trouble."

"Only because he's a peculiar character, not a suspicious one," said Lombard. "He would be dangerous if he had any concept of motive, which he doesn't. He knows how to make bombs but has no interest in exploding them. That would be messy and unnerving to somebody like him. He's morbid and obsessive, but he's no killer." She sighed. "Why can't everybody be as insightful into character as I am?"

"He's a creep," said McLean.

"Exactly! See? You're starting to get it."

"Well, get this." McLean gave a full account of the previous night's interview with Holliday, and Rhodes's casual mention of the photograph taken of Natalie and Holliday. "Holliday got very nervous when he heard Natalie's alias of Nadine," said McLean. "He denied she'd ever been to a party at first, and when Tyler reminded him about the picture—which, apparently, Holliday had no idea Tyler had shown you—he had a conniption fit."

Lombard silently processed what McLean had just told her, staring at Dana's art deco coffeemaker as steam rose up in narrow turrets around the basket.

"Loy? Are you there?"

"Tyler told you Natalie went by Nadine?" Lombard asked softly.

"Yeah."

"Sam, go in my office and grab all the stuff in my file cabinet related to the Wolf case. More to the point, there's a picture in there—the Immigration shot of Natalie I got off the TV news Web site and had printed for our records. I need that picture."

"What do you want with it?"

Lombard opened a cabinet door and looked for a to-go mug. "As soon as I can get home for a quick shower, I'll call you. We're going to Wolf Branch Farm."

Gussie Wolf was sitting forlornly on her back porch, staring at the charred wreckage surrounding her son's bunker downhill. The rain had stopped, and the temperature had risen enough to make porch-sitting tolerable in the early afternoon. She didn't look up when Lombard and McLean arrived, but she spoke to them. "Fire trucks was here till past dawn," she said. "Then the rain came. Fire went out, but everything's still too hot to fool with. So they left." She looked up. "When do you reckon they'll haul off all that mess?"

Lombard sat next to her. "Don't know. Have the cops got Abel yet?"

"Not yet. He's inside."

Lombard handed Mrs. Wolf the snapshot of Holliday and his Russian guest.

"Who's this?" Mrs. Wolf asked.

"That's Desmond Holliday. I take it you've never met."

"No, I ain't. What does he have to do with anything?"

"Well, he was a friend of Natalie's, judging by that picture, wouldn't you say?"

Mrs. Wolf handed the photograph back to Lombard. "Wait a minute." She got up and opened the screen door. She hollered for Abel to come outside and sat back down.

A minute later Abel examined the photograph and denied having any past or present acquaintance with Holliday. "Or for that matter," he added, "the young lady standing next to him."

McLean cried out—a weird, choked little sob of surprise. "What?"

Lombard said, "Sammy, we got taken in by a couple of jet-set, world-class dykes. They *wanted* us to think we were dealing with one redhead, that she was Natalie, and that she was dead."

She pointed at the picture. "Abel, I believe this woman's name was Nadine Gromyko. Are you sure you never met her?"

"No. That is a Russian-sounding name, though," he said. "But I've never seen this woman before."

Lombard whipped out her print of the photograph of Natalie Wolf circulating in the news media. "There's a resemblance. Only someone who knew her would notice that from this distant angle, the woman with Holliday isn't Natalie."

Abel was closely examining the snapshot. "This woman isn't Natalie. How can you not see that?"

"It's a profile shot at a distance, Abel. You lived with her for two years," Lombard said. "Red hair, white skin, pretty face." She eyed McLean again. "Very similar looks, but different people. We've been chasing an optical illusion."

McLean said, "There are no other pictures? Surely you took wedding photos."

"Natalie didn't want any," said Abel. "She was very camera-shy."

"She had good reason to be," said Lombard. She flapped the snapshot at McLean. "We took this photograph for granted. I've looked at her real picture in the news day after day, and never compared it closely to this snapshot only you and I had access to. I've spent my whole career trying to avoid making assumptions about anything. But who the hell would think two Russian redheads were on the make in a small Southern town?"

McLean said, "It crossed your mind in the beginning."

"But then the evidence brought them so close together," said Lombard. "It was easier to assume we were dealing with one woman. It made sense to merge them, so to speak."

"Why didn't you show us the damn picture in the first place?" Mrs. Wolf demanded.

"I wish I had," Lombard said acidly. "But it wouldn't have solved anything then, and it still hasn't. Now we have a dead stranger and two missing murderers."

Lombard looked at Abel. "Sit down, Abel. I've got some news. The good news is: I think your wife is alive. The bad news: If she is, she's a killer on top of being a thief."

Abel's face was childlike with wonder. "Then whose body got cremated?"

"If my thinking is correct, it was Nadine Gromyko's," said Lombard.

"Why?" asked McLean.

"That's what Holliday will tell us."

Mrs. Wolf spoke up. "You mean to tell me we paid Blanchard Mortuary to cremate some tramp we didn't even know?"

Holliday was supervising the packing of his BMW when Lombard and McLean drove up. When they got out of the Pathfinder, Holliday stepped back. "I had nothing to do with that bombing!"

"Nobody thinks you did," said Lombard.

"And I don't know where Attila is. She's probably long gone."

"I don't doubt it." Lombard put her hands on her hips. "You're not going anywhere just yet. And the police are already involved. So the more you tell me, the better off you'll be. Let's go in the house."

"I'm going to tell you what I know," said Lombard once they were inside. "I know Natalie Wolf left Abel, and she was working with or for Attila. I know Nadine Gromyko was working as a stripper and/or hooker, and she was hanging around here often enough to get her picture taken and make an impression on visitors. I know she was smart enough to run a Web site for Attila, and one for herself." Holliday's complexion waned, and Lombard said, "In other words, I know we're dealing with two different Russian ladies, and one of them is dead. I think it's Nadine. Am I right?"

Holliday's eyes lowered, and he drew his lips in an O. He seemed incapable of speech. Lombard pressed him for an answer, and he finally nodded.

"Now we're getting somewhere." Lombard stood up and began pacing. "Let's see, according to what you've told me and Sam, Natalie showed up in North Carolina, posing as a Russian bride. It was a good cover for her larger assignment, which was to bleed you dry for debts owed to Attila. Attila herself never made an appearance until just a few weeks ago. She meant to pick up Natalie and leave the country, or so you told Sam. But this was a bit premature, wasn't it?" Lombard sat next to Holliday and patted his knee. "She had to come up to take care of an unexpected problem." Lombard whispered in Holliday's ear, though loud enough for McLean to hear. "And the problem's name was Nadine Gromyko." Holliday smiled at Lombard. "Nadine," Lombard went on, "was part of a strange international sorority of sorts. She was a Blue Scorpion, an operative in a bizarre cult of cuties run by Attila. They had their own stylish tattoos, and even their own Web site—well, for a while…" Lombard looked at McLean.

McLean said, "But it had to be taken down recently."

"Thank you," said Lombard. "It was taken down around the time a couple of men died, men who had employed Nadine Gromyko as a dancer and, probably, as a prostitute. They knew all about her. They knew about her business. One of them got a little more attached to her than he should have, and his boss knew about it. They, and the Web site, and Nadine, all became extinct almost simultaneously."

Lombard stood up and resumed pacing. "Attila had to kill Nadine. That's why she came up here. Yeah, she was gonna pick up Natalie and blow this hick town, but only because she had to. The arrangement she'd worked out for Natalie against you should have gone on for a long time, if you owed her a lot of money. It had to end when Nadine showed up and made things uncomfortable for Natalie. And why did Nadine do that?" Lombard gave Holliday a stern look. "That's not a rhetorical question."

Holliday cleared his throat. "I asked Nadine to help me."

"You used Nadine against Natalie. How did you find her?"

"She was a Blue Scorpion," said Holliday. "I've known about them for years, ever since I met Attila's brother. You see, he was their pimp, originally. Now the sister Attila runs them. They're known for their white skin, blond or red hair. They look alike. Except, of course, Attila, who towers over them in more ways than one."

McLean had quietly been observing the unraveling mystery. Then he offered, "As long as you paid Natalie—and through her, Attila's organization—Attila left you alone. Otherwise, she'd kill you."

"That, or worse," said Holliday. "She might have set me up for racketeering. She knew my dread of prison."

"So you got Nadine to come here," said Lombard. "How?"

"I have to explain Natalie first. Natalie was in the European outfit, and she was—well, is still, apparently—Attila's favorite. The bride bit was the only way she could get in the country, into this part of the country for the kind of long-term job Attila had her doing. Nadine, on the other hand, had come here pre–9/11 and easily obtained residency. She worked the Miami area, and I knew her through my contacts there. I got her to come up here when I realized she wanted to break free of Attila. So we could help each other: I could help her set up business here, away from Attila's grip, and she could keep Natalie off my back with the threat of exposure."

"But that would work against Nadine as well," said McLean.

"Natalie had more to lose, more at stake. She was fronting a huge organization that Nadine wanted out of. So Natalie had to be careful."

"How many girls run in that Blue Scorpion racket?" Lombard asked.

"I don't know," said Holliday. "It's a multimillion-dollar business. They're all over North America and Europe."

"And they've all got those scorpion tattoos on their backs?"

"Yes."

Lombard arched her eyebrows. "Damn. I must live in a small town."

Holliday's explanation went on. "Nadine was different from those others. She was ambitious and smart. You're right: She ran the Web site for Attila before she decided to break loose. She encoded it before she left so she could use it for her operation here. She wanted out from under Attila's wing, to start her own organization. I was the only ally she could find." Holliday shook his head. "Nadine was smart, but she wasn't smart or strong enough to fool Attila. Few people are."

Lombard said, "Nadine blackmailed Natalie, then? Threatened to blow her cover. In the meantime, Nadine had a home base here, and you kept her up while she tried to break out on her own. But she rattled Attila's cage a little too loudly. Mama Scorpion had to take care of her and get Natalie out of here with one sting." She snapped her fingers. "Just like that, a plan was set in motion. Natalie left the farm for good to carry it out. Once she got her hands on Nadine and held her captive at that cabin across the river from the Wolf farm, she called Attila. Attila came into town, and the next night, Nadine was dead. They shot her in the face so her features would be obliterated, but her tattoo was intact, unusual enough for a positive identification. They waited a day or so before floating her body over to the campground. They dumped it in a very public place, where they knew it would be found. Its proximity to the farm would cast suspicion on Abel, and the corpse would be decayed enough to make her body hard to ID, but fresh enough for him to ID the mark on her back.

"But just for good measure, they left ballistics proof laying around the corpse that would match an antique gun owned by Wolf. Abel made their job easier by being creepy enough in his own right to salvage one of her body parts before Nadine was cremated. It made him look guilty, but it will now have the ironic effect of exonerating him."

"How?" asked Holliday.

"Tissue preserved from the body matched DNA from the thumb. But now it will be compared to DNA taken from Natalie by Immigration when she legally entered the country, post–9/11. New immigration policy: The immigrant's DNA info gets entered into a database, and if the immigrant ever causes any trouble and there's a need for DNA comparison, the feds have it." Lombard stretched and yawned. "So the thumb will, at last, prove that Natalie Wolf's body wasn't dumped at the Apple Creek Campground." Lombard eyed the photograph. "Appearances can be deceiving, but genes never lie."

Holliday looked relieved for the first time since Lombard had known him. "Good. I'm glad the truth is out. I'm sorry for everything."

"Then help me out," said Lombard. "You called the police after Natalie's disappearance, but before Attila got to town. So you knew something was up. How?"

"I told you that night at my party that Natalie and I had made an appointment and she'd missed it. It was Nadine who was supposed to meet me that day. Natalie showed up in her place. She told me to call the police and report her, Natalie, missing. She said Attila was on her way to town. I knew I was in danger, so I called the police and told them what she asked me to. I knew I was being played as a pawn, but I had no clue why or for what." He drew a deep breath. "Then, Attila showed up, and I was just blown away by how intimidating she can be. My God, her brother was tough, but her!" He chuckled. "I thought I was going to come unglued. I asked Tyler to stay with me at the house, which I lease from him. He's a fatuous ass, Tyler, but he's a good friend."

"You didn't know he came to my office with that picture."

"No."

"Did you know the two clients of Nadine's who were killed?"

"No."

McLean said, "We think Nadine's personal relationship with Seth Agee made him a target. He likely knew about Nadine's problems. When I met him, he seemed to think Natalie and Nadine were one and the same, but in hindsight I think he knew better. He wanted to tell me, and later the police, what was on his mind. But he was too confused and scared to come clean. He was a risk, though, and Attila eliminated him."

Lombard added, "Natalie had wanted to know who Nadine's associates were, and probably tortured the information out of her. After Attila took care of Agee, she tormented Tony Coburn with a lot of threatening phone calls until he agreed to meet her. Phone harassment was one of her M.O.'s. When he showed up, she killed him."

Holliday rolled his shoulders. "I never asked Nadine about her private affairs. But that would explain why Attila overstayed her welcome. She had unfinished business to take care of."

So did Gussie Wolf, Lombard found out early that evening when Mrs. Wolf called her back to the farm. When she arrived, Lombard heard a loud engine rumbling from the direction of the creek behind the farmhouse. She walked around back and spotted Mrs. Wolf in the driver's seat of a backhoe, downhill next to the Abel's old bunker.

Mrs. Wolf turned off the engine and waved at Lombard, who trudged down to meet her. "What are you doing, Mrs. Wolf?" she asked.

"Burying the bunker," Mrs. Wolf explained, pointing to a pile of dirt rising up from the bombed-out cavity. "As soon as the sky cleared, I had some old hands deliver a few yards of fill dirt and this backhoe, and did the job myself," she boasted, hopping down from her seat. She dusted off her overalls. "The ATF hauled Abel off today. Mashburn says I can post his bail later. They got him for bomb possession, but he'll get probation. Mashburn swore."

"What do you need me for?" Lombard asked.

"I owe you," said Mrs. Wolf.

"No, you don't. I never found your money."

Mrs. Wolf grinned. "It worked out fine. You found out who was causing all the trouble, and you know, they'll never get away with it."

Lombard looked out over the creek and downstream, where in the distance it flowed into the river. "What makes you so sure?"

"That detective, Church. He told me this morning you thought those two whores had been hiding out on that old logging property across the river. They'd even made a nest in the old cabin."

Lombard squinted against the setting sun at Mrs. Wolf. "Something tells me you knew more about that property than you admitted when we went down to the boat launch together."

Mrs. Wolf shrugged. "That's not important now. What's important is you thought to check the place out. So. I think you were right. They were hiding out there."

"What makes you think so?" Lombard looked sidelong at Mrs. Wolf. "Did you go over there?"

"I thought maybe there would still be police hanging around," Mrs. Wolf said, "but there sure weren't any when I visited a few hours ago."

Lombard wasn't really surprised to hear that. Church had told her the night before that he thought the cabin was a red herring, and the fact was, nobody other than McLean had ever seen anybody there, and Church hadn't been convinced the woman McLean had spied was Attila. Lombard and McLean were certain, but Church had called the police off as soon as the place had been cleared of any signs of Dana or Attila.

But Lombard was surprised to hear Mrs. Wolf had gone to the cabin. "How did you get there?"

Mrs. Wolf was silent. She glanced at her truck, parked in the grass a few yards from the backhoe, near the burned-out carcasses of a police cruiser and her ATV.

Lombard eyed the truck. "What's in the pickup?"

"Ah, ain't nothing." Mrs. Wolf looked down at her boots.

Lombard walked over to the truck and looked in its bed. There were several garbage bags, stuffed nearly to bursting and tied at the tops. There was also a high-powered rifle with a scope gleaming on top of the bags. "That's a pretty mean piece, Mrs. Wolf."

Mrs. Wolf went over to her truck and reached inside. She pulled out a bulging, wrinkled manila envelope, sealed at the top and stapled, and handed it to Lombard. "Don't open it till you get home. That's all. Go on, now. You're snooping around too much, and I've got chores to do."

Lombard stared at the envelope for a moment before walking back up the hill. When she'd reached the crest, she turned around and looked at Mrs. Wolf again. The old lady hollered for her to get off her land and to sleep well that night.

Lombard felt perfectly safe staying home alone that night. Even if Attila and Natalie were still in the country, surely they were smart enough to be far away from Asheville. Plenty of time had elapsed between Attila's escape the night before and Lombard's realization that Natalie was still alive. But the authorities had begun searching for

Attila very soon after the explosion. Federal agents secured the international airports in Raleigh and Charlotte, faxing sketches based on descriptions of Attila and now Natalie's Immigration photograph. The women were now hunted fugitives: State police had blocked every highway leading into and out of North Carolina, and even the Coast Guard had ordered checkpoints in the harbors.

It was very unlikely that Attila was still around to cause trouble, Lombard thought as she poured her fifth cup of strong tea around 10 o'clock. She eyed her empty liquor cabinet and sighed. "All this caffeine will keep me up till dawn," she mumbled to herself. She went into the living room, nestled in the sofa, and clicked on Turner Classics. *Walk on the Wild Side* was coming on, part of a Barbara Stanwyck movie festival airing through the night, and Lombard was prepared to stay up watching all of them.

Lombard's mind wandered as the opening credits rolled. Where was Attila? That had to have been her in the motorboat Lombard had seen winding upriver before the explosion. Dana had told her about the cell phone call Attila had taken in the bunker, and how she'd spoken Russian. That must have been Natalie calling, telling Attila where to meet her. Maybe Attila had piloted the boat by herself, or maybe Natalie had picked her up.

She brought her mug to her lips as the movie began. "Relax, Loy," she said aloud, and petted her cat Romeo as he curled up next to her. "Watch the movie."

Then she thought of Mrs. Wolf. Why had she looked so jubilant when Lombard had called on her that evening? And what was she hiding in the bed of her truck, along with that rifle? Lombard wished she'd asked to open the bags. Something was going on. Had the old woman found something at the cabin? If so, what? It crossed Lombard's mind that she had found Attila and Natalie. But there had been no trace of them when Lombard and Church had raided the cabin the night before. They had cleared out by then, and had moved on to the next stage of their plan: to kill Dana, blow up the bunker, intensify the heat on Abel, and get out of the country.

But had they gone back? Had they run into a roadblock and gone back to the cabin to regroup? Church had called police away from the cabin when nothing had turned up, though Lombard had warned him a watch needed to be put on the place. But would Attila do something that risky? Maybe, if she were desperate, and if the cabin had been the only safe place she could think of. Attila would have had no idea that Lombard or the police had found out about the place.

Just then, the glare of car headlights panned across her blinds. Lombard heard an engine idling in the driveway for a few seconds before it was cut off. She searched her mind for who it could be. McLean never came over without calling first. Nobody ever came to Lombard's uninvited, with very rare exceptions—most notably, Attila. A car door slammed. Lombard's heart fluttered. *They've come to finish me,* she thought. She sprang off the sofa and made for her bedroom, where the gun was. But she stopped halfway down the hall and reprimanded herself for panicking. Of course it couldn't be Attila. Lombard went back to the living room and peeped through the blinds.

It was Dana's car. Lombard opened the door before Dana had a chance to knock.

Dana said, "I hope I didn't scare you."

"Scare me?" Lombard said wryly. "Why would I be scared?"

"Well, *I* am," said Dana. "She's still out there." Lombard gave a start and glanced over Dana's shoulder. "Not back *there,*" said Dana, waving her arms wide. "You know, just out there somewhere, still on the loose."

"Come in out of the cold." Lombard closed the door and locked it once Dana was inside. "I thought you weren't afraid."

"That was last night. I thought Attila would be caught by now. Besides, I've had time to process everything, and I'm totally freaking out."

Dana followed Lombard to the sofa and sat down with her. She glanced at the TV. "Oh, that's a great movie. I think Capucine is so hot."

"She's a prostitute in this picture," said Lombard. "Barbara Stanwyck is her madam."

"And she's in love with her," Dana added.

"Yeah." Lombard spread the quilt over both of them and put her arms around Dana, whose eyes were fixed on the TV.

"Will the cops catch them, Loy?"

"Yes."

"And if they come back here—"

"They won't," Lombard whispered, brushing her lips against Dana's ear.

Dana faced Lombard. "But if they did, we could handle them."

"Certainly." Lombard looked at the coffee table, on top of which lay the manila envelope Mrs. Wolf had given her earlier that evening but which Lombard hadn't intended on opening until McLean was around. A thought entered her mind now that made her want to open it.

"What's up? You look weird," said Dana.

"I don't know," Lombard said. She grabbed the envelope and opened it. She pulled out a stack of cash.

"Oh, my God," said Dana. "Where did you get that?"

Lombard counted the money. It was $20,000, ten percent of the 200 grand Mrs. Wolf had promised her if she found the money Natalie had stolen from Abel. Awestruck, she looked at Dana. "They went back to that cabin. Oh, Attila, that was stupid."

"That is some serious cash, Loy," said Dana.

Lombard didn't hear her. "They're dead, all right," she marveled. "Gussie, you tough old bitch."

"They're dead? How?"

"They underestimated the situation," Lombard smiled. "So did I." She took Dana into her arms. "The money is from a client, baby. Watch the movie."

"Well, until we know for sure they're dead, can I stay here?"

"Certainly," said Lombard. She stroked Dana's curly hair and kissed her. It was going to be a long, passionate night. Lombard wasn't the least bit tired.

Outside, wind rose through the branches of trees and tickled the chimes on Lombard's front porch. There was danger in the night as a blood-red harvest moon hung over Asheville, but only for the prey of bats and owls hunting amid the pines all the way to Wolf Branch Farm, where Gussie Wolf was tamping down the earth that now filled Abel's ruined bunker. "Rest in peace, ladies," she said, blowing out a deep breath and pitching her shovel at the backhoe that had spilled dirt into the bunker earlier that evening. She took off her gloves, spit in the palms of her hands, and rubbed them together. "If you're going to get anything done, you'd best do it yourself," she muttered. She turned around, picked up a leather attaché case from atop a pile of women's clothes and luggage she'd dumped out of the garbage bags from the bed of her truck. She pulled a block of bills out of it. She packed them back among 17 other blocks of cash—10,000 in each block, $100 bills.

Mrs. Wolf carefully placed the leather case in the cab of her truck and shut the door. She threw kindling over the clothing, poured lighter fluid on it, and struck a match.

October was a fine time of year for bonfires.